Ran off on da Plug

Lock Down Publications and Ca$h
Presents
Ran off on da Plug
A Novel by *Paper Boi Rari*

Lock Down Publications
Po Box 944
Stockbridge, Ga 30281

Visit our website @
www.lockdownpublications.com

Copyright 2022 by Paper Boi Rari
Ran off on da Plug

Lock Down Publications
Like our page on Facebook: Lock Down Publications @
www.facebook.com/lockdownpublications.ldp
Book interior design by: **Shawn Walker**
Edited by: **Tamira Butler**

Stay Connected with Us!

Text **LOCKDOWN** to 22828 to stay up-to-date with new releases,
sneak peaks, contests and more...
Thank you.

Submission Guideline.

Submit the first three chapters of your completed manuscript to ldpsubmissions@gmail.com, subject line: Your book's title. The manuscript must be in a .doc file and sent as an attachment. Document should be in Times New Roman, double spaced and in size 12 font. Also, provide your synopsis and full contact information. If sending multiple submissions, they must each be in a separate email.

Have a story but no way to send it electronically? You can still submit to LDP/Ca$h Presents. Send in the first three chapters, written or typed, of your completed manuscript to:

LDP: Submissions Dept
Po Box 944
Stockbridge, Ga 30281

DO NOT send original manuscript. Must be a duplicate.

Provide your synopsis and a cover letter containing your full contact information.

Thanks for considering LDP and Ca$h Presents.

Author Notes

"Stop deceiving yourselves: If you think you are wise by this world's standards, you need to become a fool to be truly wise. For the wisdom of this world is foolishness to God. As the Scriptures say,

'He traps the wise
in the Snare of their own
      cleverness.'
And again,
'The Lord knows the thoughts of the wise;
he knows they are worthless.'
So don't boast about following a particular human
leader, for everything belongs to you—"

                 1 CORINTHIANS 3:18-21, NLT

I'm just here to deliver the message, fast:
That's why I'm PAPER BOI RARI.

Acknowledgments

First and foremost, I'd like to give all praises to God in Jesus's name! Without them none of this would exist. Next up are both of my mom dukes. Thank y'all for all the love y'all make me feel. For being my cornerstone. It's a lot of faking going on during my absence of freedom, but y'all aren't one of them.

Arianna (Lady Bugg), I love you, daughter. You are growing up fast. You will be eight years old this year, by the grace of God. You are so smart, and you amaze me with each of our conversations. You are a princess grooming to be a queen. Your mental is boss status! You already know what you're going to be doing in life and with God's help, I'm going to make it all possible. Trust and believe, you have the DNA of a thoroughbred champion! All we know is WIN!

Mookie, welcome home lil' bruh! Glad you made it out! Now it's time to take control of life, know what you gon' do and do it.

Donnie, a hard head makes a soft ass! When you make your bed, you have to lie in it. That's what I'm doing, bruh. Die laying in a bed that I hate I made, but oh, if God allows me to make it out! all who faked gone hate!

Shawnta and Tee, I love y'all! We gone be straight sisters. I just have to get there.

Aunt Shea, Big L, Tanisha, Black Jesus, T-Roni, Troy, TC, Slimm G! Y'all know what it is.

It's a lot of names not included. I ain't doing no fake kickin'! Fuck all that! If you didn't keep it real with me, it's a no deal with me! You shouldn't have crossed me because that's when you lost me. The months are coming to an end, y'all! When they do, I can promise you this, y'all ain't gone like this. What's gone be revealed, y'all haven't seen before! Until then, let's just say I'm the best kept secret.

To my fans, thanks a lot, sincerely. I do this for y'all! You locked in, there aren't any door handles to get out. Once you came in you were stuck with me. Now your job is to just continue reading these stories. Watch as they unfold that each one grows and gets

7

better and better. Each one will be different from the last. Hood stories. Reality fiction with a message. I'm here to deliver the message to y'all. PAPER BOI RARI here on the job.

Lastly, I'd like to thank LDP: Ca$h for all the insight and wisdom to this art. Thanks, big bruh, I took everything to heart and striving for betterment with each stroke of the pen. I'd like to thank Cassandra Sims for the edits. Thanks a lot. Your wordplay like DAT! I'd like to thank Shawn Walker for the book interior design. Also, I would like to thank the cover designer and layout, Dynasty's Cover Me: SRT -8 Gas: Keep 'em coming! Y'all killing the game!

Now I can't sleep if these shoutouts aren't included. Oh now, big bruh Freak Zeenie! This one for you. Oh now, Big Ced (Lenox), you already know! Hot Boy, Blazay, Dude, JB, Pitts, Bo, Stace Money, BD, King Nate, the one and only, Flav, and Thug! I appreciate y'all boys, we the family! Blood thicker than water! I can't forget you, Ms. Lois! Love you!

Thank everyone for considering me as their author of choice. Welcome to Hood Dreams Reality Fiction, where shit gets top-lip deep quick! Where the decisions have to be made in some of the worst situations, but it's your decision to decide it right. Where no one is frontin' shit, because everyone running off on the PLUG!

Enjoy the story.

Contact me with all feedback at:

Levi Maddox 118-7-002

Federal Correctional Complex USP1

P.O. Box 1033

Coleman, Fl. 33521

      Or

Facebook: Levi Maddox or

PAPER BOI RARI

Dedications

I dedicate this creation in the loving memories of my father! a love and bond that could never be broken. I miss you, Old Boy! Trust and believe I'm going to rep us to the death of me!

RIP

Levi Larry Maddox Sr.

SUNRISE 7/7   11/14 SUNSET

1955-2020

Chapter 1

As if times weren't hard enough doing time in the concrete jungle, COVID-19 hit USP Coleman 1 like a Mack truck doing a hundred miles per hour with no brakes. Not only USP Coleman, but the whole BOP was under modified lockdown.

It was now close to a year into the pandemic and prison had changed from worse to worst. The phone calls were now no longer charging, they were free. This was a blessing and at the same time, a curse on the flip side, bringing all kinds of disagreements between different cars about who would use the phone, how it would be used and what not. Cars were labeled by different states. Whatever state you were from, that would be your car, or which gang you affiliated with, you dig?

Now, on the compound, the dorms no longer interacted with each other. The administration had it where even inside your dorm it would be released in sections at a time for social distance purposes and to contain the violence.

No matter how it was done, the tension stayed thick in all the units. Inmates were allowed to come out of the cells three times a week, Mondays, Wednesdays, and Fridays, for showers, phone calls, emails, and to sanitize their cells. They were afforded two hours at the most. With that being said, *frustrated* would be a poor example of how one would feel.

Today, though, it was a prison full of happy faces. It was the first day in at least a year since any inmate had smelled a whiff of fresh air. The warden had finally granted each unit one hour of outside rec since the CDC claimed it was becoming safer to ease the restrictions due to the vaccines that were slowly being distributed into population, even though they weren't FDA approved, yet.

Freak Zeenie was on the yard in full workout gear. A sweat suit, skull cap, and a trash bag under his sweat suit, along with his MP3 player. Freak Zeenie had been going hard for the last twelve years straight. He was determined not to go out the prison gates the same way he had entered: two hundred forty pounds overweight on a five six, stocky frame.

When Freak Zeenie first came in, it took him thirty minutes to complete fifteen burpees. He would take a two-minute rest break between each burpee. Now, though, that wasn't the case by far. Freak Zeenie was burning the competition up, young or old, it didn't matter. If they jumped out there, then they were good as cooked, and Freak Zeenie was in his forties. Not only did he love competition, he thrived off it. The harder one would go, the more it pushed Freak Zeenie. Just imagine, twelve long years ago you wouldn't believe this was even the same person. Freak Zeenie had gotten his weight down to a healthy one hundred sixty pounds. He had every health book out stored in his cell it seemed like.

Freak Zeenie went over time to maintain his health. Working out twice a day and eating healthy had become routine for him. Freak Zeenie was at his best. Like T.I. once said, he got better with time. Freak Zeenie was on a mission.

"Come on, nigga! Let's go! You thought it was a game, huh? Nine eighty, nigga! Twenty more to go!" Freak Zeenie yelled, joggin' in place, after coming up pouring in sweat from the one thousand one jump burpees he and his partner BD were doing.

"Look her', Jo'. Work time! I know what you tryin' to do! I'm hip to you, Jo'. You tryin' to rest! I'm tryin' to work!" BD said, coming up pourin' down with sweat, talking workout trash right back as Freak Zeenie went right back down.

"Inmate Barber, from B-unit! PLEASE REPORT TO THE NEAREST STAFF! Inmate Barber, please report to the nearest staff!" a female voice came loud and clear over the loudspeaker.

"What you waiting for? Let's go! Two more!" he said, pointing to BD, signaling for him to go. Freak Zeenie was in a zone. He had his earbuds lodged in with the volume to the max.

"Aye, aye, aye, man!? Them folks just called you over the loudspeaker, bruh!" one of the inmates said, getting Freak Zeenie's attention, breaking his workout up, which was one thing he didn't play about.

"Huh? Say what?" Freak Zeenie said, snatching his buds out his ear, frowning up, looking 'round real fast trying to see what happened. He hated to be disturbed doing his work outs.

"They calling you over the speaker to report to the staff, bruh," the inmate said again, frowning back up, matching Freak Zeenie's expression. The inmate kept walking, continuing his laps with another inmate. They looked back a few times at Freak Zeenie and conversated lowly but kept it moving.

"For what? Hell they calling me for?" he asked, putting his arms out animatedly, looking 'round for a CO.

"What's up, Freak?" BD said, wiping his face with his face towel.

"Shh... Man, I don't know! Hold on!" He took off running toward the gate. "Oh now, Officer Johnson! Aye?" He was waving his arms frantically, trying to get the staff's attention.

"Yeah, what's up, man?" CO Johnson said, stopping in his tracks.

"The folks just called me over the loudspeaker for somethin'. I don't know what they want, man," Freak Zeenie said, still breathing hard from the intense workout. His eyes moved back and forth searching the officer's eyes, trying to get a feel or some kind of reaction from him.

"Alright, hold on right quick," CO Johnson said, getting on his walkie talkie calling it in. After a few seconds, he was unlocking the gate to let him out.

"You straight, bruh?" BD said, coming to the gate.

"Shit, we 'bout to find out," Freak Zeenie said, power walking to the unit with a zillion thoughts running through his mind. *Fuck goin' on! Hell I done did? Man...I'm tellin' you, them folks bet not be wit' the bullshit now. I ain't got time for this shit. Damn!* he was thinking to himself as he made his way up the walk.

***
Minutes Later...

Knock, Knock, Knock!
Freak Zeenie knocked on the counselor's door.

"Come on in, Mr. Barber," Counselor Bowers said, motioning his hand for Freak Zeenie to enter. "Have a seat," Counselor Bowers said, as soon as Freak Zeenie walked in, then went silent for an uncomfortable second.

"Man, what's up, Bowers? What's going on?" Freak Zeenie said, breaking the silence, not able to stand another second of the intense anticipation.

"You tell me, Barber," Counselor Bowers said, scratching his head and adjusting his hat. Putting his hand on his forehead looking at the computer, he pressed the keys swiftly. Counselor Bowers was typing away, making it hard for Freak Zeenie to read him. Freak Zeenie was thinking of all the shit he had done wrong. He couldn't come up with what he could have done. Since he couldn't come up with nothing, he chose to remain silent. "Barber, Barber, Barber un-hun, un-hun! Just can't do right! Boy, I tell yah, what's wrong with y'all, man?" He looked up from the computer monitor into Freak Zeenie's eyes.

"Huh? Y'all don't like pussy or somethin'? Man, see me, I love me some pussy too much to fuck up. All these women out there and y'all tryin' to stay up in here. Damn, I just don't understand y'all," he said, as he returned to typing away.

"Shit, me too, Bowers, that's why I'm tryin' to get the hell out of here! I don't know what you talking 'bout now, 'cause I know I ain't did shit! Man, I got a life sentence, been gone for twelve years, got six kids, Bowers, four girls and two boys. A mother and father with a big, God-fearing family who loves me, man, so I—"

"Alright, alright, Barber, I get it, man. Congratulations, they just granted you compassionate release! Gone pack your shit! I was just messing with you, man. You finally got your second chance! Don't go out there and fuck it up now, 'cau—"

"What?" Freak Zeenie jumped up, tears flowing freely down his face without shame. "Stop playing, Bowers," he said the first thing that came to his mind. This was so unexpected, but really the only thing that should have been expected, being that all his co-conspirators had already been freed. Freak Zeenie was the last one. To his family, he was the missing link. To his co-conspirators, he was the last person they wanted to see again. Before Freak Zeenie knew it, he reached in, shaking Counselor Bowers's hand. "Thank you. Thank you, man! I can promise you this, ya won't see me no more behind a prison wall, that's on my life!" Freak Zeenie said, turning around running to his cell to pack up the few belongings that he was going to take with him.

BD met Freak Zeenie on the stairs. "What's up, bruh? Where you going, Jo'?" BD said, concern written on his face.

"Boy, compassionate release, my nigga! They done finally freed a real nigga!" he said, moving in high speed down the stairs. talking the whole time.

"For real, Jo'? Man, that's good, bruh! Congratulations, my nigga! Shit, I know I'm next, Jo'. They letting everybody out now, 'bout time." BD was right behind him.

"Hell yeah, I'm 'bout to make my phone call right now to let my people know. Then I got to quarantine for a few days. Then I think I got to go to the halfway house first, my nigga. I left all that shit up there in the room for you, bruh. Everything, I ain't fucking with these niggas." Freak Zeenie had a cell full of shit from Versace glasses, Cartier glasses, better known as buffs, Timberlands, to all the latest shoes and a locker full of food, to say the least.

"Yeah, alright, 'preciate it, Jo', but man, damn bruh, I'm gone miss yah, my nigga." BD reached in, giving Freak Zeenie some dap, pulling him in embracing him in a brotherly bear hug. "Stay up and go out there and take care of your family and do everything we talked about now. Don't side track out there. Stick to the script," he said, stepping back looking at Freak Zeenie one last time.

"Man, you already know I got you till you get there, nigga! My word law, BD! Watch this! I'm 'bout to show you how this shit go for real! The rest of them niggas playing! I'm that nigga for real! Pressure! Straight drop! A'ight, watch this one! Gone get something to write with and take this number down right fast. The folks on the way to get me now, bruh." Freak Zeenie picked the phone up and started dialing numbers to place his last prison call. Freak Zeenie talked his ten minutes to his brother Levi. He hung up the phone and wrote down his brother's number for BD.

"So when you want me to call, Jo'?"

"ASAP, nigga! I'll have a number soon as I touch! I don't play, BD. Bowers said I'll do like four days in the M unit, then…Skurr! I'm gone!" He made the sound effect of a tire spinning off. BD laughed a bit.

"Alright Jo', I gotcha!"

"Nawl, I got you!"

"Earle Barber! Let's go, grab your things," the CO said, pushing the cart toward Freak Zeenie.

"Alright, this it, my nigga, you up next." Freak Zeenie dapped BD up one last time. He hated to leave his man, but he had to go. "I gotcha, BD, I'm 'bout to get on top of everything soon as I touch. That's my word, my nigga." He looked BD in his eyes.

BD knew it was real from the seriousness in Freak Zeenie's eyes. He just nodded his head, no more words needed. Freak Zeenie dropped out the unit, head high, chest out, smiling like the boss he was. Never looking back, not once, or speaking to anyone else.

Chapter 2
Four Days Later

"Earlie Barber! all the way!" the CO said, unlocking the cell for him to come out.

"'Bout time!" Freak Zeenie said, damn near knocking the CO down trying to get out the cell, out the unit, and off the prison grounds. He had been up waitin' to leave since 4 a.m.

"Damn, watch out! They gone let you go!" the CO said, stepping back.

"I'm gone make show, shiiid. I just gave back a life sentence. I ain't gone be happy till I get the fuck off the premises," he said, already down the stairs and waiting by the door. Everyone was bangin' on the doors and trying to holler at Freak Zeenie, but he was too amped to talk. Freak Zeenie wanted to see his family. He had been around them niggas for twelve years too long.

Due to such short notice and the pandemic, the postal service was behind across the nation. Freak Zeenie had to dress out in prison-issued clothes. He didn't care, though. As long as he was free was all that mattered. Freak Zeenie was dressed in the blink of an eye. Next, he was signing all the release papers that were to be signed before one could leave the premises.

"Ok, Mr. Barber, here you go," the CO said, handing him his debit card and his bus ticket. "It will be a two-hour delay before your bus arrives, so don't get into any trouble, ok."

"Aight, aight, man, I understand. I don't mean to be rude or nothing, but I got this. I'm ready to get to that world! I don't know what trouble is if y—"

"Freak Zeenieee..." CO Willis said, coming in for his shift, calling Earlie Barber by his alias that he had overheard someone call him in the unit on several occasions.

"Who you talking to, Willis?" Freak Zeenie said, frowned up at the CO.

"You! They done released the wrong person, ain't it?"

Freak Zeenie stuck his middle finger up at CO Willis and silently mouthed fuck you. "Alright, Rue Paul, stay up. I see you

17

forgot your wig today! That baldhead a good look for ya!" The female CO burst out in laughter, as did Freak Zeenie.

"You got me, you got me with that one, Barber. Good luck," CO Willis said, knowing he favored the drag queen. CO Willis went on his way as Freak Zeenie was being released into the parking lot. A cab awaited Freak Zeenie's presence to transport him to the bus station in Orlando, Florida.

***

Forty-Five Minutes Later…

Freak Zeenie stepped out the cab with his few belongings. The Greyhound bus station was on 555 N. John Young Pkwy, in Orlando, Florida. First thing he noticed was a burgundy Rolls Royce parked out front.

"Damn! That bitch bad right there! I got to get me one of them," he said, to no one in particular.

"Which one? Me or her?" the dark-skinned stallion said, pointing to herself then to a short, thick yellow bone who was standing next to her. They both seemed to magically appear out of thin air.

He looked at the both of them head to toe, giving a silent approval. The dark-skinned stallion was tall with curves that graced her in all the right places. She was designed from head to toe by Fendi. The yellow bone could have passed for a supermodel. She was just on the short side for one, standing at 4'11 bare feet. Dior acuminated her elegant skin. They both had a show biz smile as they stood there pigeon toed.

"Shiiid, all three of y'all to be for real, for real, hell yah talkin' 'bout!" Freak Zeenie said, the two women looked around for the third female but didn't see one. When they looked back to him, he was pointing to the exotic sedan that he was originally speaking of in the first place.

"Freak Zeenie, huh? How you come up with that name?" the dark-skinned stallion said, pussy oozing from the thought of getting her back blown out from the boss she'd heard much about. On top of that, prison dick was the best dick, which all her home girls had been telling her. She was desperate to find out.

"How you know me?" a surprised expression plastered onto his face.

"Levi," the dark-skinned stallion said, which made Freak Zeenie a bit suspicious. Knowing how much dirt he had committed in the past caused him to stay paranoid and highly alert. On top of that, Freak Zeenie was far from being slow. He knew that a bitch was the fastest way to trick a nigga, and before you knew it, you would have a bust down shelf getting dirt thrown on top of your casket in someone's graveyard.

"Levi?" Glancing 'round, Freak Zeenie didn't see Levi anywhere in sight. "Levi who? I don't know no Levi, fuck you talking 'bout?" he proclaimed.

The ladies wore a serious expression as the tension became thicker by the second from the silence that enveloped them. "Levi Maddox, your brother. You do have a brother by that name, right? Or have you been absent from society that long that you forgot?" the dark-skinned stallion said, staring deep into his eyes.

Freak Zeenie wasn't going, though. He just scratched his head for a second. "Um... Let me think. I know so many people I—" Before he could finish his sentence, the dark-skinned stallion's phone interrupted him as it came to life with a rap ringtone.

"Hello? Yep! Acting like he don't know you for some reason or another." She looked at Freak Zeenie as she continued to talk ghetto-like on the phone, rolling her eyes and neck. "Hold on. Here." She reached out, handing the phone to Freak Zeenie.

"Who this?" Freak Zeenie took the phone reluctantly after looking at it in her hand a split second.

"Surprise! Man, get your ass in the car, bruh! Nigga, we ain't got all day, fool. You know damn well we couldn't let you ride no motherfuckin' bus home, nigga! You a boss, and bosses get chauffeured and charter on PJ's, you heard!" Levi said on the other end of the phone.

Freak Zeenie laughed at his little brother. "I know that's right! Where you?"

"In Tampa at the clear port, gettin' domed up from a Spanish flight attendant. Waitin' on you, bruh. Come, come! all your wardrobe here waitin' on you. I sent two of my hoes to come slide on you real fast while I put some shit in motion on some more shit. I'll see you when you get here!"

Freak Zeenie was smilin' ear to ear 'cause he could hear the slurpin' sounds from the flight attendant as she served his little brother. "Aight b—" The line went dead. Levi had hung up on him already.

"I'm Poochie," the dark-skinned stallion finally introduced herself.

"I'm Remy Red, let's get the fuck out this joint," she said, and headed toward the 2021 Phantom Rolls Royce struttin' her ass off.

"That's right! What that juice box hittin' foe what I'm talkin' 'bout, though... Shiiid." Freak Zeenie was behind them admiring the sight that was being displayed. Their ass cheeks were dancing to their own beat with every step, causing all eyes to watch the show until the chauffer got out, opening the back suicide door for them to enter.

"You gone find out," Remy Red looked over her shoulder replying.

"Nawl, lil' mama, you cool, but I was talking to her. What's 'er name?" Freak Zeenie waved his hand as he slid in the car.

"Poochie!"

"Yeah, Coochie!"

"Poochie, nigga!" she said, looking back, smiling.

"That's what I meant...Poochie. I want some coochie." He shook his head as they all got in and got seated for the hour and a half trip to Tampa Airport.

"Like I was sayin', I don't do red, h...oes—ok...ok. Shit now, for real." Before he could finish talking, Remy Red had his dick in her wet, hot, watery mouth, giving Freak Zeenie some fire head, and he couldn't protest. Freak Zeenie put his hand on the back of her head and laid his head back, reclining in the captain seats enjoying the sensation. All the while, Poochie directed her home girl on how to serve him. Poochie fingered herself to the same rhythm until she creamed over her two fingers as Freak Zeenie blew Remy Red's wig off. Literally.

When she finished, Freak Zeenie opened his eyes, face balled up like be bit a sour lemon, fist clenched with a red wig in between it. "Got damn," was all he could manage to say, breathing hard like he had just run a marathon. Freak Zeenie looked at Remy Red, noticing she only wore a stocking cap on her head. Then he looked at his hand and smiled. "My bad, here." He gave her wig back.

***
An Hour and a Half Later

The burgundy Phantom Rolls Royce pulled into Tampa Airport. Levi stood outside the private jet talking into his iPhone 12. He was draped in all-white linen with white Gucci loafers, wicks hangin' to his waistline, seemingly havin' a serious conversation. Once Levi spotted the Phantom, he hung up without further instructions. "Yeah, yeah, yeah. Just line everything the fuck up and do what I say… Damn!"

Before the car could stop, Levi was opening the back door. First thing he noticed was Remy Red's wig was on crooked. "Damn! What happened to you? Levi studied her as he teased her a little.

"Nothing!" she said, getting out headed toward the awaiting jet. Levi watched her for a split second.

"Welcome home, bruh!" Levi helped Freak Zeenie out, and they embraced in a brotherly hug. "'Bout time they release a boss! They done let all them lames go." They walked slowly toward the private jet, and Poochie was trailing right behind them.

"Hell yeah, that bitch ass nigga Big Man been out when he was the main reason all this shit happened. Lame ass, snitchin' bitch! Then I heard gotdayum E-Dub's pussy ass been out here too on a 5K1. Bitch ass nigga had thirty years and did eight years. Got a rule thirty-five." 5K1 is a downward departure, meaning you worked for the government on their behalf for your behalf. A rule 35 is when an individual cooperates after sentencing, to get a downward departure.

"Yeah, I heard 'bout that fuck nigga. The word is, he all the way up too, bruh. How the fuck is anyone still fucking with his Stewart Little ratting ass.

"He a bad motherfucker, ain't it?" 'Cause money make niggas blind to the fact of reality. They have no principle or morals, my nigga." Freak Zeenie shook his head, getting mad from the new information. He was having a hard time hearing about his once longtime partner, E-Dub, whose government name was Eric Horn.

"Nawl, he should be a dead motherfucker you ask me." Levi wore a scowl expression, entering the jet as the door vacuum sealed shut behind them.

"You know they let sis go a few months ago on compassionate release too." Freak Zeenie got comfortable in the plush seats, strapping himself in with the seat belt.

"Yeah, I saw the homecoming party on the Gram. They went all out for her too. Like the queen she is. It was well deserved," Levi said, strapping himself in, preparing for takeoff.

Once the plane was safely in the air, Freak Zeenie got up and went to get Poochie.

"Come on, Coochie," he said, pulling her by the hand. "Let me show you what these burpees did to a nigga." Freak Zeenie jumped down and did one burpee. He looked back. "We'll be right back." Remy Red started to get up too. "Where you going? I told you, well, I tried to tell you, I don't do red hoes no more. Done that already!" The bathroom door shut strongly right in her face.

The sound of a sex episode could be heard loudly throughout the private jet. Freak Zeenie mutted Poochie's back out, getting twelve years of pressure off his chest. Levi welcomed Freak Zeenie home to the Mile High Club.

When Freak Zeenie came out, Levi had it all laid out for 'em. A forty-one MM Skydweller Rolex, all gold. The white buffs sat on the coffee table in its case. Next to it was a cool honey bun (a hundred thousand cash), all blue-face hundreds. There were high-top Saint Laurent sneakers, white Balmain shorts, a Saint Laurent belt, and a fitted V-neck Saint Laurent tee shirt. A small black velvet box with 5-carat solitary VVS earrings was the last thing he examined.

Freak Zeenie went and took a shower, getting that prison smell off his skin. When he stepped back out, he had shaved his head. Had it *Mr. Clean* shining with a thin mustache. The nigga was clothed in so much white he looked like a thousand grams of pure white cocaine.

***

Minutes Later…

"Please remain seated and buckle up. Prepare for landing in the next fifteen minutes! Clear skies today, temperature is at a mild 73 degrees. Winds calm in the city of Montgomery, Alabama," the pilot spoke over the intercom as they approached the Montgomery skyline.

"Shiiid, I still got plenty time, bruh. What we gone do for the next six hours?" Freak Zeenie asked, looking at a city he hated but loved to see after twelve long years of his absence.

"We'll figure something out, nigga!" Levi said bluntly. He was in deep thought, thinking 'bout all the people who had counted his brother, Freak Zeenie, out.

"I'm with ya, bruh, you got it," Freak Zeenie said, looking through his white buffs, seeing the world through new lenses.

"Oh yeah, bruh, I damn near forgot! You know your gurl done moved back to Dothan from the 'A,' nigga?"

"Who?" Freak Zeenie said, taking his attention off his touch screen phone that he was desperately trying to operate.

"Khashia," Levi said, smiling nonchalantly.

"Khashia? When?"

"Shit, 'bout six or eight months ago, and been worrying the fuck out a nigga 'bout ya." Levi unbuckled his seat belt and got up, then stretched while waiting for the door to open up on the jet.

"Yeah…That's my bitch, got to get me some of that pussy now. Gurl got that pook on 'er. What else she said? Who she been fucking with? How the bit—"

"Nigga, fuck I look like? Call 'er and find out! Fuck wrong with you?" Levi said, not wanting to tell him that she was fucking with the opps, but giving Freak Zeenie Khashia's number before stepping off the jet.

"Who you talking to like that, nigga?" Freak Zeenie said, right behind him, after putting the number in his phone. They talked shit all the way to the silver 63 G-wagon. Freak Zeenie got in the luxury Jeep and felt comfortable. He was back in his element like he had never left. If you didn't know him, you wouldn't have known he just did twelve years in a federal VSP.

It's on!

Levi sent a text before pulling off out the parking lot.

Chapter 3
Two and a Half Hours Away...
Tallahassee, Florida

A triple-white Range Rover pulled slowly onto Holton Street, coming to a stop behind a pineapple-gold, '71 donk (Impala) sittin' on 30-inch Forgiatos. The streets were filled with old skools and foreign cars on both sides.

Heavy traffic continually moved through back and forth. Stopping at different houses, staying at some longer than others, people were standing 'round talking all kinds of shit. A dice game could be seen going on in the distance of one yard. Just two yards over was a dog fight, a bunch of loud talkin', and big old bettin' going on. Dirt bikes were zipping up and down the street catwalking. The hoes were damn near naked walking through the hood popping their asses, mingling with different types of niggas trying to get chose.

After a few minutes, E-Dub finally ended his call, stepping out of the white Range Rover.

"Lil' Tee, what they do, my nigga?" he said, dapping Lil' Tee up while scanning the area at the same time.

"Ain't shit! Aye, Dub, I was just tellin' Main 'bout them lil' bad ass hoes we snatched from FAMU," Lil' Tee bragged, waving his hands 'round animatedly.

"Boy, you know I already done hot god that hoe and her home girl, bitch!"

"Noooo!" Lil' Tee said, steppin' back in surprise.

"Boy, hell yeah, bitch, you know the Dub don't play, boy. Had to double back on you before you got me. Smoked them hoes right quick. And guess what?"

"What?"

"I got the keys to the cribbb!" E-Dub held the keys up in his hand for them to see. "You know how the Dub do. Just another spot we can use to handle some shit from, stash some shit at, all that and some more shit! Ain't no pressure," he said, putting the keys back in his pocket.

"Bitch, you a dirty dog!" Lil' Tee said, shaking his head, looking at E-Dub through hateful eyes.

"On some other shit, bitch, I need to holla at ya right fast! Come hop in the truck with me." E-Dub put his arm 'round Lil' Tee's neck, walking him back to the Range Rover. He missed the jealousy in Lil' Tee's eyes.

"What the business is?" Lil' Tee leaned on the door, looking at E-Dub.

"Check it out, I just touched a thirty piece of that good ice cream, bitch! All I want is seven apiece for each of 'em. I don't care what you make, nigga. I already know you gone go off." E-Dub rubbed his nose after he finished. Ice cream was the code for meth.

"Hell yeah, bitch, you know Lil' Tee gone get 'em gone in a New York minute. Ain't no pressure."

"A'ight, I'll get 'em to you later tonight then, and we'll go from there."

"Bet that."

"Gone get us some extra play money for the Sunshine State concert T-Pain 'bout to throw for um, Kodak Black. Know Trump freed that boy before they got his fuck ass up out of office." E-Dub checked his mirrors out of habit.

"Yeah, they been promoting the fuck out the concert, giving free tickets away and shit all month."

"Bitch gone be lit now! T-Pain got everybody performing, City Girls, Trina old ass, and Trick Daddy, Poppa Duck, DJ Khaled mixing it up. Pitbull, Blood Raw, Kodak Black, with Uncle Luke hosting that bitch! A'ight! Shit, at Club Moon? Nigga, this city gone be live!"

"Hell yeah, bitch, already," Lil' Tee said just as a black four-door Porsche pulled up alongside them, tapping the horn twice. The passenger window came down on the Porsche.

"Say, who need some money! It's help the homeless day, poor ass nigga!" Horse Head said, showing a black duffel bag full of blue benjees (hundred-dollar bills), leaning over his homie, Paco, to flex on E-Dub and them.

"Nigga, if that's the case, you better keep that shit then, bitch!" 'Cause we all know you still leasing that baby mansion, bitch," E-Dub said, dapping Lil' Tee up to flex back on Horse Head and Paco.

"Got me fucked up, bitch! I run this shit, boy! Fuck you talking 'bout?"

"Since when? You know this my city! And don't ah bitch eat unless I say so, fuck wrong with cha? Now come on with that lil' bread you owe me, bitch! So I can fix your broke ass a plate!" E-Dub was holding a serious facial expression but couldn't hold it. He bust out laughing hard. He knew he had gotten under Horse Head's skin. Even though E-Dub was dead ass serious, he lightened the matter, and his words were true. They all knew it. E-Dub had the city talking.

"M-M-Man, w-when y-you g-got th-that b-bitch right t-there, H-Horse Head? Th-that bitch c-clean as a m-mutherfucker b-boy!" Main said as he walked over stuttering his ass off.

Horse Head let his window up. "Paco? You heard this slow ass nigga? Talking 'bout he run the city? Slow ass lame bitch! Nigga from Mariana."

"Yeah, I heard that bitch! They shoulda been done killed that nigga!" Paco said, clutching the Draco that sat between his legs.

"This bitch ass nigga sweating me 'bout ten bands for a dog fight. 'Fore I pay that nigga, Jesus gone rise from the dead. He can chalk that!"

The black Porsche squatted down in the back, catching a tire as the tail lights got small to E-Dub and them and just like that, Horse Head was gone, never answering Main's question.

Two black motorcycles pulled off right behind Horse Head, who had been in the cut silently waiting, weaving in and out of traffic, trying desperately not to lose sight of the Turbo S Porsche. Just as the motorcycles were gaining on Horse Head, he veered off, turning into the gas station pulling up to pump three.

"Damn!" Lil' Tay said, bringing his bike up on its front tire in the middle of the street before turning around and zooming back in the direction they had just come. His partna did the exact same stunt.

They had been going way too fast to make the sharp turn into the gas station the first time.

Horse Head sat there texting while Paco twisted up a cigarillo. Horse Head looked up suddenly from the loud roaring sound the powerful engine made just as Lil' Tay pulled up to pump four right beside them. Lil' Tay's twin sister pulled up behind him and dropped her kickstand. She got off her bike, walking toward the entrance of the store.

"Damn, that bitch bad! Who that?" Horse Head said, finishing his text and getting out the car hastily, en route behind the twin. "Aye, miss lady?"

Shawnta turned around swiftly, Glock 40 in hand.

Blocka, Blocka!

At the same time, Lil' Tay commenced to hitting at the passenger side of the Porsche.

Blocka, Blocka!

Horse Head took off running, dropping his phone and all, caught completely off guard. Shawnta was right behind him. Horse Head was zig zagging good, looking like a modern-day Randy Moss trying to shake his opponent. "Fuck!" he mumbled as a bullet whizzed by his head, barely missing him.

Blaka, Blaka!

Paco let off a series of lucky shots, luckily tearing of half of Lil' Tay's helmet, taking some of his head along with it, stopping and dropping him in his tracks instantaneously, but not before Paco took an arm wound in the midst of it all. "Bitch ass nigga!" Paco crawled into the driver seat, throwing the car in drive, stompin' the gas to the floor. Fishtailing out the gas station onto Tennessee Street, he left the clerk on the phone in shock.

Horse Head was running out of breath, so he began to slow down, regretting the whole time leaving his pistol in the console of his car before getting out. Shawnta was persistent as she paced herself like a pro. As long as she didn't lose sight of Horse Head, she was sure she would get her man. In broad daylight, she was still shooting at him every few seconds. Shawnta had a 30-round clip slapped up under her 40 Glock.

Horse Head did something he didn't usually do. He gave up. Horse Head turned around, hands on his knees, out of breath. Shawnta steadied her aim. Their intentions were to rob him at first, but now it was murder since Horse Head ran, causing a scene. Horse Head closed his eyes. He didn't want to see death coming.

Paco came flying out of nowhere, slamming the car into Shawnta, knocking her fifteen feet into the air. She collided with a power line, and the massive current knocked her motorcycle suit and helmet completely off. The electricity killed Shawnta instantly. The power shut off all down Tennessee Street.

"Nigga! Got damn! You a motherfuckin' life saver! I love yah!" Horse Head said, all out of breath. He rushed to the back door, getting into the backseat as Paco stomped on the gas, rushing from out of harm's way to safety.

"I told you long ago, pussy gone be the death of you!" Paco said. Horse Head closed his eyes for the remainder of the ride home.

***

Later That Night...

Horse Head and Paco listened to the news anchor after the veteran finished sewing Paco's wounded arm up, quickly leaving as fast as he came.

"Earlier today, a horrific shooting took place on Tennessee Street at the Amaro gas station, leaving two dead and a male who was partially decapitated from a series of gunshots. Further down the street, a female was found with her clothes blown off after being knocked in the air into a power line, which caused a power outage throughout half the city. Video footage captured most of this among other eyewitnesses. The suspects are still at large. If anyone has more information, please call 1-800-tips. A black Porsche, license plate #—" Horse Head cut the TV off, lit the blunt, and inhaled it, blowing out a rich, thick cloud of weed smoke. Eyes lowering almost instantly, Horse Head knew that he had to lay low for a minute and either paint his car or sell it.

***

E-Dub dropped off the 30 bricks of ice cream to Lil' Tee just as promised. While they sat in his truck discussing the business, E-Dub noticed the news alert illuminating his phone, which caught his attention. "You see this?" he asked, passing his phone to Lil' Tee. "Should have killed his clown ass! Ain't paid me—" E-Dup stopped mid-sentence, keeping the rest of his thoughts in his mind.

"Damn! They put that bitch on the power line, dog! I was wondering what the hell the power was out for earlier," Lil' Tee said, finding the situation a little funny.

E-Dub wasn't laughing at all. He wished that all of 'em were dead if it was up to him. He already felt played by Horse Head and was beginning to think that Horse Head wasn't going to pay him for real. Especially after the way Horse Head had fronted on him earlier that day.

"A'ight, bitch. I got a date with a playmate. Too bad I can't say the same for your no pussy gettin' ass. Don't you trip, though. I'm gone fuck something for the both of us. I'll fuck witcha a lil' later, partna!"

E-Dub dapped Lil' Tee up and hit the unlock button on the truck. He waited until Lil' Tee made it safely in the house with the duffle bag full of product. E-Dub pulled off with Horse Head on his mind heavily.

Chapter 4

Freak Zeenie sat in the back of the halfway house enjoying the spring sun at Dismas Charity. A few of the housed inmates were still there, either because they didn't have a job or they had to wait until their three-day probation period was up. That's exactly why Freak Zeenie was there. He was patiently waiting for his three days to be up. Freak Zeenie had only been at the halfway house for a day. He was just dying to experience his shot of freedom.

Freak Zeenie had witnessed all the mask-wearing stuff on CNN News, but being out in it in reality was as surreal as it would get. He was sitting quietly observing and absorbing his surroundings from behind an expensive Gucci COVID-19 face mask.

Ms. Netta came walking out the back door hauling that big ole mule ass on her back. *Damn! She toting that big ole ass*, Freak Zeenie thought to himself, eyes glued on Ms. Netta until she stopped directly in front of him.

"Mr. Barber?" she said, one hand on her hip, the other hand holding on to a chip board. Ms. Netta was Amazon thick with a mocha skin complexion to compliment her beauty. A real country woman from out of Haynesville, Alabama.

"Yeah, what's up?"

"Today is your lucky day."

"Nall! How you know that? You sho' right now? It is Wednesday, what you got going on, Ms. Netta?"

Ms. Netta smiled, but she didn't know what Freak Zeenie was talking 'about exactly. So, she just nodded her head anyway. "Because, due to the COVID-19, sir, we need extra bed space. Your name is one of the people who came up on the list to be able to go home on leg monitor. So, you need to come in so you can sign these papers. Then you need to call someone to come get you where you will be staying. It had to be someone with a landline too," she said, turning that mule ass 'round for him to get a full view as she headed back inside the building.

"Thank you, Jesus." Freak Zeenie was right on her heels, dialing numbers on his track phone, the ones without cameras and internet.

"Oh now? What's up with it, bruh?" Levi answered.

"You ain't gone believe this, lil' bruh!" Freak Zeenie said, making it to the front desk.

"What's that? What happened?" Levi sat up in his Alaska King bed. "Hold on, hold on. Watch out for a minute!" He damn near had to pry Remy Red from off of his dick. It was like Remy Red was glued on his dick, sucking Levi dry.

"Boy, God is good! Nigga they just let me know I'm going home on leg monitor—"

"When?"

"Today! I need you to get up here ASAP!"

"Damn! A'ight, shit! I'm on it now! I'll be there in like a hour, bruh," Levi said, jumping up, rushing to put his clothes on.

"Bet that. Make it forty-five, nigga, c—"

Levi hung up on him.

Freak Zeenie was still talking until he heard the dial tone. He looked at his phone. "Nigga crazy, man." He hit redial.

"Yeah! Nigga, I j—"

"Man, what the address, ole crazy ass nigga? And do you have a landline? 'Cause I have to have one."

"Yeah, yeah, yeah, um, three, three—"

"Nigga, I know all that! What's the last seven?"

"Seven-one-four-eleven-seventy-seven, and the address is 1912 Brentwood Road," Levi said.

"Aight bruh, hurry up, I'm ready t—" Once again, Freak Zeenie found himself talking to a dial tone.

Freak Zeenie just shook his head, putting his phone in his small pocket. Thinking to himself 'about all the things he had been waiting twelve years to do, that he thought he might not get a chance to do, had finally became reality. Khashia came across his mind. I'm 'bout to fuck the shit out you, lil' red ass bitch. Matter fact, let me call 'er right quick. He pulled his phone back out and dialed her number as he pulled up a chair and started filling out the papers Ms.

Netta had sat in front of him. Khashia's phone went straight to voicemail. "Fuck it! I'll catch 'er," he said.

***

An Hour and Thirty Minutes Later…

Levi pulled up to the halfway house ridin' dolo in a triple-black 911 Porsche. Freak Zeenie came out carrying his belongings to the front of the car. The hood popped, which was the trunk.

Levi had his earbuds in talking away on one phone while texting expertly on another. "Right… yeah… Shiiid… Say no more, partna! Well, I'm outta town right now as we speak. Fa'sho. Soon, soon." Levi nodded his head in agreement as he glanced in all his mirrors.

"Later!" He hung up, finishing up his text at the same time. He cut the phone off as Freak Zeenie shut the trunk on the 911. Levi slid the phone he was texting on up under the seat.

"'Bout time you made it here, nigga. Damn!" Freak Zeenie said, opening the door and sliding in.

"Yeah, I know right. Shiiid, what? You gotta be somewhere at a particular time or somethin', nigga? I'm important! What can I say." Levi reached behind the passenger seat. "Here, put this on." He handed Freak Zeenie a black salon plastic bag.

Freak Zeenie took the bag and opened it up, studying the contents carefully for a second before a smile rose across his face. "Nigga, ya stupid as fuck! Fuck I want a got damn wig for? My hustlin' days over, lil' bruh." He closed the bag back up, sitting it down on the floorboard of the car. Then he put his seat belt on, sitting back ready to be chauffeured to Dothan, Alabama, a city he hadn't seen in over a decade.

"Nigga, that's called a disguise! Don't nobody know you home yet, and that's how I want to keep it for a while. Let me do this! I got a lotta shit going on! All that rides in my whips is bitches, big bruh. No niggas! So put that shit the fuck on real fast, and let's go," Levi said, as he finally found the song he was looking for. He touched the seven-inch screen in the center of the dashboard. The track by Pooh Shiesty, "Call See Red," came on from off of the *Shiesty Season* album. Levi started bobbing his head hard with a unit on his face as he turned it up, pulling off from the halfway house.

Everybody 'round me see red/Everybody 'round me got one in the head/Shiesty pulled up shootin' they fled/ Shiesty pulled up shootin' they were trying da play dead."

***

Cartier Jay finished reading the text he received then cut his phone off, puttin' it in the glove compartment. He clutched his FN tightly.

"Bitch ass nigga! Time is on your side...for now anyway!" Cartier Jay looked at the house as the man escorted a fine ass yellow bone in the front door. "Unk savin' your lame ass! For what? I don't know! But he better make up his mind soon before I act on my fuckin' own! Give your fuck ass a halo and frisbee that motherfucker, boy!" He talked aloud to himself as he eased off.

Cartier Jay's nuts were sweatin'. He had been waiting for a very long time to cut this man's life short. He could hardly wait to get his hands on all that cash.

Chapter 5
A Day Later

The next morning, Freak Zeenie was up before sunrise. He already had completed an hour-long workout and took a shower. Freak Zeenie had gotten approved for all the moves he needed to make for the week that he put into the kiosk before departing from the halfway house.

This morning Freak Zeenie was going to the license office, which was located on West Lena Street. Freak Zeenie was surprised when he got approved for this move because he asked for six hours, knowing it only took two tops. He wanted to use the extra time to move around a little before he headed back home. Freak Zeenie had finally reached Khashia late last night, and they had shared a bunch of explicit text messages. Now, he wanted to execute his plan smoothly and stop by her place for some good morning pussy.

Levi was up bright and early also. As Freak Zeenie exited the bathroom, Levi walked barefoot across the shiny hardwood floor toward the den.

"What's up, lil' bruh? See you up early. Fuck you got going on?" Freak Zeenie said, eyeing Levi suspiciously.

"No sleep. Way too much money to be made, bruh. Wayyy too much," Levi said. Texting, he turned into the den without looking back.

Freak Zeenie walked into his bedroom just as the screen on his phone blinked off. Thinking he got a text from Khashia, he picked it up and slid his finger in a L shape to unlock the screen. "Ump." He sat the phone down after he witnessed nothing new. Freak Zeenie began to get dressed. Little did he know, Levi had held his phone up to see Freak Zeenie's L pattern smeared on the screen. Levi had unlocked it and read Freak Zeenie's and Khashia's texts, storing the info he needed right before Freak Zeenie exited the bathroom.

By the time Freak Zeenie came out of his bedroom getting dressed, Levi was already gone. Freak Zeenie walked toward the front door to leave.

"Heyy, Freak Zeenie." The sweet sound of Remy Red caught his attention. Remy Red stood there naked in the kitchen holding a glass of orange juice.

"Sup," Freak Zeenie said, walking out the door. It automatically locked behind him. "She wants to fuck a nigga sooo bad. Why not? I'm a king." Freak Zeenie jumped in the triple-black Wraith, snatching off out of the driveway.

*****

Across Town…

"Man, Unk, today the day now. Fuck all that keep waiting shit! Been on this nigga for two motherfucken months since you put me on him. The fuck nigga strap! It's all in that house, you heard! What goes in never comes out. I been put cameras on the nigga's shit, and he don't even know it. Security, yah dig?" He pulled the house up on his iPhone. "See." He leaned over and showed it to his uncle.

"Yeah, yeah, yeah, nephew, that's neat right there now. Today he'll take a permanent dirt nap, yah diggg?"

"Hell yeah." As they watched the house on the phone, they witnessed a triple-black Wraith pull up. "Who the fuck is that? I ain't never seen that car. Now the fuck going on?" They continued to observe the situation.

A short, stocky female got out headed to the front door, holding her head down. They couldn't make out the features of the woman because the dark shades and long hair shielded the majority of her face. The front door came open, the woman quickly entered, and just like that, it closed.

"I thought you said you had everything mapped out, nephew?" he said, trying to remember where he saw that Wraith before but came up empty.

"I did, but the bitch just broke pattern right here because —"

"You can't plan for every fuckin' thing!"

They began to argue. They had been sitting there waiting for their *vic* to pull up. Marcus walked right by their car, headed inside the building he had not long ago purchased, never knowing the

Grim Reapers were only inches away sitting behind the limo tint of the car he swiftly passed.

Marcus a.k.a. Big Man held his head down. He was in deep thought, walking briskly into the building carrying an expensive briefcase. Inside were his important briefings on a new construction of an Amazon warehouse location. Marcus hadn't long inked a deal with the multi-million-dollar corporation.

Marcus had been doing wonderful for himself, especially after getting his record expunged and sweeping a lot of dirt under the rug. He linked up with a few powerful people who were 87 percent the cause for his prospering career. Marcus had his own construction company that was now number one in the Southeast region. With it being so successful, he started using it as a funneling utensil. Marcus had a mean pipeline with the brick of cocaine, locking his region down, never even having to touch one gram of it ever. Thank God for powerful people.

Everything came through the mail and his trucks. Today, Marcus was feeling himself. Since he took his business public, Marcus went from M's aka millions to low budget B's, or billions, annually on paper.

Making it to the elevator right in time before it closed, Marcus stepped on, releasing a whiff of Icy Blast breath. The elevator was packed and everyone was silent for the most part.

I can't believe she said yes! Well...yes, I can. Fuck, I'm rich! The richest nigga she know, hell. Probably will ever know, Marcus thought to himself.

Just two days ago they took out ten-million-dollar insurance policies on one another after he purposed to her. She said yes. Marcus and Khashia had plans to marry in the next six months if the pandemic allowed it.

Marcus stepped off the elevator with super confidence, headed straight into his conference room. Entering the room, it was full of all the main boss players. They all were waiting for him.

"Aight, good morning! Let's get down to business!" Marcus said, putting his briefcase down on the massive, long, expensive oakwood table. Everyone became quiet and attentive. Marcus was the CEO and his presence demanded that type of respect.

***

Across Town...

Khashia stood pigeon toed in pink, see-through boy shorts, staring at Freak Zeenie with confusion on her face. She was having second thoughts about being with him now. The wig Freak Zeenie was wearing was better than one she owned, and it was throwing her off.

"Freak, what in the world? Why are you wearing a fucking wig for? What's going on, baby?" Khashia said, studying his demeanor, crossing her arm over her chest, feeling uncomfortable.

Suddenly, Freak Zeenie wore a devilish smirk. He pulled the wig off. Never taking his eyes off Khashia, he was taking her beauty in all at once wholeheartedly. Freak Zeenie could feel his nature rising with a mind of its own. Khashia had that kind of effect on most men.

"Stop playing with me, girl. You know me better than that now! Fuck wrong with you? This for safety purposes only. No one knows that I'm out but a few very close people. That's how I want to keep it for a while. When I was gone, no one fucked with me. So, I ain't trying to fuck with no one but you. Hell you talkin' 'bout? You know what it is. I'm muthafuckin' Freak Zeenie, BITCH!" He mimicked a line of the great Rick James. Stepping up pulling Khashia to him, he rubbed her hips, reaching 'round grabbing two good hands full of soft yellow ass. Ass spilled through Freak Zeenie's fingers easily like trying to hold onto a half-full water balloon.

Khashia starting unbuckling his pants and Freak Zeenie pulled off his shirt. She grabbed his hand, leading him toward the master bedroom. Khashia entered her bedroom, stopping abruptly. She pulled her boy shorts off, wiggling her phat, voluptuous ass as she bent over, keepin' her legs straight. Freak Zeenie could see her freshly waxed pussy that resembled a ripe peach from the back.

Stepping out of the boy shorts, Khashia carefully took one foot out at a time, careful not to rip her sheer boy shorts with the expensive six-inch pink red bottoms.

"Ok, Daddy, I'm only keeping these on." Khashia lifted her leg up, showin' Freak Zeenie her smooth shaven legs and gorgeous red bottoms. "What's up? I'm ready for the Freak Zeenie show, nigga!" Khashia walked seductively over to the massive king-size bed. Pushing her phone further back on the bed, she bent over, spreading her high-yellow ass cheeks. Khashia smacked her ass a few times, causing it to do an exotic dance of its own, movin' like a Hawaiian dancer. "Well, come and get it! It's been twelve years, right? I don't think you still got it, nigga!" Khashia grabbed the massive bedpost, wrapping her arms 'round it, and made her ass talk to him.

That was it. Freak Zeenie took two steps and was knee deep in Khashia's pussy, fucking her like a porn star. "Yeah, yeah, yeah, throw that ass back! That's what the fuck I'm talking 'bout!" He was holdin' on to the pole, digging all up in Khashia's pussy like a grave digger. Every time he pumped her, the force was pushing Khashia further and further onto the bed. Freak Zeenie had gone animalistic on Khashia. Pulling her hair, smacking her ass hard. He was growling and all. They went from the pole to the end of the bed. He had Khashia crawling tryin' to get away. "Un-hun, bring that ass here! What you was just saying? Hun?!"

Khashia was trying to adjust to a more suitable and comfortable position. Her fingers accidentally brushed against her phone a few times, unbeknown to her. "Yes... ahh, ohh, yesss, right there! Beat it, beat it, beat it! Smack that ass!" Khashia was in pure ecstasy.

Marcus walked from the chalkboard as he had finished up explaining all the exhibits to the room of colleagues. Looking down, he was distracted by the vibrations of his phone.

"Smack that ass! Yeah, yeah, yeah! Oooh...sss! You going *soooo* deep!" Khashia was making all kinds of fuck faces and sounds. Marcus watched in horror, witnessing his fiancée getting her back blown out. He tried desperately to see who the man was but couldn't. Marcus could only see Khashia's face and hands clawing the bed spread.

Marcus was so caught by surprise that he didn't even notice all his colleagues had surrounded him. They were all watching in shock at how Khashia was performing like a real porn star with arousing set sounds.

"BITCH! Is you crazy?" were the words that boomed from Marcus's mouth.

Khashia's eyes popped open in complete shock. "Oh shit!" she managed to say, noticing that her phone was on, and on Facetime at that. At the same time, Freak Zeenie pulled out, yanking her head back by her hair as he skeeted his seed all over her yellow, phat ass.

"I'm gone k—" Marcus's phone went black as Khashia disconnected on him, embarrassed from being caught in her scandalous affair.

Marcus half packed his briefcase, rushing out the conference room in a blur. Pain, confusion, and anger ensconced his face as Marcus descended the steep stairs two at a time.

"Bitch got to be crazy! Got me fucked up! Got a mutherfucker all up in my shit while I'm out here *bussing* my ass making sure we live good! Ol' broke ass hoe 'bout to get the fuck up out my shit! Today!" Marcus talked to himself, making his way down to the first floor.

***

"Hurry the fuck up, nephew!" he said, as he watched out for any witnesses as his nephew slid the flat jack up out the window, unlocking the door of the black S600 Benz without triggering the car's alarm.

"Got it!" he said, sticking a thumb up at his uncle as he got into the back seat on the floor, pulling the door shut just in the nick of time. This was the perfect plan for them to catch old Big Man slipping.

Marcus sprinted to his black S600 Benz, unlocking it with the push of a button. He slung his briefcase over in the passenger seat and crunk up, squealing tires out of the parking lot, leaving a trail of white smoke behind him all the way to the highway.

Marcus's colleagues were cracking up laughing once they looked out the window and were sure Marcus was gone, seeing and hearing the squealing of tires.

"Man, that's fucked up, ain't it?" one of them said.

"Man, hell fuck yeah!" another said.

"That's why I'm single, bitches can't be trusted," another one said, bent over hands on his knees from laughter.

"Says who?" one of the females said, speaking up in defense of the other women in the room, staring holes through the accuser. Everything went silent.

"Says Marcus! Hell you talkin' 'bout, girl! Obviously, you too, 'cause you have gone from peach pie to savage dog! Ha ha." They all shared another round of laughter. Even she had to join in with them, knowing she had given the gay life up.

Man was doing 80 miles an hour in a 30 mile an hour school zone. Marcus ran through red light after red light to get home. Unk was right behind him like three car links.

"Got damnit," Unk said, knowing this could attract the unwanted attention of the law to them. Unk had hands and toes crossed, knowing his nephew was in the back seat of the car with a big old firearm accompanying him.

***

Khashia was rushing Freak Zeenie out the house.

"Listen, you better keep your word. This nigga gone try to trip on a bitch! I don't trust 'em! We just took out ten-million-dollar insurance policies on each other like two days ago. So I don't know what he may try now! But you must go, just call and check on me later, ok?"

She pushed Freak Zeenie out the house, pecking him on the cheek as he adjusted his wig. What she didn't know was how Freak Zeenie's ears went up like a deer from the mention of the policy. His mind went to work ASAP.

"Aight, I got you! Fuck that nigga! He a lame anyhow. I'll hit you once I finish at the license office, ok?"

"Do that!" Khashia slammed the door in his face. She ran up the stairs to the master bedroom, pulled out her Gucci luggage, and started slinging clothes in it left and right. She finished in record time. Khashia ran in the closet, moving the dresser. "Shit! I need to hurry the fuck up!" Punching in a four-digit code, the door came open on the mid-size safe. Grabbing fist fulls of money, she put it inside an oversized pillow case.

No sooner than Freak Zeenie turned two blocks away from Khashia's house, Marcus turned in his driveway, pressing the button causing his garage to raise up as he jetted the car forward. Marcus killed the engine and reached for the door handled.

Whack!

"Araggh, shit!" Marcus grabbed the side of his head to see if he still had his ear attached. Blood oozed through his fingers down his face.

"Shut your bitch ass the fuck up, nigga! Make another move or sound without me instructing you to! Brains and skulls ah be all over this pretty dashboard! Understand, nigga?" He pressed the barrel to the back of Marcus's head for him to get the picture.

"Damn, yeah man! Yeah, whatever you say! Just don't kill me!" *This weak bitch set me the fuck up. Low-down ass bitch!* Thoughts skipped through Marcus's mind while he also thought about all his money inside the house.

Whack!

Another thunderous hit went across Marcus's head, slightly blinding him for a quick second.

"Get the fuck out the mutherfuckin' car, pussy." He climbed over the seat, holding onto the back of Marcus's collar while he kept the pistol trained on him. "Nice and slow. Nice and slow," he said, real calm.

Unk pulled up seconds later, slamming his car in park but leaving it running. Jumping out, his pistol led the way. He sprinted in a crouching position inside the garage, up on Marcus and his nephew.

"Who else in this motherfucker?" Unk asked, knowing the answer to his question already. He pushed Marcus to open the side door.

"Just my fiancée, man, that's it!" Marcus said weakly, sticking the key into the door.

Just as he did, Khashia swung open the door carrying her luggage right behind her, catching everyone by surprise including herself. She almost got herself shot.

"Bitch, get down, get down! Get the fuck down, stupid as hoe!" Unk ran up on her, pushing Khashia down hard to the ground. "Who else in here, bitch?" Grabbing a fist full of her hair, he yanked Khashia further back into the house. Unk waved his pistol 'round, finger on the trigger.

"Nobody but me, I swear! It's just m—"

WHACK, WHACK, WHACK!

Khashia's lights went out. The pistol whipping knocked her unconscious.

"Move, nigga! Move, nigga! You know what we here for, don't it? Fuck nigga, I want it all! Money and dope, or DIE!"

They pushed him forward roughly, causing Marcus to stumble, tripping over his own feet. Marcus fell hard.

"All I got is money here, man! I-I don't sell dope!" Marcus stuttered, managing to say, as he climbed back up to his feet.

WHACK!

Only to be knocked back down.

"Oh, I'm stupid then? You got money here, but it didn't come from dope selling! Is that what you telling me, bruh?"

"Yeah, I think that's what he saying to you, nephew!" Unk said, as he finished tying Khashia up like a hog. With her hands and legs tied behind her back together, she couldn't get loose if her life depended on it. Which it did. Unk picked the pillowcase up, dumping its contents out. "Well, well, well, look ah here. Look like she was 'bout to go on a shopping spree or the run, one! What you think, Marcus?" Unk asked, placing the pillow case over Khashia's head.

Marcus's face flushed the color of a ghost, but he remained silent. *I'm gone kill this stupid bitch if we get the chance to make it out of this situation.* He kept his thoughts a secret.

They snatched Marcus up, forcing him up the stairs in search of the goods.

***

Freak Zeenie made it back home unnoticed from the license place. Sitting on the back porch watching the sunset, he was enjoying his freedom. The wind blew lightly, easing in through the screened-in porch.

The strong buzz started to creep up on him as he continued to sip Remy Red on the rocks. Even though Freak Zeenie had texted Khashia over eighteen times, she still had not replied yet.

"Now she tell me to hit her up and now her ass still won't answer. Just like a bitch," he said, then tried Levi's number again for the umpteenth time to get no answer either. "Where the hell this nigga at? Ain't no telling. Fuck it! I'm free, so let it be!"

Freak Zeenie picked his laptop up and started working on his non-profit business plan, The Change of Heart Program. This was something he longed to do. Freak Zeenie wanted to give back to the community and help as many people as he could to change their lives so they would not have to experience what he did or went through to enjoy life.

Chapter 6
Tallahassee, Florida
Club Moon

Since President Biden, Moneybagg Joe what they call him, had reached his goal of a hundred million COVID-19 shots in his first ninety days, the governor had fully opened the whole state back up. Business was booming like a box Chevy with four fifteens in the trunk with no insulation.

The streets were packed to capacity. Cars were coming into the parking lot from all sides of town to Club Moon. Club Moon was a popular club, if not the most popular club in Tallahassee, Florida.

Tonight was a Kodak moment. It was a welcome home Kodak theme going on for the Sunshine State concert. Everybody and their momma came out for it.

VIP was jam packed. Box players from all over the states showed up to show support for the homie Kodak Black. Sparkling bottles could be seen from every angle you turned your head. That mullah (money) was definitely in the building. President Biden just cut them second-round stimulus checks too. Had the females glamorized up to a tee. FAMU, TCU, TTC, and Florida State University were also in the building going hard reppin' their schools. You could feel the good vibes in Club Moon tonight.

E-Dub sat in VIP in all white, drenched in diamonds. Twinkles sparkled like a disco-ball was spinning round and round with E-Dub's every movement. He was chillin' at the table closest to the front with his homie, Lil' Tee.

E-Dub and Lil' Tee had their table covered with Ace of Spades and Louis 13. Strange thing was, E-Dub didn't even drink, though. He was settin' it all out, flexin' and flossin' hard on 'em. Surrounded by so many bitches you would have thought that the party was for them.

"I told you this bitch was gone be *live*, bitch," E-Dub said, grabbin' a Simply orange juice, turning it up.

"Man, I'm high as mutherfucker, bitch! That shit straight pressure you laid on me, you heard," Lil' Tee said, clear enough over the loud music for E-Dub to hear. Lil' Tee couldn't seem to control his knees from shaking up and down. They were moving fast from the line of all the icc he'd consumed.

"I already know! Everything the Dub drop be A-1, bitch! I'm E-Dub! Name hold weight! Literally! The E stands for everybody. Dub mean, they want to copy. Everybody want to Dub what I do, bitch, 'cause I do it well," Sitting his orange juice down, E-Dub smacked the female who sat in his lap on her ass twice. "Aye, get up for a minute. I need some me time with my dawg." The sexy female didn't move fast enough for his liking. "I said, bitch, get your funky ass the fuck up! You can't motherfuckin' hear or somthin'?" Smackin' her lips, face flushed from embarrassment, the sexy female reluctantly removed herself off his lap, making her way through the VIP. E-Dub waited till she was out of eye shot. "Man, I got somin' else for you, bitch!" E-Dub leaned in toward Lil' Tee, rubbing his hands together, making the diamond bracelet and bezel of sky dwella dance with each other.

"What? Some more of that there? 'Cause man, the streets eating that shit the fuck up, bitch!" Lil' Tee said, sticking his straw in his personal bag, sneaking a few sniffs while they were alone.

"Yeah, you know I'm still strapped up on that tip, but I just came up on some straight clean, bitch. I'm talking 'bout by the truck loads, nigga! Just met a b—" E-Dub cut his words short as the orange juice just abruptly splashed in his face and all over his fresh white fit. For a second, he thought the female had thrown it in his face, until he looked around. He was feeling very disrespected. "Aye, aye nigga?" Jumpin' up, face balled up, he rushed behind the person of interest who just kept it moving. His ten-thousand-dollar fit ruined from orange juice and a mixture of alcohol beverages all over it. E-Dub reached out for the dude's shoulder. "Aye, motherfucker! You heard me."

"Nawl nigga! I ain't heard shit but music. Heard what? Fuck should I have heard, fool?" The dude took a good look at him, then his grimace turned to a shocked expression. "Ohh shit, dawg! Look at your shit! Fuck happen to you, fool? Damn," the short Spanish dude said, with a mouth full of gold. He was smiling but broiling on the inside. He'd purposely walk by bumping into the table hard enough to knock over everything, hopin' to stir E-Dub up.

"Nigga, fuck you mean? You just knocked my shit off the table, ole clown ass motherfucker! Do you know who the fuck I am?" E-Dub pointed to himself then spread his arms out. "You just ruined my ten thousand-dollar fit plus"—he looked back at his table—"another fifteen in beverages, nigga! Who gone cover that, you?" E-Dub stood there muggin' the short, stocky Spanish guy down, waiting for the right or wrong response.

"Hell yeah, bitch! You gone pay, right?" Lil' Tee said, holding the Ace of Spades bottle by the neck as a weapon.

The short Spanish guy stared at them through a bleak expression. "No need for the disrespect, dawg. Is that it?" He went in his pocket, comin' out with a cabbage head full of straight hundred-dollar bills. "Nawl, I don't know who you are and care not to, but my fault for the damages, partner. I'm Chico D, though, ah cash vault, homie. Here, this should cover it." Chico D cashed E-Dub out a quick twenty-five bands out of his pocket, all in hundred-dollar bills. "You should be careful how you talk to people. You never know who you might bump into." He looked in E-Dub's eyes then spun off.

E-Dub looked at the bills, inspecting them all in the same. Nodding his head, he looked at Chico D's back. "Fa'sho, partna, bet that. You good, you good," he said. E-Dub was still mad, though, because he had to leave and go change then try to make it back in time. Knowing all along that he would miss most of the performances if not all of 'em, but he had to change. He looked at Lil' Tee. "Aye bruh, look at this duck ass Chico. Introducing himself, talkin' all that gangsta shit like he livin' like that! Nigga, who give a fuck? Nigga don't even know a nigga and came off twenty-five bands." They both bust out laughing. "Look bruh, shiiid, I got to go change right fast, a'ight?"

"Yeah, I gotcha, bruh. Be safe and hurry back, bitch! This bitch 'bout to sauce up!" Lil' Tee dapped him up then made his way to the stage where the City Girls were twerkin', performing their latest songs after JT was recently released.

Chico D pulled his phone out, making it back to his table.

He on his way out now! All white with orange juice all over him! Chico D pressed send, sending the text out.

Bet. We on it.

A text came back, and Chico D read it then put his phone up.

"Now, where was I?" Chico D smiled a gold-toothed smile at the two fine Spanish women, getting his mack on in the pandemic.

E-Dub made it to the parking lot. It had started drizzling lightly. That didn't stop nothin' or slow nothin' up. The cut line was moving along at about the same pace as the regular one. They were just wasting money to prove that they weren't regular.

"Damn, E-Dub, what happened to you?" a female said, noticing the stains on his clothes as he passed by.

"Girl, ain't no telling. Probably done got a drink thrown on him from getting caught up with his hoeish ass self!" another female said, standing behind her getting rained on.

E-Dub kept it pushing past them, trying to ignore everyone who was fighting for his attention. "Fuck y'all broke ass hoes. Bitch can't even afford the cut line, know y'all ain't hitting on shit, ole regular ass thots!" he said, briskly walking to his Range Rover.

Approaching his truck, E-Dub hit the alarm unlocking the doors. Parked right beside his truck sat a navy-blue Dodge Charger with the scat pack. The Spanish female was struggling with her keys, desperately trying to get her passenger door open. E-Dub noticed how phat her ass was as her mini-skirt came up, teasing whoever was looking. Making it to the driver's side of his truck, he had to squeeze through because they were rather close. The keys slipped out of her hand, falling right in front of E-Dub.

"Damn," she said, drunkenly turning around and bending over in her high heels, no panties, just naked ass and a bare coochie.

"Ssss, got damn! I mean, don't trip. I got 'em, ma," E-Dub said, grabbing himself before bending down to retrieve her keys for her. E-Dub grabbed the keys quickly and was coming up.

Whack!

"Ar—" E-Dub tried to holler, but was cut short. A heavy nap sack covered his head to his chest, smothering most of his sound.

He was snatched backward, blinded from the bag. E-Dub tried to struggle out but was overpowered by the four arms that punched him in his torso and head. Before he knew it, he was being stuffed inside a trunk that slammed down violently. Surprisingly, no one saw a thing.

Next thing E-Dub knew, he was being slung side to side from the car turning hard lefts and rights. E-Dub knew the city well so he was actually trying to keep up with where they were headed. He managed to shake out of the nap sack. It was dark except for the taillights providing a little light for him. E-Dub reached for his cell phone but couldn't find it. He must have dropped it during the kidnapping. "Fuck!"

Now he didn't know what to think 'cause he knew he had been living a very adventurous lifestyle. E-Dub prayed his past hadn't caught up with him. He strained to hear, listening for any form of recognition from his enemies or surroundings, because now they had done so much turning that he had become confused on location. The loud pipes made it difficult, though, so E-Dub could barely hear.

The driver was now speaking Spanish back and forth. The female passenger pulled the phone out and started texting.

We got that bitch ass nigga bruh, meet us there.

Already, I'm leaving now as we speak.

"Bruh said he on the way now, so step on it."

The conversation was barely audible, but E-Dub was able to make out some words.

"The homie on the way," E-Dub mouthed silently. Instantly, E-Dub started fumbling with the tail lights at first. Then he thought a second about that when his supervised release came across his mind, knowing if he hit Leon County Jail he'd never make it out from there. It was field bound. E-Dub went to work seriously on the trunk latch. The car made a sharp left, throwing him to the back of the trunk. "Fuck!" Scooting forward, E-Dub moved back toward the latch. Not knowing his outcome, E-Dub started to sweat profusely. Panic made him work that much harder.

"Can't wait…Kill this pussy, mutherfucker! Ole tellin' as—"
The music mixed with the loud pipes caused E-Dub to miss the last
part. His eyes grew the size of silver dollars hearing *kill* and *telling*.
This made it that much harder for E-Dub to figure out who it could
be. Thinking it could have been a robbery at first went out the door.
E-Dub had dropped all kinds of dimes on so many different people
he could have started a wishing well or a tella tell-free from jail. All
he did know was his past had caught him slipping.

"Shit, shit, shit! I got to get the fuck outta here, lawd!" E-Dub
talked low.

"See, those black folks got the game fucked up! Always want
to enjoy the fruits of another motherfucker's labor. But don't want
the down side that comes with it. Making deals and shit with the
DA and shit to stay with their family while taking away from
another person's family," the Spanish person said real sad and
feminine. "Know what I mean, bruh?" she said, looking toward her
brother.

"Come on, sis, stop playing!" he said, coming to a red light.
"All of us just reunited after what? Twelve, thirteen years of forced
separation. Living in different motherfuckin' foster homes and shit!
We lost our parents to the system because this fake ass pussy
motherfucker right here." He pointed his thumb in the direction of
the trunk. "Dad got life, he is USP1 Coleman. Mom too, she at the
camp with twenty years. For not telling. How gee is that! Bitches
going harder than most niggas out here and she what, sixty-seven?"
he said, tapping the steering wheel. The lights on Tennessee took
all day to change.

"First, I'm cutting his tongue out, ole talking rat ass bitch!" she
said, slicing her hand through the air, imitating a knife impression.
"If it wasn't for bruh coming to get us, bringing us back—" Her
eyes grew the size of golf balls. E-Dub had managed to pop the
trunk and climb out, running through the streets like a crackhead
who just snatched a forty rock without paying. His head was reared
back, chest stuck out as rain pounded down heavily. Horns blared
as people could be heard cursing after him. "Nooo! Go, go, go! He

getting the fuck away!" the Spanish female said angrily, pounding her fist on the dashboard.

"Fuck!" he said, then started speaking in Spanish, pressing down on the gas causing the car to spin 'round in the middle of the street. Intending to run E-Dub down and over, hoping to kill him right there now like a dog in the streets. His face was flush red with a satanic expression on.

E-Dub made it onto the sidewalk, running in between Campus Walk apartments, coming quickly out the back on Baser Street. He managed to shake them with that move. Campus Walk was one way in one way out with only a gate to walk through the back. E-Dub didn't stop for a breather until he was deep into the hood and sure he had lost his kidnappers. E-Dub was a dirty mess.

After walking a while to catch his breath, E-Dub came across an old abandoned house. He posted up on the porch until sunrise. E-Dub got lucky slipping through the cracks like grease. A slick, slimy motherfucker. His thoughts ran wild trying to think of all the people he had crossed in his career. It had become hard to keep count.

"Fuck it! I got away to snitch another day. It's a dirty game. The grimiest ones always win! That's why I'm winning! Shit, ole stupid ass niggas don't want to get dirty, they too fresh! Somebody got to play the part. Fuck all that, I signed up for it first." E-Dub talked to himself until he got tired.

Once the sun was up, E-Dub jumped up and stretched then headed back to his side of town, footin' it. Making it slowly down Tennessee Street safely, he crossed the street walking over to the bus terminal and waited for the bus. The bus terminal sat directly across the street from the Greyhound bus station.

Five minutes later, E-Dub had boarded his bus and found a seat in the back. He sat down and lay his head back, closing his eyes. E-Dub said a silent prayer and started formulating his next moves with his new plug he'd recently found out of town.

He didn't forget what had happened last night, but he pushed it far in the back of his mind. E-Dub was a catch me if you can type of person. If you didn't, then he would just continue his tactics.

Chapter 7
Dothan, Alabama

Three days passed by without Freak Zeenie hearing a word from Levi or Khashia. It had him bruising his brain focusing on his Change of Heart non-profit program, draining Freak Zeenie of pain, sweat, and tears. Sitting in his La-Z-Boy chair that sat to the far right in the corner by the window of his bedroom.

Freak Zeenie rubbed his shiny bald head from the back coming down over his face. Taking a deep breath he hoped to subside his anxiety with a whiff of relaxation. With the Bible within arm's reach, he had his laptop resting on his lap. Reading carefully over everything he'd put together, a smile finally crept across his face just as the sun sneak peeked through the wood blinds. Freak Zeenie knew it was his time to shine bright as the phoenix sun. Just a few more tweaks and he would be ready to present it all to his cousin and aunt in ATL.

This nigga ain't answering a niggas texts or calls and shit. I pray everything straight. Remy Red said he'll go absent from time to time, though. Niggas! I have no choice but to assume he's good, probably just don't want to be bothered. Nigga play too much! Freak Zeenie just shook his head, pushing away the thought that something could gravely be wrong with his little brother. *This nigga got a whole lot of foreign cars too. I got to ask him how he got all this extra expensive shit next time we choppin'.* Freak Zeenie just made a mental note of the topics he wanted to present to Levi.

Damn, I hope my baby Khashia's a'ight. She hasn't answered for a nigga either. That pussy ass nigga Big Man bet not have hurt one hair on her head. Got somethin' for 'em anyway, he a dead man walking. How he got me a life sentence while he out getting money? That shit don't add up. He may have lived to talk about it, but not for long though. Freak Zeenie looked over at the Bible then to his indictment papers. His thoughts were everywhere.

Rubbing his face once again, Freak Zeenie blew out a strong whiff of frustrated breath. Sitting the laptop to the side, he said, "I know, I know, Father God! You got to forgive and don't wish no harm on your enemies. But Lord? How do I turn the right cheek to the left and receive the exact same slap? Knowing that one is coming! Ain't that's folly? I need your guidance, Father God, 'cause I'm hurting badly. Even though I forgave these people who done me wrong, punishment must be inflicted. It's a time for everything, Ecclesiastes, Chapter 3!

"I'm a sinner, please forgive me, Father God, but they took me from my family, and these crimes have to be paid for. In blood! Snitching is intolerable! Amen," Freak Zeenie ended his prayer. After examining the names in the indictment papers , he had a hit list to go by.

Frank Zeenie walked over to his bed carrying the laptop with him. He sat down on the edge of the bed and began to type then scroll until he was satisfied.

"All y'all rat bitches gone pay! Snitchin' mothafuckers."

Freak Zeenie hit play on his music playlist on his laptop. The song "Snitching" came on by Pop Smoke, Quavo, and Future, off the *Shoot for the Stars Aim for the Moon* album.

"So, you got the job doing what?"

"Bruh, I get paid to snitch now. Nigga, it's really classified. I can't really even talk about this shit, my nigga."

"Oh my God."

"Only reason I'm tellin' you this shit 'cause you my boy, but don't fuck with me. You seen what I did to Rogers, you seen what I did to Rogers! Forty years!"

"He had forty years?"

"Forty years, bitch! He ain't wanna sign that plea! Forty years! Don't fuck with me!"

"Bitch ass niggas need a whole fifty round of a seven six point twos in his bitch ass face!" Freak Zeenie said, speaking on the intro of the song as they began to rap. I still haven't gone to see Mom Dukes yet. Got to go by there and peep on her a little later. Nigga not 'bout to keep being couped up in this house like this.

Knock! Knock! Knock!

Soft taps on the door broke Freak Zeenie's train of thought.

"You busy, Freak?" Remy Red stuck her head in the door, not waiting to be invited.

"What's up?" he asked, waving his hand, motioning for Remy Red to enter the room. Remy Red strutted in seductively, wearing a see-through Gucci sheer nightgown. She gave Freak Zeenie a small peek of her freshly shaved pussy with every step she took.

Remy Red's perky C-cups sat up like ripe grapefruits, softly jiggling as the delicate fabric tickled her nipples. This caused her luscious C-cups to enhance in size, lookin' lustrously delicious to Freak Zeenie and activating a very horny sensation deep within Remy Red. Molly was the instigator, which was a stimulant abused as an upper, or just to enhance emotions basically. Remy Red had been on Molly all night and had damn near masturbated herself to death and had now become bored with the self-pleasing issue. She wanted and needed her hot wet tunnel to be felt. Levi's absence had her going nuts.

Freak Zeenie's eyes had fucked Remy Red in a coma already. Remy Red equally eye fucked him the same. She held his eye contact without answering him on the what's up part. Once she was only inches away from Freak Zeenie's face, they both knew by now what was up.

Freak Zeenie was already in fiend mode for some more of Khashia's pussy but couldn't reach her for the life of him. Even though Freak Zeenie had a dark-chocolate fetish appetite, lately yellow or red was doing just as good, and Freak Zeenie made an exception for Khashia due to past history. Now here he was, finding himself fighting with temptation. Temptation was what it was. Temptation. The flesh weaker than tap water. Plus, thirteen years of prison will show you a different view than the one you thought you had anyway. Oh, if you think it's a game, let's see you do it. Then tell me 'bout it.

Freak Zeenie made a gesture to speak.

"Shhh!" Remy Red shook her head no, putting her finger to his lips, hushing Freak Zeenie before his words could form in his vocals. "No need for any words, when we both already understand our desires must be satisfied." Remy Red stared in his eyes. "You know?" Remy Red grabbed Freak Zeenie's hand and led him over to the La-Z-Boy chair.

Putting her delicate hand on his chest, she eased Freak Zeenie down into the chair. Remy Red pulled Freak Zeenie's pants off, taking her time folding them neatly, laying them over the arm of the chair. Getting comfortable between his legs, Remy Red pulled Freak Zeenie's dick out his gray Gucci boxer briefs through the dick hole.

Greedily taking his whole shaft into her wet mouth, she left a trail of warmth saliva behind. She sucked on him slowly, making her jaws close firmly around him as her lips pulled up to his tip.

"Mmm," Remy Red hummed around his dick head, before sinking her head back down to his nut sack. She made her lips kiss his sack lightly as her eyes watered up when Freak Zeenie's dick head teased her esophagus.

"Ssss, shitt!" escaped from his mouth without his permission. Contracting her throat muscles, Remy Red paused, allowing it to massage his dick head as she stared into his eyes. Freak Zeenie's whole ass straight left from off the chair's cushion, causing his back to arch on its own. He pushed more dick into Remy Red's throat, which she accepted proudly as it came with a highlight of pre-cum in the process. Remy Red allowed it to glide down her throat before pulling up off of Freak Zeenie, causing a popping sound just as she released him. Freak Zeenie's eyes shot open, not knowing that he even closed them. "Hold, hold, I was just 'bout to n—"

Remy Red pulled the lever on the side of the chair. The chair went back, pulling Freak Zeenie back, placing him in a laying position. Remy Red got up, walking 'round crawling onto Freak Zeenie's face without warning. She clamped her knees to the side of his face.

Freak Zeenie began to flick his tongue over her clit in a rhythm to the beat on the laptop. She started poppin' on his tongue, putting her hands on his legs riding that tongue reverse cowgirl style. "Olee." Remy Red came quickly with words coming out in their own language, because what she met to say was ow-wee. Remy Red was turnt up like a fifth of Bumpy Neck gin in the hood. Leaving

56

over, Remy Red stretched her neck until she was able to swallow Freak Zeenie's dick again. This time she sucked him with a different style. She was going fast and powerful.

Freak Zeenie never stood a chance. He was out of there like a back in the day Tyson fight. He came, releasing a healthy, thick load down Remy Red's throat after fifteen seconds of her throat game. "Yeahhh! Ummm! Suck-that-dickkk!" Sounds of pleasure came from them both, but if he thought Remy Red was finished, he would have thought wrongly.

Sliding down on Freak Zeenie, still in reverse cowgirl position, Remy Red placed her hands on the floor. She was as freaky as she wanted to be. Remy Red rode Freak Zeenie like she was a jockey in a Kentucky Derby race in the lane by the fence.

Freak Zeenie was gritting his teeth, biting down hard. He was desperately trying hard not to bust again so fast. Remy Red's pussy felt like silk brushing up and down on him. She was super wet and tight. He saw why his brother chose her. Remy Red would have a nigga like the Beyoncé song. Drunk in love off her sex game.

Freak Zeenie was smacking Remy Red's soft red ass, causing her to leave a white film up and down his shaft. He stuck his index finger into her ass hole. "Aha…A-A-A Ah-ah! Sheeitt…I'm-I'm c-cu-cumming." Remy Red started going up and down on him with her hands pushed deeply into the carpet. She was arching and rotating her back, milking that dick for all it had, holding her tongue out looking back at him. Freak Zeenie grabbed her ass cheeks, slamming Remy Red to him powerfully, releasing his last bit of seed into her hot tunnel.

"Ump, ump, ump!" he said, out of breath as he laid back to catch his breath. Remy Red was so hot and still horny that she was still grinding on him, slowly milking him. She was making all kinds of sexy sex sounds, hoping he would remain hard. "Hell nall, get up, get up! Freak Zeenie leaned up, pulling out of her oozing pussy. She had him tender while she continued to move, had his member feeling all tingly. "I'm cool, I got some shit to do. Is ya crazy? 'Preciate that though!" Freak Zeenie was looking at her as he put his dick back in his boxer briefs.

"You got that come back on you now!" He smiled, heading toward the shower.

"I know, right? I thought you were through with the red bitches though? Red is in right now, if you don't know." Remy Red turned on the balls of her feet, leaving him to his own thoughts.

That bitch crazy. With some crazy head and circle K pussy. Straight gas, Freak Zeenie thought about Remy Red as he hit the shower.

***

Forty Minutes Later…

Freak Zeenie sat outside in the parking lot of his mother's daycare. He just wanted to see his mom, the reason his heart beat. They held a bond that couldn't be broken.

Ms. Lois pulled in driving a big boy, black-on-black 500 Mercedes Benz. After parking, Ms. Lois got out, going inside the daycare to sanitize it before everyone arrived. Even though COVID-19 had declined in cases, it was still very much alive. Ms. Lois was in good spirits, humming a church tune as she made her way.

"That's right, Momma, God is good. God is good," he said, as he crunk up, backing out, knowing she was humming a Godly tune without even hearing her. Freak Zeenie knew his mother like the back of his own hand. "Now, my heart is at ease with that. Let me go put somin' on bruh books and shoot these pictures right fast. Shit, I ain't got shit else to do right now since this bitch ain't fucking with a nigga." Freak Zeenie checked his phone as he pulled out. He headed to CVS to put some money on his partner BD's books and print out some pictures for him.

Chapter 8
Webb, Alabama
The Same Day

Five minutes outside of Dothan, Alabama, Levi and Cartier Jay were in Webb, Alabama. Levi took Cartier Jay to his grandfather's hog farm that sat on Webb Road. Levi made sure to explain to Cartier Jay about throwing his phone away and why. It was only a select few people who knew of this spot, including family members. Levi was one of them, and that's how he'd plan on keepin' it.

His grandfather, OG Barber, had been an entrepreneur as late back as the mid-1940s. First, OG Barber co-founded a transportation business that he called the Quick Service Cab, located on Cherry Street in Dothan, Alabama. That was changed later to The Cherry Street Cab. In the late forties, he also had started a grocery store business, The Barber Grocery, on the land acquired by his father, Jason, in Dothan's Lakeview community. In addition to the cab service, and concurrently with the grocery store, OG operated piggery (hog) and vegetables farms on rented and/or personally owned land in Dothan, Alabama.

OG Barber's self-owned and operated grocery was the only food store in the Lakeview community for many, many years. The store provided affordable food (meat, poultry, homemade smoked sausage, beef, pork, fresh vegetables, etc.). The businesses had been passed down the generations, creating generational wealth.

Levi had been maintaining and taking the businesses up the charts since his big brother Freak Zeenie's absence. He had opened a barber shop and a successful Smoky Pigs Barbecue Restaurant that he had their uncle James running.

Cartier Jay was ready to get from 'round there. This was super country to him. Dothan, Alabama and Webb, Alabama were only five minutes apart, but different, just like night and day.

"Man, Unk, what the fuck you brought me out here for?" Cartier Jay was looking around, checking out how country it was out there. He could see trees for as far as he could see.

"'Cause I'm 'bout to show you the most important part of the game, besides keeping your mouth shut!" Levi looked at Cartier Jay, studying him a second. He knew this part that was 'bout to be revealed, if used wrong, could get him a five-star cell at West Jefferson Alabama Corrections Prison, on death row.

"Man, fuck all that, we shoulda just smoke this pussy ass nigga at his crib! Him and his bitch, and let 'em share it as a graveyard. Right now, though, we have a gain of evidence here with us, Unk. You know what I'm talking 'bout?" This is like a million years now." Cartier Jay pointed to Big Man. Smacking him across the head with the butt of his pistol, he instantly woke Big Man back up.

Whack!

"Got yo' fuck ass up, bitch ass nigga! Yeah, you thought you were scot free, hun? Ole dumb ass bitch nigga!" Cartier Jay was grittin' on him. At first, all this time Levi had led him to think that Big Man was just a come up, but he found out on the way to Webb that Big Man was the reason behind his step-pops doing a life sentence. Now he was fucked up behind this and super mad.

Big Man was hog tied with a big strip of duct tape over his mouth, lookin' like the elephant man. Head the size of a navel watermelon. Big Man's eyes were now swollen shut from the beating he'd taken over the past seventy-two hours. He could only hear them, and that was out of just one ear 'cause the other had been busted from a powerful impact blow from Cartier Jay. He was taking all his anger out on him for ruining his life by taking his father and role model from him.

Big Man did get to see his kidnappers' faces before his eyes were swollen shut. This made him that much more nervous. He knew Levi but very little 'bout Cartier Jay. Big Man smelled of urine mixed with defecation.

Levi walked off to go to the shed, only to come back with a five-pound sledgehammer. Levi hadn't fed the hogs in over two and a half weeks. They were going crazy out in the hog pen since he came three days ago.

"Nephew, this where you separate yourself from your peers right here. Y'all youngstas are too sloppy. Always shooting shit, leaving your victims to be found. Only to let the cops find out who did what, then come take your life from you too. Now both of y'all dead! Fuck all that!" He paused. "I'm the clean-up man for real! Mop a nigga ass up, boy! I make the germs disappear. Forever!" Cartier Jay was all ears now. "See, your great-great-grandfather left us this farm, to continue to be able to feed the family. I have brought a lot of undiscovered bodies here." Levi waved his hand 'round.

Levi pointed to the hog pen. "You see them there hogs over there, nephew?"

"Yeah, what about 'em, though? 'Cause I ain't got time for no pigs, Unk! That's why this nigga is in the position he in now, he ah gotdamn pig! Oink oinkin' an shit!"

"Right, right, right," Levi said, nodding his head in agreement.

"I know right! Pussy ass nigga got a got damn siren on top his motherfuckin' head, boy." Cartier Jay hit Big Man again, damn near knocking him back out. "Pussy! You got my dad a motherfuckin' life sentence, bitch! Got the audacity to be in our hood like ain't shit happen, gettin' money, living life all wavy and shit! Oh, you got balls, hun?" Cartier Jay took off toward the shed, sprintin'. Moments later, he returned with a pair of hedge clippers. "I'm 'bout to clip them bitches for you today, 'cause you a bitch anyway, nigga!" Tears of anger blinded his sight. Cartier Jay loved his dad more than life itself. Now that he finally had the person who was responsible, Marcus (Big Man) had to die.

Cartier Jay snatched Big Man's pants down to his knees.

"Hold on, nephew, you right now. When you right. Listen for a second, though. See, them hogs got to eat! If we don't feed them, eventually they will start to feed off each other, yah dig?"

"Yeah, so what you saying?"

"I'm saying they will eat anything nephew. Everything will digest, except teeth." He paused, letting his words sink in.

"So what? We gone feed this pig to his parents, the hogs? Is that what you're trying to tell me, Unk?" Cartier Jay let everything process. "Ok, Unk, boy, you ah dangerous ass nigga now! Boy, you ah motherfucker!" He smiled, shaking his head in disbelief.

"Right, then we slaughter the hogs and make sausages, pork skins, etc. Sell that shit to the community, getting rid of all evidence." Big Man released his bowels hearing this. There were many times that he had eaten at Smoky Pigs. This didn't bother them. "So, first you have to take all the teeth out." Levi lifted the five-pound sledge hammer. "Huah!" Swinging it as hard as he could, he smashed it into Big Man's jaw. He broke both jaw bones, knockin' majority all Big Man's teeth out with just one swing.

Big Man passed out from the pain as Levi beat his mouth in. Putting on a pair of leather gloves, Levi reached in Big Man's mouth, moving his fingers 'round smoothly, feeling for any teeth that could have been still intact. Pulling his fingers out, Levi was content with his work.

"Wake this fuck nigga back up." Still heaving from putting in work on Big Man's jaw, Levi had knocked down his teeth with the sledgehammer like a bowling ball did to the pins.

Cartier Jay broke a stick of methadone, wavin' it under Big Man's nose, instantly waking him. "Wake your ass the fuck up, bitch boy!" Sounds came from Big Man's throat that weren't understandable.

Levi slung the sledge hammer again, this time breakin' both of Big Man's legs at the knees. Then he broke his arms. Big Man felt every bit of all that pain. "A'ight, we done, nephew, let's get 'em over there to the hogs. He'll be good and devoured by tomorrow. You better believe it. The head also supposed to be crushed from them to able to consume it, but we gone crush his shit in the morning because his bitch ass gone get ate alive. So, we here for tonight then clean up tomorrow and clear it," he said, dropping the sledge hammer.

"Right. But, no, we ain't done just yet! I got to clip this fuck nigga nuts first." Cartier Jay aimed the hedge clippers toward Big Man's nuts. Since they had Big Man hogtied, his shit was sitting out in plain sight. Cartier Jay snapped 'em close as hard as he possibly could, cuttin' dick, balls, and clothes all at once. Big Man's member fell as blood instantly rushed out, soaking the surface under him.

"Arrrgh! Mmmm!" Big Man screamed through the tape as tears squeezed out his swollen eyes right before he passed back out from shock. Cartier Jay waved the stick under his nose once again. Big Man hollered again once he stirred.

Levi and Cartier Jay began dragging Big Man over to the hog pen full of big ass male boar hogs. The hogs were going super wild. Biting each other, headbutting one another, jumping all on top of each other, trying to be first to feed. They were starving. Literally. There were at least nine hogs out there.

No sooner than they finally flipped Big Man over in the pen, the hogs were on him. Tearing flesh and bones with their razor sharp teeth. Big Man never hit the ground. The hogs were headbutting him into the air like a volleyball. They were eating his ass alive. It didn't take long before the tape was discarded, and hollers could be heard only for a second or two. The squealing and snorting drowned out his cries before the biggest hog out there crunched down on his wind pipe, ripping it completely out, killing Big Man instantly as they continued to dismember his body.

The next morning, the only thing left was a skinned skull. Levi crushed it up with the sledge hammer then cleaned the hedge clippers and the sledge hammer with an acid and added ammonia afterward.

"A'ight, nephew, let's get on out of here. This how you properly erase a nigga without a trace, nigga. Don't ever, never mention what you seen or done. Never come here without me knowing as long as I'm alive." Levi paused, looking at Cartier Jay making sure he understood him. "Understand?"

"Come on, Unk, don't try me like that. Y—"

"Understand? Fuck all that shit!" Levi said, with so much force, staring Cartier Jay down.

"Yeah, Unk, I got you, never!" Cartier Jay said, looking Levi back in the eyes. Levi turned and headed for the car, and Cartier Jay followed close behind him with his hands behind his back with his fingers crossed. He hadn't uncrossed them yet since he gave Levi his answer.

Levi stopped in his tracks. A strange feeling came 'cross him, causing Levi to look 'round making sure everything was done correctly. This made Cartier Jay feel guilty. Cartier Jay had never lied to his uncle in his life.

Levi went back, putting the fire out in the barrel where they had burned the clothes that they came with. They got rid of the last bit of evidence except the teeth that were scattered about the grass and dirt, hard to see to the naked eye.

Just like that, Levi and Cartier Jay left as quietly as they had come.

Chapter 9
Dothan, Alabama
The Next Day

The powerful wind and sounds of heavy rain drops rushing against Freak Zeenie's window pane awoke him. He blinked his eyelids a few times as his eyes roamed the ceiling of the bedroom. After a few short moments, Freak Zeenie finally noticed Remy Red and Poochie sprawled across his king-size bed, still in the nude. A smile displayed across his face as his memory of the night before slowly came visible in his mind.

Freak Zeenie sat up a little too fast for his body's liking, which clearly disagreed with that decision.

"Good God Almighty!" he said, laying back down holding his forehead. "Motherfuckin' headache, need a strong cup of coffee and two pain pills." He rolled over Poochie, smacking her on her ass softly, causing it to jiggle like a wave in the water.

"Mmm," Poochie stirred, pulling the covers over her head, getting comfortable.

Steppin' over clothes and a half-empty bottle of 1942, Freak Zeenie snatched up his phone. He walked into the hall and headed to the bathroom, closing the door behind him. After taking a good morning piss and washing his hands, Freak Zeenie stood there going through the motions of checkin' for missed calls and text messages to find none.

"Hold the fuck on now! Fuck going on? Shit just ain't sittin' right with me! Four motherfuckin' days without a word from bruh or my bitch? Shitting me. I got to find somin' out today, though," he said, talking his thoughts aloud. Turnin' the shower on, he stepped into the blistering, steamy hot water to shake back.

Fifteen minutes later, Freak Zeenie came out the bathroom refreshed in full stride. No sooner than he made it to his bedroom, his phone lit up in his hand. Looking at the screen to see who it was calling, he couldn't answer fast enough.

"Got to answer this," he said. "Hello," Freak Zeenie said, as he sprayed Bond #9 cologne into the air, stepping through the mist.

"Good morning, Mr. Barber. How you been since your release?"

"Top of the morning to you too, sir. Man, I'm blessed, don't have any complaints coming from up under the pressure that I did to where I'm at now, you know?"

"That's good, in these times that we're in, you must count your blessings. Well, I'm only calling to confirm that you have received yet another great blessing. You are no longer on probation. Due to your circumstances, having a great support system in place for you, we are clearing out our log of anyone who doesn't fit the high-risk level of recidivating. So, yeah, that's it. You should thank the lawyer really in your case because truthfully, Mr. Barber, your history showed a recidivating of drug selling, but he fought tooth and nail in your defense, sir. You're now a free citizen again," the PO said, then paused a few seconds.

"Hello," Freak Zeenie said, studying himself in the mirror as reality started to settle in on him.

"Yes, Mr. Barber, I'm here. Mr. Barber?"

"Sir."

"Stay out of trouble. God has you in his favor. Good luck and God bless, sir!" The line went dead before Freak Zeenie could respond.

Freak Zeenie dropped to his knees and went into prayer for a good five minutes. Finishing up his prayer, he stood up satisfied. Grabbing the car magazine by the name of *Autotrader* from off the dresser, and his phone, Freak Zeenie went and sat in his La-Z-Boy by the window and opened the magazine up. It only took a few minutes to find the car he wanted for some just in case stuff. He stored the number in his iPhone. Getting up headin' out the bedroom, he pulled the door closed quietly behind him. He left the women sound asleep and headed to the den.

"So, while I'm gone, you just decided you just was gone fuck the shit out my hoes, hun bruh," Levi said, taking a sip of the hot coffee before placing the mug on the coffee table. Then he picked up the remote controller.

Freak Zeenie stopped in the doorway, staring at Levi for a split second. "Hell yeah! Fuck talkin' 'bout. and what? I did what was supposed to be done with 'em. Dick 'em down then get 'em the fuck from around, you heard, shiiiid," he said nonchalantly, then walked into the den taking a seat in the recliner to the far right.

They shared a good laugh for a second.

"That's what you better did. The same thing I would've done, shiiid, you ain't do nothing wrong," Levi said, flicking through the channels.

"You *shole* know what to say." Just as Freak Zeenie was about to continue, his phone came to life interrupting him. He checked the caller ID. "Must be my lucky day, I guess! First bruh pops up, next my bitch callin'." He looked at Levi before answering. "S'up? What the fuck took you so—" He was stopped in mid-sentence. His facial expression had changed as he listened. "A'ight, a'ight, calm down. I'm on the way as we speak." Hanging up, Freak Zeenie stood up.

Levi was lookin' at him. "What's up, nigga? Fuck that's all about? Everything good?" Levi asked, acting like he wasn't already hip.

"That was Khashia's mom, saying that they had found my baby bound and gagged and some more shit. That's all I know," he said.

"What about her nigga?"

"I don't give no fuck! What about him?" Freak Zeenie rushed out the house into the stormy rain, jumping into the Wraith and peeling out the driveway in a blur.

Levi looked out the window just in time to see the car, and that's when he realized where he recognized that car from. *Damn, bruh was at the bitch's house moments before we got there. How could I have forgot that when I had just saw his text that same morning? I'm slippin'!* Levi thought to himself before turning back to watching the CNN program.

Freak Zeenie turned what usually took fifteen minutes into a six-minute drive. The rain couldn't even slow him down. Pulling up into Khashia and Big Man's driveway, Freak Zeenie parked, killed the engine, and jumped out, rushing inside the house in the spring thunderstorm.

Khashia's mom stood in the foyer, and beside her stood Khashia's older sister.

"Hey, Deacon, long time no see! It's good to see you. I'm glad that God saved you from out that Devil's mouth. Come on, Khashia's in the kitchen. Right this way. The police haven't long left, but she'll explain all that to you," she informed him of a few small details, as she should. Freak Zeenie listened, consuming as much info as he could. Knowing Big Man was a marked man for one and he was still top-lip deep in the streets, meaning anything may have happened. At this point, nothing could be pinpointed.

Freak Zeenie stepped into the kitchen. Khashia was sitting at the island nursing a hot cup of tea as she listened to CNN News. Finally, Khashia looked up from her deep train of thought, meeting Freak Zeenie's gaze.

Noticing the bruise on Khashia's forehead as she leaped off the bar stool, he embraced her into his arms. Khashia squeezed him for dear life, sobbing something awful as Freak Zeenie rubbed the back of her head and neck. Khashia's whole body trembled with fear. She was overwhelmed with the joy of being alive. Knowing just how close she had not long encountered with the angel of death. Before her fresh experience, Khashia had known life to be super amazing. That was up until four days ago. Now, she wasn't all so sure anymore if she could respect it the same.

"Baby, soon as you left, it all happened so fast, baby. I was just about to leave his ass like we planned. But when I made it to the side door—" Khashia began to weep even harder. Flashes of the assault violated her memory, causing Khashia to witness it all over again vividly. "I believe he's behind all this, baby! He set it up like this. They were beating him and all of a sudden, I got knocked unconscious.

"When I woke up, I was tied up and couldn't move or see nothing. I didn't know how long I had been here. If it wasn't for Mommy coming over here checking on me." Khashia paused. "I probably would have died in here. Which I truly think was their intention."

"Yeah, after trying over and over to reach Khashia to no avail, I decided to come over to make sure everything was alright. After arriving, I knocked on the front door and got no answer, so I checked the door. It was locked. I went in the garage to the side door and it was unlocked. This raised my intuitions, so first I pulled my mace out as I called the police, before entering the house. As soon as I got through the door, I find my baby in a pile of fecal matter and urine. My heart dropped, automatically thinking the worst first. Until I came closer to her was when I could hear faint mumbles coming from Khashia," Khashia's mom explained. Freak Zeenie released Khashia and took a seat at the island, still listing attentively.

"So, where Big Man at now then?" Freak Zeenie finally got the chance to ask, as he rubbed his chin. Thoughts were running through his mind. Freak Zeenie was thinking of all the things he was going to do to Big Man once opportunity presented itself. Big Man would pay for his betrayal. Playing a major part in helping the feds take his life from him. Freak Zeenie wouldn't be satisfied until Big Man was six feet deep in the ground somewhere.

"That's the thing. No one has heard from nor seen him since. I know Marcus is behind this stunt. All the money is gone, and the demo too. I called and checked the bank account transactions too. There hasn't been any in the last four days." Khashia took a minute to sip her warm tea. "I already filed a missing person's report on his ass, though, with the police.

"So, if Marcus don't turn up before long, then I'm going to file to claim the insurance policy on him. I do know that. Since he want to play," she said, turning the volume up on the TV.

The news anchor, Abby, was giving a breakin' news report.

"Well, good evening, everyone. The jurors just came back with the verdict on Officer Derek Chauvin, who kneeled on George Floyd's neck for over nine minutes. Wait, here we go right here, let's listen," Abby said, as the judge began to speak after asking all twelve jurors some questions. "Yesss! Guilty! All twelve jurors made a unanimous decision of guilty, folks." Tears ran down

Abby's face. "Thank you, Lord." CNN started showing different cities around the world going crazy, chanting "guilty" with joy.

Khashia turned the TV back down.

"That's right! 'Bout time!"

"Hell yeah, that's good for his racist ass! Fuck wrong with that stupid ass motherfucker! Fuck that cracker! They got us fucked up! I love my beautiful black peoples! Done killed that man like that for nothing! This shit is crazy." Freak Zeenie's face was balled up tighter than a hedgehog.

"Come here for a second. I need to talk to you in private." Khashia grabbed his hand, pulling him with her out the kitchen, out of ear reach of her mom and sister. "So, Freak, what we gone do? You think he gone come back?" Khashia searched his eyes for answers.

I mean, it's too early to tell. Fuck that fuck nigga. Shiiid, you already know what's up with us." Freak Zeenie stared into her pretty, dreamy eyes. He pulled her in with his hands on her soft, fat ass.

Khashia melted under his touch.

"Well, if he don't show up in a few more weeks, like I said, I'm going to file the claim on the policy, and gone take over all the assets that I can. 'Cause even though we're not officially married, he did have a few things in my name. Like I know this house is, the cars, and a tree farm." Khashia rubbed her hands up and down his chest.

Freak Zeenie nodded his head, agreeing as Khashia brought memories back to him about the tree farm. He remembered how back in the days, Big Man always had his money in the trees and would mark 'em the exact same way each time. He was willing to bet anything this was the reason for Big Man purchasing a tree farm.

"Everything gone work itself out, bae. Don't worry 'bout nothing. God got it. On another note, I'm glad you are okay, though. I would have lost my mind if something had happened to you, girl." They headed back toward the front of the house. "Another thing too, my PO called me right before your mom. I'm now a free man!"

Freak Zeenie smiled for the first time since he'd been there. Khashia was the first person to receive the good news.

"For real, Freak?" Aw, that's great! So is that's the reason why you got rid of the wig now?"

"Oh, hell nawl! Once I heard what your mom said, I flew out the house in such a rush. You right, go grab me one of yours, though, before I go, 'cause I can't get caught slipping like that," he said, cheesing as he waited for Khashia in the kitchen.

Freak Zeenie made sure that they felt safe before his departure. Khashia had promised him that she would be staying with her mother until they figured things out with Big Man, just to be safe about it. They all felt content with that decision.

Freak Zeenie left, riding through the rain with all kinds of things running through his mind. Freak Zeenie found himself on the side of town where Big Man's tree farm was located. He drove by the tree farm trying to see if he could see anything unusual. *Everything looks normal to me*, he thought to himself.

Freak Zeenie decided to head on back home. He had two things on his mind as he thought of all the success Big Man had obtained while he had rotted away in a USP maximum cell.

Revenge and millions of dollars.

Paper Boi Rari

Chapter 10
Marianna, Florida
11:00 a.m.
5001 Tall Pines Drive

Remy Red pulled into the parking lot at BJs beauty supply store in a silver 550 Benz. The parking lot was rather empty besides a doo doo brown 550 Benz that was the same make and model as hers. Bringing the sedan to a stop right beside the doo doo brown Benz, Remy Red threw her car in park, killing the engine.

Remy Red stepped out in a pair of navy-blue red bottom high heels, wearing an identical navy-blue, pinstripe, mini-skirt business suit. Remy Red pushed a button on her key ring causing the trunk to glide up smoothly as she made it to the back of the sedan. Remy Red reached in the trunk, coming out with a tote bag, sitting it down on the pavement as she closed the trunk.

Remy Red sold hair supplies to beauty supply stores nationwide as a side hustle. This was her way of staying busy besides getting high. Remy Red didn't need money, thanks to Levi. He provided her with everything she needed by request. Remy Red's loyalty gained her security, money, love, and protection. Must I keep going?

Whenever Remy Red became bored from being spoiled, she would go out on her own and get her hustle on. Today was one of those days. Being that Marianna, Florida wasn't far from Dothan, Alabama, that's where she landed.

Remy Red walked inside BJs beauty supply carrying her bag full of samples. The store was poorly lit. Remy Red quickly glanced 'round the store looking for an employee. There was no one behind the cash register.

"Hello?" she spoke loudly, hoping to alert someone to her presence.

Seconds later, a slim dude came from out the back of the store. The lack of light made it hard for Remy Red to make out his features at first, until he came very close. She could see the guy had 'bout three days of facial hair along with the same on his head. Brown skin, athletic build with the height of B. Armstrong, the basketball player. The guy walked right up to Remy Red, extending his right hand.

"Hi, I'm Brandon, Brandon Johnson, but everyone calls me B-Love," he said. Remy Red accepted his hand, shaking it after sitting her bag down.

"Nice to meet you, ah B-Love. Where is the help 'round this joint? For a minute, I thought this was a self-checkout joint or something," Remy Red said, cracking a smile.

B-Love looked around.

"Nawl, well, due to the pandemic, I had to cut loose a lot of my employees. This my place of business, and for the last eight months I been running it by myself. Like mostly everyone else, business been slow with all the restrictions, but now it's starting to pick up again. I was just in the back doing inventory, that's all. So, how may I help you today?" B-Love's eyes roamed the fruits of Remy Red's body, admiring everything that they took in.

Remy Red noticed the thirst in B-Love's eyes.

"Well, B-Love, I'm what you would also call self-employed. No doubt business has been slow for everyone, with the exception of truck drivers, hun? I'm a private beauty supplier distributor. Most of my business sales come from online. It's very profitable, but there's nothing like the old school way of hands on, you know?" Remy Red kept her eyes trained on his as she spoke every syllable while she used her hands to help explain. She was being flirtatious while they carried conversation along.

B-Love nodded his head in agreement.

"A'ight, so what you got to offer that's hot that I may not have but need? I'm talking trending and flying off the shelfs for me?" B-Love rubbed his hands together like he was trying to warm them up.

"Well, I have a few choices in this here goodie bag of mine." Remy Red looked around. "Do you have somewhere I can prop my bag up so I can pull a few of my best top-shelf sellers out for you?"

"Yeah, as a matter of fact, I do. Back here I'm 'bout to turn into a beauty salon. I just have a few more adjustments to make but for the most part, it's almost complete," B-Love said, leading the way through the store. *I hope she offers some of that fire twat she got along with it,* he thought to himself. After a few seconds, they were in the beauty salon section with mirrors surrounding the walls, floor to ceiling. There were six beauty salon chairs and six chairs with dryers attached on 'em that sat in the far right corner of the room. Two 42-inch plasma TVs hung from the ceiling. B-Love waved his arms around the room. "So," he paused, "sorry, I just realized, I didn't get your name."

"Oh, I apologize. How unprofessional of me. It's Shonna, Shonna Pitsman," she lied through a Colgate smile.

"Aight, Shonna, you are the first person who has witnessed this. So, what do you think? Is it a comfortable spot for the ladies, or what do I need that's missing?"

Remy Red let a few seconds pass by on purpose.

"For the most part, it's good. Only thing missing that I see is customers and employees," she said, as she found a spot, walking over to the counter placing her bag on top of it. Remy Red unzipped the bag, taking her time to study the contents in it before taking out a few different items after she was satisfied with her choices. "So, first, I have this new hair remover cream here." Remy Red held it up for B- love to see before placing it back on the counter. "It's one of my best sellers too! It has a foul odor to it, but it takes all the hair from anywhere it's placed smoothly with no after burn, and it moisturizes the skin also.

"Best thing about this product is it lasts for seven days before one inch of hair even attempts to grow back, guaranteed or your money back! And I promise you this. The population is eating it up without complaint!" Remy Red said, patting the top of the container. She moved to the next item. "This ri—"

"So, let me get this straight," B-Love said, cutting Remy Red off. "The hair remover keeps the hair off for a full week straight! Guaranteed? Or your money back? Can you prove this?"

"Yes, I can." she pulled out her phone, pulling up a demonstration of the process on YouTube. She turned the phone around so B-Love could see it. A woman applied the cream up her legs. She let it sit for two minutes tops then rinsed the cream off with a shower head. Then she showed a set of pretty, smooth legs.

Next, a black dude applied the cream to his face and head. Minutes later, he rinsed it off, revealing a clean face and Mr. Clean-looking bald head. Each example showed a before and after date up to seven days later, showing that the hair didn't grow back. By the time third person came on, B-Love was sold.

"A'ight, I'm convinced. I definitely want an order of that. Matter fact, could you do me up right quick?" He paused, looking at her. "I mean, if you have time, that is." He rubbed his head, looking in the mirror. "I'm 'bout three days late now."

Remy Red looked at her watch for a second, buying time before she answered. *I thought you would never ask*, Remy Red thought to herself.

"Well, truth be told, B-Love, I have a few more stops to do here in Florida, but if you apply the cream in time, I'll rinse it off for you," Remy Red said. Truthfully, she never planned on touching the cream in the first place. Remy Red pulled her mask on that could pass for a Corona mask, but it had a special insulation for hardcore fumes that could be harmful and contaminating.

B-Love grabbed the hair remover cream and stood in the mirror as he began to apply it to his face, mustache, and head. After he finished, B-Love took a seat and looked in the mirror.

"I covered everything, didn't I, Shonna?"

"As I can see, you did! That's very good."

B-Love started fanning his face and head with both his hands. He noticed even the palm of his hands had also become inflamed.

"Whew, this shit getting kinda hot! They didn't say shit 'bout that on there. What's wrong?"

"It probably is hot. But not as hot as your low-down rat ass, motherfucker!" Remy Red said, with a menacing grimace on her face.

"What you just say?" B-Love jumped up out the chair, knockin' it over.

"You fucking heard me, bitch ass nigga!"

B-Love's face and head were making a sizzling sound, like bacon frying in a skillet.

"Bitch! What the fuck you put on me?" B-Love rubbed his face, trying to remove the cream. The skin came easily away with the slightest touch on his face and hands. B-Love let out a wincing scream. He ran to the sink, grabbing the sprinkler hose. B-Love's head and face had begun to release a heap of smoke, like they were on fire. The skin started to quickly melt away with each second, causing flesh to fall in watery chunks to the floor.

"Anthrax! With your hot ass! Freak Zeenie sent his blessings! Word of today, play with fire and it's just a matter of time before you get burned! Ole stupid, goofy ass nigga! Oh yeah, they freed him too, he out! But he couldn't make it here, so I'm here representing him," Remy Red said, watching the Anthrax eat through his face and skull.

B-Love was on the floor crawling, leaving flesh and bone behind until he finally fell flat in a puddle of body fluids. He couldn't believe his ears, hearing Freak Zeenie's name for the last time before he slowly slipped into a dark place, promising never to see the light again. The reaper had come to collect. B-Love's whole face had melted to the bone gristle. Even his eyes had evaporated.

Remy Red walked carefully around all the human waste before making it to the counter. She placed all the contents back inside her bag and wiped down anything she may have touched. After she finished sanitizing everything, Remy Red went to a room in the far back and found what she was searching for.

"Need this, look at you! Still tryin' to tell some shit!" she said, in a baby-like voice. Placing the tape inside her bag, Remy Red left out walking hastily. She glanced at the remains of B-Love on her way past. "Dead men can't talk, fuck nigga!" Keepin' it moving, she walked carefully to the front of the store, not leaving a trace of evidence behind.

Remy Red made it to the door and peeped out first. After making sure the coast was clear, she came out, got into her Benz, and pulled out of the parking lot just in time. She passed a white Tahoe that was turning in, but the driver couldn't see her behind the tint of her sedan. Remy Red drove back to Dothan, Alabama, proud of her work.

Remy Red had canceled one of Freak Zeenie's co-defendants who was responsible for helping place a life sentence on him. She did this free of charge. Just for the love of a real nigga and the hate for a fuck nigga. She was thorough like that. Females like Remy Red were unheard of and hard to come by in these days and times that we lived in.

If you happen to find one, it's a must you keep her happy and on your team like Levi did for her. Freak Zeenie had benefited because of his brother. As the saying goes of the great Jonny Taylor, it's cheaper to keep 'er.

Chapter 11
Dothan, Alabama
Early Sunday Morning

Freak Zeenie, Khashia, and Levi sat inside the tiny office at the tree farm. They made small talk over freshly roasted coffee prepared by Khashia as they calmly waited for one of the many resourceful friends of Levi's to show up. Freak Zeenie had both Levi and Khashia convinced that the tree business was the business to be in. They had been there for about forty minutes going over different prices on the sales of pine trees.

Levi glanced at his watch for the third time within twenty minutes.

"This nigga Snoop always late, man! That's why a nigga like him you have to give a thirty-minute head fuckin' start for anything that's going on. Shiiid, nigga probably gone be late for his own damn funeral, you heard?"

Levi had Freak Zeenie smiling, shaking his head. Levi had just brought Freak Zeenie out of a mean thought that was playing vividly in his mind. Remy Red had brought back the video footage showing him the B-Love incident. This had Freak Zeenie feeling quite groovy in itself, knowing one of his frenemies had been canceled on his behalf. Freak Zeenie was now at full attention listening to Levi.

"Nawl, for real! The nigga gone be dead, scheduled to be buried at such and such time. Everybody gone be already there to show the nigga their respect. See, when it's time to view his body, the motherfuckin' nigga ain't gone even be in the got damn casket!" Levi was on his feet demonstrating the act. The coffee had kicked in on top of the Molly. Combined, it had him super hyped. "I don't know what's so funny, bruh? You's ah used to be late ass nigga too! Prison got you on point now! But for real, though, not to get off subject. I really have seen a nigga late for his own funeral before! I couldn't bel—"

"Fuck outta here with all that shit, Levi!! Boy, you'll say anything. Ain't nobody trying to hear all them damn lies early this morning, nigga!" Khashia said, getting up cutting his story short as she collected all their Styrofoam cups and threw 'em away.

"Yeah bruh, fuck all that. How many trees y'all think out there, though?" Freak Zeenie said, changing the subject.

"Well, from the log book, it says here twenty-five hundred, bae." Khashia held the log book up for them to see.

"Oh yeahh." Freak Zeenie dragged his words, rubbing his hands together. "Meads says they give seven hundred per tree. So, let's just do a load first to test it out y'all. Then we go from there," he said, as he crunched the numbers in his head.

"Sounds like a plan to me." Khashia sat the log book down on the desk and walked to the window. "This must be Snoop here." She let the blinds go after seeing a white truck pull in the parking lot with all kinds of tools on it.

"Yeah, that's his lanky ass self out there," Levi said, just as his phone lit up displaying Snoop's name across the screen. Levi hit ignore as he was walking out the front door. Freak Zeenie and Khashia were right behind him.

"Oh now, what's up with it, fool?" Snoop said, dappin' Levi up. Snoop was rockin' a navy-blue monkey suit. You know, the Dickie mechanic full jumper is a monkey suit. Snoop was skinny and tall as a tree.

"You late, fool, that's what's up, nigga!" Levi wore a fake mug.

"Yeah, I know, I had to go the long way, though. It was a fucked up wreck coming the short way, yah dig?"

"Un-hun, right, right. Excuses are like ass holes, everyone got one!"

"Fuck you, nigga! How you know?"

"How I know what, fool?"

"How you know everyone has a ass hole?"

"Bitch, because they got to shit! And you full of it! Fuck you talkin' 'bout?"

"Yeah, good answer. But people have shit bags too, fool, just to let you know," Snoop said, headed back to his truck. "Y'all come on. I'm ready to work! Levi, your broke ass better have my bread too, nigga, 'cause ain't shit free, fool," he said, getting into his truck and crankin' up, not waiting for a response.

"Damn you! How much you need? With yo' super poor ass, bitch! And, just 'cause they have shit bags, don't mean they don't own an ass hole. You ass hole!" Levi made sure to get his point across as they all climbed into Snoop's doolie truck.

Snoop was laughing at his longtime friend.

"Man, which way, ole crazy ass nigga? This nigga wild, y'all know that, don't it?" He looked at them, waiting for directions.

"Got to know it," Freak Zeenie spoke for the first time since Snoop's arrival. "Drive 'round back, make the first right." Freak Zeenie had been to the farm just the day before searching for the marks on the trees that he was sure Big Man used. Just like his mind told him, after a short while, he'd located 'em. So, he knew the ones he wanted cut down. They drove for a couple minutes over the wood-chipped trail.

"Right here, bruh," Freak Zeenie said, pointing out the window. Snoop stopped the truck and they all got out. "These are the ones we want cut right here, homes." Freak Zeenie walked down the path showing Snoop ten pine trees. They were on the same side in a neat row with red X's on 'em.

"Why these, bae? Are they any different from the others or somethin'? Khashia asked curiously.

"Yeah, they are very different in size but are the same kind." Freak Zeenie left it at that.

"A'ight, I got the location now. Y'all want to watch me work or take y'all back?" Snoop asked.

"I don't know 'bout them, but I'm going back!" Khashia blurted out, making it very clear.

"Yeah, me too, how long will it take?" Freak Zeenie quizzed him.

"Ten trees?" Snoop paused, as he estimated a timeframe. "I should be finished in like a hour or so," he said.

"Make it thirty minutes, nigga! I got shit to do! I ain't fina be out here all day with no motherfuckin' trees, fool. Ole tree house building ass nigga!" Levi said, killing himself laughing at his own joke as he went and jumped in the truck.

"Man, shut up! This nigga stay on joke time," Snoop said. He turned his truck around and took them back to the office. "You just have my bread ready when I'm done. That's what you do. I ain't doing shit on no credit either, with your slick ass." Snoop laughed, 'cause he knew his dawg well. Everyone knew Levi would use his credit card in a minute to the very end. He would save his cash for dear life, and the crazy thing was, Levi always wanted credit or consignment, but he wouldn't honor it on his end. If you wanted credit from him, you were dead. Levi was cash only if you were trying to get what he had. Snoop waited 'til everyone was all out of the truck. The driver side window came down. Snoop leaned his left elbow out the window seal. "Oh now, Levi?"

Levi stopped on the third step going to the office and looked back.

"Oh now, what's happen?"

"Count them ten racks out, 'cause I'll be right back! I'm going to put that on a trailer for my big rig, nigga! You need to get the CDLs fool," Snoop said as Khashia and Freak Zeenie kept walking on into the office.

"Nigga, nigga, I drive big rigs without one! Why would I do that?"

"'Cause I'm making seven bandz a week, nigga! Just having seven cars to Texas and back. Thirty-five going and the same coming back. In only two days, fool." Snoop eased off the brakes, causing the truck to creep forward. "Think about it." He hit the gas, going into the tree farm, leaving Levi to his thoughts.

Who 'bout to give you ten bandz when Meads ain't paying shit but seven hundred a tree, nigga? Got to be on that spice, Levi thought, headed into the office.

"Man, Snoop a fool, bruh! Where you meet fam at?" Freak Zeenie asked soon as Levi stepped through the door.

"Yeah, Snoop silly as hell. He ah real one, though. I met him on a fed beef a while back. Bruh had a bank robbery case. Homes from that north side of Monkey-Town. He fucks with them dogs

82

and shit. When we got out, we linked up like a Cuban link and been locked in ever since. Stupid nigga ain't got no filter on his mouth now! That's bruh," Levi said, sitting down reading a text on his phone. "Well, that's it. I done my part. I got to get going, y'all. I'll fucks with y'all in the later hours, I guess." Levi jumped up, headed toward the door.

"Oh, yeah. I forgot all 'bout you hit the feds before, bruh! But the hell you did? What part? Where that man's bread at?" Freak Zeenie said, and Levi stopped.

"Oh, yeah, that part. It's on you this time. I got the next one. You know how it goes. This was your idea, wasn't it? Just keep my cut of the Meads part!" Levi said, walking out the door and closing it back before Freak Zeenie could get another word in.

"Nigga, that ain't shit but seven bandz for the trees, fool!" he yelled behind Levi for the hell of it. Got damn nigga chargin' more than we making, hell!" His face balled up, but Freak Zeenie couldn't hold it. He burst out laughing at his brother. Levi had pulled it on him. Khashia was looking crazy 'cause Levi's voice was sounding like the one who put the pillow case over her head on the day of Big Man's disappearance, but she didn't see their faces, so she quietly dismissed the thought.

"What you gone do with him, baby?" Khashia asked, kissing his forehead. "And what's the purpose of Meads then, if we losin' three bandz and makin' no profit at all?" She stood up with her arms folded, poutin' while staring at Freak Zeenie.

"It's not 'bout the profit this time, bae. It's 'bout the relationship. As we get to doing business with one another on the regular, then the profit will increase. That's how it goes. First lost is on us. After that, it's gains from then on, feel me?" He reached out, smacking Khashia's ass.

"Yeah, daddy, I understand," she said, putting her finger to her temple in thought. "On another note, I went on and filed for the insurance policy too, baby. The people said everything should be ready within six months from now, unless Marcus shows up. As of now, though, still not a word a word on him," Khashia said, waving her hands for emphasis.

Let's hope he's a no show then, hun?" Freak Zeenie moved his arms like an umpire did when a baseball player's safe.

Khashia smiled at him.

"Can you lock up when you leave, please? Sorry, but I have to get ready to go and take Momma to church." She looked at her phone's clock. "Damn, it's seven forty-four already? Time is movin', baby."

"Yeah, I got it since everybody all a sudden have this or that to do. I'll arrange for the trees to be picked up tomorrow morning too. Gone and get that shit did. Make sure to put a prayer in for me too. Let Mom Dukes know I send my love." Freak Zeenie got up, walking Khashia to the door.

"Awl, don't be like that! I'll see you tonight and put this kitty cat on you, bae." Khashia batted her eyes seductively, then she turned around and left out the door, leaving him to attend to the business.

Freak Zeenie stood in the doorway watching until Khashia left. Closing the door, he went to the TV and turned it on. CNN was already on, so he placed it on mute and took a seat.

"Shit going even better than I planned it," he said, speaking out loud to no one. Freak Zeenie pulled his phone out, dialing his favorite cousin's number, who resided in the Atlanta, Georgia area.

After a few rings, the phone picked up. "Hello?"

"What's up, cuzzo? Top of the mornin'," Freak Zeenie said, amped up.

"Who this?"

"Freak! Freak Zeenie, nigga! What's crackin'?"

"Nawl, you out? I'm lookin' at a cell number on my end, cuz."

"You better say it!"

"Nawl, how long, when did, how did, what's going o—"

"Compassionate release, Funk! Don't nobody know I'm out! I touched down like a cool month ago or so. Just been puttin' everything in motion before I pop out like a jack in the box! You know how I do," Freak Zeenie said, getting to his feet, walking toward the front door. He opened the door just as Snoop was pullin' back up. "So what's in motion on your end, cuzzo?"

"Man, I got my label up off the ground. I been lacing you 'bout my clothin' line already in rotation. Plus, I'm working on a movie right now as we speak. What about you? How you comin'?" Funk asked.

"My nigga. I'm on top of my A-game. I got this non-profit organization in motion called Change of Heart. But I'm starting to run into a few roadblocks that's trying to slow the motion of it. I ain't trippin, though, 'cause I'm going to bring Cuz and Aunt 'em in to oversee it anyhow. Then I got a T-shirt line I'm putting together, and last but not least, I have this record label I want to crank up ASAP! You know it's no biz without showbiz, cuzzo!" Freak Zeenie stopped onto the front porch of the small office.

"You need to come up here ASAP, cuz! Ain't shit in no Dothan, Alabama for you, nigga! Don't worry 'bout that rap part. I got that part handled already. My hands are in the cookie bowl, you just need to get up here! A'ight, cuz, do that. For real now!" Funk said.

"Come on now, cuzzo, this *me*! Say no more, bruh." Freak Zeenie motioned for Snoop to come in as he turned, going back into the office. "Check it out, though. I'm in the middle of some business, so I'll check in on you later, cuzzo. And cuzzo?"

"Yeah, what's up?"

"Don't let no one know I'm out, nigga! No one!"

"A'ight, you got that."

"Bet, I'll holla." Freak Zeenie ended the call, puttin' his phone back in the front pocket of his pants.

"So, you just came home, hun? State or feds?" Snoop asked, since he couldn't help but hear the convo.

"Feds. Just beat a life sentence by the grace of God, my nigga!"

"God is good!"

"All the time!" Freak Zeenie walked over to the desk.

"So, what's my tab?" He looked at Snoop, waiting for a price he already knew.

"Where's Levi ass at?" Snoop looked around the small office.

"They had to run. Nigga left the bill on me," Freak Zeenie said, shaking his head side to side with a smirk.

"Just like his ass too. Since you just came home, bruh, I tell you what." Snoop paused in thought a second. "Just shoot me twenty-five hundred. I can't do you like that. If it were Levi, though, he'd have to give me every penny! Nigga know he already owe a nigga. That's why his country ass cleared it before I finished, ole slick ass nigga!" They both laughed.

Freak Zeenie quickly counted out twenty-five hundred dollars for Snoop neatly on the desk.

"'Preciate that, bruh. Real talk!'"

"It ain't nothing, welcome home. Just keep it that way. Prison not for no real man, partner," Snoop said, snatchin' up the money from the desk and stuffing it in his pocket on his monkey suit.

They both walked outside. Snoop walked to his truck preparing to leave. Freak Zeenie looked at all the tools on Snoop's truck.

"Good looking, my nigga. I'll be in touch soon 'cause I'm gone be probably doing business with Meads on a regular if he cashing out right." He had a thought come 'cross his mind. "Aye, you wouldn't happen to have a big boy ax on there you could sell me, would you?"

"Nawl bruh, I don't," Snoop said, even though Freak Zeenie had just spotted one. "I have one I'll give you, though, my nigga." Snoop got out and grabbed an ax from the back of his truck.

"Here you go, homes." He handed Freak Zeenie the ax then returned to his truck. "Well, that'll do it for me. Guess I'll gone get going, homes. Call if you need me. Levi got the number. Tell that nigga he still owe me too, then again, never mind. I'll tell 'em my damn self." Snoop crunk up, threw up the deuces, and pulled off. They had formed a brotherhood of respect for one another in a short matter of time.

Freak Zeenie didn't waste another second. He locked the door to the office and jumped in his car, taking the ax with him. He headed down the trail to where the trees were cut down. He parked, grabbed the ax, and placed it up against his car for a second while he pulled his shirt off then grabbed a pair of work gloves from out his glove compartment. Pulling the gloves on, Freak Zeenie snatched up the ax and walked over to the first tree.

"This is going to take a while, but as long as it adds up in the end, I gives a fuck!" he said aloud as he aimed the ax for the red X on the tree. Freak Zeenie went to work.

***

Ten Hours Later...

Just like Freak Zeenie said it would, it took him all day to finish what he started. Once he finished, he was drenched in sweat, like he'd just come from off the Alabama prison farm plowing up a five-mile-long corn field.

Hungry and tired, Freak Zeenie bent down retrieving the last paint can from out the inside of the tree. This made paint can number ten that he placed by the other nine on the ground. It was now six o'clock in the evening. The sun hadn't begun to set yet and it was still producing plenty of heat.

Freak Zeenie ended up picking up the paint can that he had just sat down, walking to the driver side of the car. He opened the door, taking a much-needed seat. Pulling his knife from off his key chain, Freak Zeenie began to pry open the paint-can lid. After a few good minutes of elbow grease, the rusty, crusty lid finally gave, falling to the ground.

Freak Zeenie smiled a big ole smile that outdid the Kool-Aid man by a landslide. Reaching inside the can, he pulled back a fist full of crisp, blue hundred-dollar bills. Instantly, he went to counting the bills.

"A hundred thousand? Yes sir, right on time!" He jumped up and went to scoop up the remaining nine cans, bringing them within arm's reach. He repeated the same pattern until he finished, coming up with the same results.

Freak Zeenie had a pile of empty paint cans in front of him on the ground along with a passenger seat full of hundred-dollar bills. "A motherfuckin' million dollars! Ha! Do it, Freak Zeenie! Just killed these niggas! A million dollars in less than two months! Who else could do it, but me? And just think. I said I would have one point seven six months after my release," he said aloud, jumping up picking all the paint cans from off the ground, placing 'em in the back seat. "Bitch ass nigga! Got me a life sentence. Now I'm back to take yo' life savings, nigga! And everything else you got, pussy ass nigga! You can't hide forever! You done all this work to give it to me, hun? 'Preciate it! Oh yeah, I got yo' bitch with me, nigga!" Freak Zeenie said aloud, looking 'round at all the trees. *I got to come back and check all these shits! It got to be some more*, he thought to himself.

Jumpin' in his car, Freak Zeenie left the tree farm a million dollars richer than he had been. Freak Zeenie was cheesing so hard it was like he had a permanent smile plastered on his face.

Freak Zeenie hadn't made it up the highway good before his phone lit up.

"Yeah, what's up?" he answered.

"You ready for this kitty cat? She need to purr one time," Khashia whined through the phone.

"On my way, baby. Just give me 'bout a hour tops and I'm there to 'tend to Ms. Kitty-Kitty." He put his phone on Facetime so he could see Khashia naked, playing in her pussy with an illegal snub-nose black and brown revolver dildo, making all kinds of sexy moans. "Got damn! You just got my dick harder than a Flintstone newspaper, woman!" Freak Zeenie said, pointin' the phone screen toward his joint showing his print to her.

"You crazy, baby, just hurry up, okay?"

"A'ight, you ain't got to tell me. I'm on the way, as much fun as that dildo having, shiiid," Freak Zeenie said, hanging up the phone. He cut it off completely, not wanting any more distractions.

Freak Zeenie drove out to Kinsey, Alabama. Another town that sat on the outskirts of Dothan, Alabama. Which would be considered country compared to Dothan. He had a piece of real estate property he'd purchased before his incarceration. The house sat on four acres of land with an underground safe inside it that was located in the basement. Freak Zeenie never told a soul about this residence.

Pulling up, killin' the engine, Freak Zeenie grabbed his shirt and tied a quick knot in the neck, making it like a bag. Placing all the money inside it, he got out, looking around and listening for a second for anything out of the norm. After feeling content, he went 'round to the back of the house, letting himself in.

The house was dusty as hell inside from the absence of life but still in great condition. Wasting no time, Freak Zeenie took the stairs down to the basement and found what he was there for. He input the code, unlocking the safe. The only thing inside the safe was a black book. He pushed it further back inside then quickly began placing the money inside the safe from the shirt.

Once he was finished, he secured it then made sure it was secure a second time for good measure. Getting up, he left without a trace and headed back to Dothan, Alabama.

"That's what you call bag talk. Securing the bag! Real FREE BANDZ!" Freak Zeenie said, talking aloud as he piloted his way home.

After making it home without incident, Freak Zeenie went straight toward the shower. He freshened up and got dressed in a flash. He headed out the door, picked up Khashia, and took her to a hotel to satisfy their sexual appetite. One thing he wasn't doing was fucking her in Big Man's house again, taking a chance to get caught slippin'. As far as he was concerned, Big Man was somewhere lurkin' out there waiting to get revenge. Freak Zeenie wasn't trustin' shit.

Paper Boi Rari

Chapter 12
Atlanta, Georgia
The Weekend
McDowell Street/The Old Bankhead

E-Dub cruised up the street on the Westside in his Porsche Cayenne Turbo SUV. The Westside was one of the roughest sides in Atlanta. Home to D4L, RIP Lil' Marlo, and if you gone mention Bankhead, you bet not forget the infamous RIP Shawty-Lo!

E-Dub had his cousins Kendall and Reneesha with him along with Reneesha's homegirl, La-La. E-Dub turned the music down, grabbing his phone from the console.

"Hold up, y'all, for a second." He pressed the speed dial.

"Hello!?" Denise answered on the fourth ring. She had one finger in her ear, straining to hear over the loud music.

"What's up with it? I'm—"

"Hun!?!!" Denise screamed.

"I-I said, what's up with it? I'm up here just pulling into the Flame thang now, you heard? Sounds like that bitch jumpin'," E-Dub said much louder for her to hear him.

"Oh, yeah. A'ight, shit come on in. I'm in this bitch! Got a section. Poppin' bandz and bottles on some freaky models! You'll see me when you enter," Denise said, ending the call.

E-Dub laughed a bit and pulled up to park. They all were inside the strip club known as Blue Flame.

***

Atlanta, Georgia
Highway-85 North

Freak Zeenie and Levi were in Atlanta, Georgia with one of Freak Zeenie's longtime partners, Carlos. Carlos was driving Levi's 2021 black-on-black Escalade truck on Highway 85.

"Damn shawty, it's been a long time, dang! Shawty, look at you. Shawty, you look young as a motherfucker, shawty!" Carlos

91

said, smiling as he kept looking over at Freak Zeenie, glad to be reunited.

"Yeah, yeah, boy, you already know! I preserved reserved, lookin' like a few mega-ton of birds without sayin' one word," Freak Zeenie said, solitary diamonds gleaming in the dark with his every move.

Carlos busted out laughing.

"Shawty, you still crazy, shawty. Man, the streets miss you, I'm telling you! Hold on, shawty. I got to hit Lil' Fred up, shawty!" Carlos said, picking his phone up from his lap. Finding the number, he pressed the speed dial.

A few rings later, the phone picked up. "What's up, shawty? What's goin' on?" Lil' Fred answered.

"Man, where you at, shawty?"

"I'm on Old Nat, headed to the fifty yard line, and after that I'm going to the Ritz, shawty. What that?" Lil' Fred said, navigating his way through traffic.

"Nawl shawty, meet me at the Flame, thang! I got a gift for you, shawty," Carlos said.

"Say no more, shawty, I'm in route!" Lil' Fred hung up and changed routes.

***

A Couple Minutes Later…

Lil' Fred called Carlos's phone.

"Yeah shawty, what's up? You here?" Carlos answered on the first ring.

"Yeah, I'm over here, shawty. Where you at?"

"In the back. You'll see the black Escalade, shawty." Carlos hung up.

Lil' Fred pulled up beside the truck, parked, and jumped out. Carlos stepped out, dapping Lil' Fred up.

"Shiiid, what's goin' on? Where the gift at? This truck? Shole 'preciate it!" Lil' Fred said, looking 'round, only seeing the truck and assuming it had to be what Carlos was talkin' 'bout.

"What's up, shawty?" Slow it down, shawty, damn! You taking me fast," Carlos said, putting both hands out in front of him, signaling for Lil' Fred to slow up.

The back door on the Escalade opened up, and Levi stepped out fresher than a kilo straight out the wrapper.

"Shawty, shawty? What the fuck? I know damn well you ain't just call me over here, shawty, talking 'bout no damn gift and this supposed to be it? Nigga, I just saw this nigga Levi ass last week, shiiid shawty!" Lil' Fred said, eyes squinted as he took a step back, scratching his head in frustration.

"Nigga, nigga, yeah! Surprise! Fuck you talking 'bout. Anytime I'm 'round it's a fight just to witness my presence, you heard? Act like you know!" Levi said, his diamonds sparkling with his every move.

"Shawty, all I know is—" Freak Zeenie walked 'round the back of the Escalade truck, causing Lil' Fred to stop mid-sentence. "Awl man, shawty! What the fuck? Cuz, when did you touch? Nigga, I know we 'bout to turn up!" Lil' Fred rubbed his hands together fast. "Shawty, oowl woo, I know we 'bout to get so much mutherfuckin' money, Shawty!" Lil' Fred went and embraced Freak Zeenie in a brotherly bear hug.

"You know what to say, Lil' Fred. Yeah, back from the dead, fresh out the feds! I'm here, but you ain't never saw me, 'cause no one knows I'm out, cuz," Freak Zeenie said, while the diamonds on him danced like Mike Jackson moon walking.

"Fa sho', shawty! Now come on, let's go in and fluddah! Throw some bandz on these hoes, shawty!" They all footed it to the front door.

Izzy was at the door on security, and Carlos spotted him first. "What's up, shawty? What's goin' on?" he said.

"FOE, shawty! Family over everything, shawty. The money gone come regardless, yah dig," Issy said, dappin' Carlos up.

"Mann, what up with Izzy?" Freak Zeenie said, making his way to the front of his circle.

"Oh shit! Shawty, when you get out? Man, hold the fuck up. Get shawty a section ready! Bottles on me all night, shawty! Got damn infamous Freak Zeenie in this bitch!" Issy said, dapping him up.

"Man, compassionate release, bruh. Just gave a life sentence back. You know, I'm just breezing through the city for a minute, lettin' my nuts hang, dawg. Check it out, take my number down right fast. I'm 'bout to jump this music off, Izzy! Got some gas 'bout to come out!" Freak Zeenie gave Izzy his number, then they all stepped inside the Flame thang.

***

On the Other Side of Blue Flame...

E-Dub and Denise were making it hurricane at the stage. The strippers were chunkin' ass and pussy everywhere as the bills rained down on stage as "Said Sum" by Moneybagg Yo played.

Hun, I thought a broke nigga said sum/talking shit but they still ain't said nuttin'/we gone trap it out to the feds come.

The DJ was cranking it up for the dancers. Freak Zeenie was bobbing to Moneybagg Yo, getting into his element.

"Aye, let me get a fifty piece (50 thousand)," he said to a passing waitress. He turned up his cup of Remy Red, draining it before grabbing another from off the table.

Levi silently watched his older brother. *Hell this nigga snatch a bag from like that to blow this fast?* He kept his thoughts within as he ordered up a platter of ones for himself.

"Yeah, I'll take a thirt- piece for now," Levi said.

"Anything else?" the waitress smiled and asked.

"Damn cuz, you still got that bag reserved for real, ain't it, shawty?" Lil' Fred said, after placing an order of his own.

"Yeah, shawty, we 'bout to chew, nigga!" Carlos said, placing his order too.

Freak Zeenie just laughed at them.

"Ain't shit changed! I am money? Come on, y'all know that!" He reached out, grabbing his platter full of ones soon as they arrived.

On the other side, which wasn't far from Freak Zeenie 'em, Denise and E-Dub eyes had followed the platter full of money. They could see it was four dudes, but the poor density of light made it hard for 'em to recognize 'em.

"Ok, them niggas eating right there! That's 'bout a cool two hundred thousand alone," Denise said, nodding her head up and down.

"Easily," E-Dub commented and went back to chunking ones into the air.

Denise was buzzing hard now off the Ace of Spades. "Damn, E, you looking good tonight. Keep fucking with me and you gone be looking great!" She giggled a little from her own statement.

E-Dub looked out over to his cousin 'em, who Denise didn't allow in her section. They were all looking salty at him. He paid 'em no never mind, though, and gave Denise his undivided attention.

"You know we locked in, D! You got straight pressure with non negotiable prices, yah dig?" he said, and released a fist full of ones toward the stage.

"Make sure you do that. So...what we talkin' 'bout tonight then?" She looked over at E-Dub through lustful eyes. Denise was becoming attracted to E-Dub but fought against the temptation.

"Something like a light fifty, for now, ah be cool." E-Dub looked her in the eyes, liking what he saw but keeping it professional. He knew one thing. Once you start to mix business with pleasure, that's when the bullshit starts and your money will decline instantly along with some more shit to come along with it.

E-Dub let a few seconds pass to think about what shouldn't have taken any thought at all. Plus, he had to regain his composure.

"Most definitely," he said, taking a peek at Denise's apple bottom, which was poking out like a sore thumb as she stepped back, putting some space in between them. *Damn, that shit super phat!* E-Dub kept his thoughts concealed.

"A'ight. I'll put that together for you. We'll go to breakfast in the morning and go from there. Now enough of that, let's enjoy the rest of the night. Oh, next time, come by yourself. Leave your company elsewhere, please," Denise said firmly enough that E-Dub understood it. She went on to order another platter of ones then made Hurricane Ida look weak with how she blinded the stage of women from all the ones that flooded the floor of the stage. Drenching the dancers a whole hour straight, non-stop.

Freak couldn't see the dancers from where he was at from all the dollar bills raining down on the dancers.

"Who the fuck that bitch up there throwing all that stuff like that?" Freak Zeenie said, after trying to get a better look at her, but still couldn't see from the poor lights illuminating almost none' at all. He had the thought to go up there and greet her, but second-guessed it then disregarded it. All of a sudden, Freak Zeenie had to piss like a Russian race horse. "Man, I'll be back! I got to piss like a motherfucker, boy!" Walking off, Freak Zeenie headed to the bathroom.

No one knew how Denise was because whenever she was in Atlanta she kept mostly to herself. She was a Detroit, Michigan resident and liked her low profile to remain low.

Soon as Freak Zeenie was out of sight. Levi had been spotted E-Dub but didn't lace his brother up but he didn't know the female he was with. And didn't give a fuck either. Levi leaned over tapping Lil' Fred on his arm.

"Aye, Lil' Fred?"

"Yeah?"

"See that nigga right there?" He pointed to E-Dub's back.

"Yeah, I see homes. What up?"

"I want you to GPS that nigga for me, bruh!"

"Say no more, I'm on it!"

"Bet dat! Don't lose 'em," Levi said. *Boy, boy, boy, the world is small. I want to blow this nigga's candles out right mutherfucking now!* Levi was thinking to himself just as Freak Zeenie was making it back to their section. "You ready bruh?" Levi asked Freak Zeenie, ready to leave before his brother noticed E-Dub and they had to do something that would land them in jail tonight with an outstanding bond or No bond at all.

"Yeah bruh, let's gone hit it," Freak Zeenie said, dapping Lil' Fred and Carlos up before he left. "Y'all stay up, I'll be in touch."

"Bet that up shawty, you stay cool!" Carlos said, he was gone stay with Lil' Fred and finish the night up.

"Yeah y'all boys be safe shawty!" Lil' Fred said.

"Already," Levi said, as he and Freak Zeenie headed out the Flame thang. Levi looked back to Lil' Fred. He pointed toward E-Dub signaling for Lil' Fred not to forget what they had discussed moments ago.

"I'll take you home," Lil' Fred said.

"The hell you will shawty, I'm leaving with one of these phat booty strippers tonight shawty!" Carlos said.

"Say no mo'," Lil' Fred said, then he reverted his attention to E-Dub. Watching his every move. I'm on you suck. He thought to himself.

***

The Next Morning...

Lil' Fred called Levi bright and early the next morning.

"Hello?" Levi answered.

"Shawty, I been on that nigga all night! I just left the W downtown, shawty. Right now I'm on Northside Drive, at Restaurant Ten, parked in the back. You'll see my car.

"A'ight, say no more, I'll be there in like ten minutes." Levi hung up, jumped up, and got dressed, leaving out in a hurry. Freak Zeenie didn't hear a thing as he was sound asleep.

***

Northside Drive
Ten Minutes Later...

Levi pulled 'round back on Northside Drive at Restaurant Ten parked. He got out and hopped into the car with Lil' Fred.

"What's up shawty?" What's the lic' gon' be? You know I got that dirty Glock forty right here now, we can end his career today shawty," Lil' Fred said, all amped up, pattin' his black Glock forty with the leg (extended clip) stickin' out if full of red tips.

"Let me think a minute, just waking up!"

"Just wakin' up, *just wakin'* up, shawty? Man, a nigga ain't trying to hear all that shit, shawty! You need to hurry the fuck up shawty, hell you talking 'bout?"

"Yeah, yeah, yeah, I got this shit!"

"The nigga in there catting with the exact same bitch from last nigga. Might have to down both of 'em! No witnesses shawty, you already know!" Lil' Fred said, even though he didn't have the slightest clue of what the real purpose of him keeping eye on E-Dub was all about in the first place. All he knew was homes was throwing a hellava lot of money in the booty clue and that's a fact.

"Yeah, so a'ight. Check it: when they come out then. I'm gone run down on 'em dome his pussy ass and we outta here!" Levi said, looking 'round getting a visual of the surroundings.

Lil' Fred looked Levi up side his head crazy as hell. Because he was expecting to at least get some money out of E-Dub. Now that Levi was talking about a homicide with no robbery made him feel some type of way. His love for Levi made him go against his better judgment of the situation.

"A'ight shawty, no mistakes," he said, disappointedly.

"Already," Levi responded, never catching Lil' Fred's expression.

They sat calmly waiting for E-Dub to come out.

"They should be on their way out any minute now!" Lil' Fred said. While they continued to wait. A black Impala pulled up. A fine sophisticated elderly female jumped out simultaneously as E-Dub trunk popped open. She carefully placed a black duffel bag in it then closed the trunk back. Making sure the trunk was secured before stepping quickly back to the Impala And pullin' off quietly as she came. "Oh shit, shawty! I know that move from anywhere! That's bag talk right there now, shawty! That's what that is!" Lil' Fred said, getting super excited from the opportunity to grab some free bands.

"I'm already hip," Levi said. "But this is body bag talk right here now," he held his pistol up after finishing tying the T-shirt around his face. A couple minutes later. E-Dub and Denise emerged, strolling out the restaurant laughing and talking in deep conversation. Not knowing that death was just a foot away on the same turf as them. Levi grabbed the door handle to get out. A patrol car pulled up parking two cars down. "Ain't this 'bout a bitch?" Levi said, frantically, looking up at the sky. "For real Lord?" "Man, shawty ya tripping now. Don't question gods work shawty." E-Dub got into his car but sat here a few minutes. He crunk up and eventually pulled off. Lil' Fred and Levi followed him a couple car links behind. E-Dub led them to Lenox Mall on Peachtree.

E-Dub pulled up paying the attendant for valet parking. *Damn, I should have went on and placed that shit in the stash box. Fuck it, it'll be straight. I'll do it when I come out or make sure cuz do it before we pull out,* E-Dub thought as he went on in the mall.

Lil' Fred looked over to Levi.

"What now, shawty? We wait him out?" he asked.

"Hell nawl! We get that bag! Fuck that faggot! I'll catch him, sooner than later!" Levi said. Lit Fred finally found a close enough park then parked. They hoped out moving with precision went and located E-Dubs car. "Bingo!"

Making it up on the car unnoticed while the attendant was occupied with oncoming customers, Lil' Fred went to work. Within seconds the trunk was popped, bag retrieved, trunk was closed back and Levi and Lil' Fred were back on 285.

Lil' Fred weaved in and out of traffic with finesse. Levi unzipped the bag. Lil' Fred couldn't help but peek over at the exposed contents. "Now that's bag talk shawty!" Levi smiled. It was something light to him. He wanted E-Dubs life if anything but time wasn't on Levi's side at the moment it had sided with E-Dub once again. Levi sat quietly plotting his next move.

***

Back at Lenox Mall...

E-Dub came out of the mall and waited for his car. Once the car showed up E-Dub jumped in and hit the highway headed straight over to the W hotel. By the time he made it there E-Dub was so anxious he hoped out giving No directions for real. He switched cars. Giving Kendell and Roneesha 'em the car with the bag that was supposed to be in the trunk but should have been in the stash spot. E-Dub hopped back in his Range Rover pulling out hastily wasting No time to get back down the highway back to Florida.

E-Dub was so eager to get to his city and flood the streets with his product that he even forgot to turn his phone back on. Assuming Kendell 'em knew to check the car and protect the brand. He was so wrong. At the moment all he could think about was how fast his return would be. Promising Denise he would do this once a week with her and on the next time purchase some straight ether cocaine. That, if cooked up, would be considered straight drop that Denise promised him she would provide with their next meeting.

***

Back on 285

Lil' Fred zipped up 285 while Levi went through his call log. Finding the number he was searching for Levi pressed speed dial.

"Yeah, yeah, shawty, what the move is?" Carlos answered.

"What's up with it, homes? Where you at? What you got goin'?" Levi said, putting the phone on facetime.

Carlos's fade showed up.

"Over here on Cleven Ave, at the Gold Rush, shawty! Trying to get a shot of this breast milk to go with this brunch shawty!"

Levi and Lil' Fred were cracking up laughing.

"Boy, you a wild nigga homes!"

"Nawl, for real shawty! These hoes on one up in this bitch shawty! Early bird gets the worm shawty, y'all know that!"

"Fa' sho', ain't that's the truth. Check it though. I need you to meet a nigga over in college park on Creel Road right fast, yah heard? I'm talkin' like right now over at the club house nigga!" Levi peaked in the rearview mirror a split second before diverting his attention back to the screen. A state trooper was trailing them.

"Don't panic shawty. We good," Lil' Fred said, turning the right signal light on. Navigating the car into the right lane allowing a few cars to get ahead of them including the state trooper. "Told you, shawty, we straight! This my city shawty!" he said, getting off on Old National Blvd.

Carlos had hung up. Levi's phone lit up as Lil' Fred came to a traffic light on red.

"Yeah, what's up with it bruh?" Levi put the phone to his ear.

"Man, gotdamn, nigga! You then got your ass up and crept up out this bitch. Leaving ah nigga and shit! Where the hell you at bruh?" Freak Zeenie said, looking out the window of his loth. That was downtown on 18th Street close to Atlantic Station. A well-manicured area in downtown Atlanta. "Shiiid, you know I got to meet Funk at Restaurant Ten on Northside Drive in a hour!" Freak Zeenie was going on one.

"Yeah, yeah, yeah, nigga. I already know! That's why I got a Uber on the way for you. Just chill, I gotcha, my boy!" he said excitedly.

"Who? You got who a Uber? Nigga, you got me fucked up! I don't ride Ubers. Shit! I'm Mr. Presidential! Better have me a gotdamn chauffeur! Fuck you takin' 'bout?"

Lil' Fred and Levi were cracking up laughing! Levi put his finger to his lips for Lil' Fred to keep quiet. He knew he had Freak Zeenie goin' now. "Right, right. I'm already hip! But see, it wasn't none available bruh, so shiiid, I got you the next best thing. Just look at it. It's really the something for real. You still being driven somewhere by someone else. Feel me though?"

"A Uber? Nigga, the hell it is." Freak Zeenie shook his head in aggravation.

"Nawl bruh, I'm bullshittin', you know I got you. I'll be there in a minute nigga. Soon as I handle this," Levi said.

"Nigga, ha-ha-ha! You always playin' and shit! Hurry up! You know how I am. I don't like being late nigga!" Freak Zeenie said.

"Already bruh, look, I got to go! I'm on the way!" Levi said, disconnection' just as Lil' Fred pulled up at the trap known as the club house. Lil' Fred cut the engine off. Levi grabbed the black duffel bag off the back seat. They both exited the car and went let themselves into the trap and waited for Carlos to pull up.

***

A Few Minutes Later…

Carlos pulled up and parked. He got out and went inside the trap. Levi and Lil' Fred were both standing when Carlos entered.

"What's up shawty?" Carlos said, dapping them both up. "So, what's the business shawty?"

Levi wasted No time.

"I'm gone get straight to it? How many blues you got nigga?" Levi rubbed his hands together looking at Lil' Fred.

"Hun?" Carlos said, looking dumbfounded at the both of 'em.

"How many hun-duns…you got niggas? Say the right amount and I'm gone bless yah! What you got? Both y'all. Twenty, thirty, forty? Talk to me," Levi said, showing a sinister smile.

Lil' Fred looked at Levi in disbelief.

"Who?" Shiiid, shawty. I know I get a discount ain't it?"

"Stop fuckin' round Lil' Fred. I'm gone bless you regardless."

"Why shawty? What you got first? Carlos said, rubbing his chin in thought.

"Nigga-Levi-Mister Ice Cream Man…Mister Ice Cream Man…!" He sang his words out like the Master P hook on the song.

"Shiiid shawty, I got a cool honey bun (100 thousand) shawty! What you sayin'?" Carlos said, staring Levi in the eyes pulling fifty thousand out his pockets showing him. "Yeah, another fifty in the whip, shawty."

"A'ight, naw. I don't need the whole thang. Y'all give me a thirty count apiece. The discount already included. It's fifty of 'em right here!" Levi paused for a second. "A'ight now, y'all should be on like a motherfucker from here, right?"

Carlos And Lil' Fred counted out sixty-thousand for Levi placing it on the counter.

"Yeah shawty, This a jug right here shawty! That's love right there shawty! Good looking," Carlos dapped Levi up.

"Hell yeah…Shawty, I'm 'bout to snap! Straight turn up!" Lil' Fred said, He couldn't wait. Already making plays in his mind. He pulled his phone out texting, putting things into motion for later on. He dapped Levi up too.

"A'ight y'all I got to clear it. It's been fun though," Levi looked at Lil' Fred. "Come on bruh, shoot me to my whip right fast so I can gone take bruh to meet cuzo," he said, walking out the door.

**

Forty Minutes Later…
Northside Drive, Atlanta

Freak Zeenie and Levi walked through the doors of Restaurant Ten. Freak Zeenie saw Funk sitting at the table reading something on his phone.

"Check him out, bruh, looking all professional and shit." Freak Zeenie tapped Levi on his chest, pointing at Funk, who didn't recognize Freak Zeenie right off as they were approaching him, since Freak Zeenie had lost a lot of weight on his decade-plus-something bid.

Funk was looking like a Dapper Don Manikin. He was Gucci head to toe. Once Freak Zeenie was within inches of Funk's table was when he finally realized who Freak Zeenie was.

"Freak?" Funk said, jumping up embracing his favorite male cousin in a brotherly bear hug.

"Who else?" Freak Zeenie said, embracing him back. Releasing one another, they all took a seat at the table.

"Damn, cuz, I been waiting on you! You been the missin' piece to the puzzle, cuz. I'm talking 'bout for real! So this what it do," Funk got right to it. "I'm working on a movie, a documentary called the *Too Funky Era*! Recently, though, I been in the music business. Yeah, cuzo, I'm in the field like a scarecrow! Everybody rubbing elbows with me, cuz," Funk paused, letting his words sink in. Freak Zeenie and Levi were like jack rabbits sensing danger in the jungle. All ears. "I have a few artists of my own who been doing shows and walkthroughs, well until the China virus slowed shit down for a minute. But Lil' Durk, French Montana, Rick Ross, Future, just to name a few of 'em who on speed dial, cuzo." Funk clapped his hands together on the table and went quiet.

Freak Zeenie remained in thought for a few seconds.

"I know how you do, cuz. Well, like I explained to you over the phone, I have my Change of Heart program, which is a non-profit org! I have a bunch of different branches built around it that will benefit the community as a whole, you know?"

"Right," Funk and Levi said simultaneously.

"I also have my own T-shirt business I'm bringing to the table, cuzo, but the music." Freak Zeenie paused. "Is where me and bruh will shoot past the stars, Funk! I'm tellin' you now!"

"A'ight, I see! So, what's it called?" Funk asked enthusiastically.

"Duffle Bag and Hustle Mode Records, cuz. You know 'bout the duffle bag, cuz. It's no telling what's inside that motherfucker, hun?" Funk just smiled, knowing his cousins were one of one. They couldn't be imitated or duplicated.

Now that Freak Zeenie was free, they could all finally come together like Voltron and take over. Funk and Freak Zeenie went on to discuss the zillions of dollars they were about to confiscate from the world in itself. Funk knew Levi could talk that shit but not like Freak Zeenie. Freak Zeenie was the Don King of shit talking. Everybody and their mama knew this, and if not would eventually in the near future. On God.

They all left Restaurant Ten with 2020 vision on them, Benjamins, big blue daddies.

***

Later that Night...
Tallahassee, Florida

E-Dub pulled up on Lil' Tee, who was at the trap. Lil' Tee had been anticipating his arrival all day. He couldn't wait to get his hands on the A-1 bricks of ice. Lil' Tee had run into a few rich preppy white guys who went to Florida State University, who could move a whole glacier of ice in just a cool day or two.

Lil' Tee never revealed this secret to E-Dub, he'd just stretched it out for almost a week, finishing in time to pass E-Dub the re-up so he could go cop on time. Lil' Tee would use the money from the ice to purchase bricks from a side resourceful dude out of Dothan, Alabama. Then sell 'em to Horse Head on the low behind E-Dub's back.

E-Dub had just missed Lil' Tee's side plug by only minutes before he pulled up. If he didn't have to switch vehicles, then he would have caught Lil' Tee in the act. Lil' Tee came right out, walking to the passenger side of the car.

E-Dub had just shut the stash spot after he didn't find his products inside. Just as Lil' Tee attempted to get in, E-Dub jumped out, rushing in the middle of a conversation on his phone.

"Yeah, man. I hear you! Okay, yes, I'll be there in hun..." He looked at his watch. "Thirty minutes, tops!" E-Dub hung up, as he made it to the trunk. "What's up, bitch?" E-Dub dapped Lil' Tee up. "Man, these stupid motherfuckers ain't even put the shit up!" He popped the trunk of the car. "Look, come on 'cause I'm in a rush! Mom Dukes just hit me up all hysterical and shit, talking 'bout the crib been broke into or some shit s—" E-Dub stopped mid-sentence. "Hold up, I'm trippin', ain't it?" E-Dub pulled up the spare tire, thinking that's why Kendell them thought the product was already put up. "Man, what the fuck?"

Lil' Tee was clueless.

"You need me to roll with you, bruh?" he said, while observing the empty trunk faking concern.

"Man... Hold the fuck on now. Where the fuck my shit at, dawg?" E-Dub rubbed his head, puzzled, after he had searched the trunk frantically. Whipping his phone back out, E-Dub pulled his call log up then pressed send so hard he damn near crack the screen.

"Hello, what's up, cuz?" Kendell answered.

"Where the shit at, cuz?"

"What you mean? It's where you put it at, bitch! We ain't touch shit! Fuck you talkin' 'bout?" Kendell said defensively.

"A'ight!" E-Dub hung up on him. Then he found Denise's number and called her 'cause he never checked the trunk.

"Hello? What's up, E? You made it back safe, didn't it?" Denise answered.

"Yeah, I'm back, but…where the fuck my shit at, Dee?"

"What you mean?"

"I mean ain't shit here! That's what I mean!"

"Well, we both witnessed the demo as it was being dropped. So, now I'm confused. What are you trying to insinuate, E-Dub?" she said defensively.

"My shit's not here, but I did see the demo. I'm as confused as you, Dee." E-Dub slammed the trunk closed. Lil' Tee stepped back onto the curb, shaking his head, disappointed.

"E-Dub? Where did you go after our departure? Straight home?"

"I went to Lenox Mall, got valet parking, then I came out driving straight back to the W. Did the switch and hit it!" he said.

"Lenox Mall? Valet parking? E-Dub, are you serious? You did what?" Denise chuckled a little.

This caused E-Dub to become heated.

"Fuck so funny? I'm missing a fifty and that's funny to you?"

"I'm sorry, baby… But I thought everybody knew 'bout valet parking 'round the whole world. They'll rob your ass blind. You never do that. You would have been better off parking regular, E! The game cost now, honey. It's to be sold not told. Count this as a lesson for the future.

"It just cost you a light one twenty-five, you'll be okay. Just come back up and I'll look out on a little somin, somin extra on whatever you spend. Now I must be going." Denise disconnected.

E-Dub looked at Lil' Tee, who stood there with a poker face.

"Ain't that 'bout a bitch?" E-Dub was mad as hell, but he knew if he tried to catch the valet attendant the chances were slim. "Fuck! I got to go, fool. It ain't 'bout shit! I'll charge it to the game! Just gone have to shoot back in a few days. Right now, though, I got to go check on Mom Dukes, bitch. Be safe, I'll holla later on, my nigga!" E-Dub said, speed walking to the driver side. E-Dub got in, crunk up, and hit the gas, leaving a trail of white smoke behind him fishtailing up the highway.

Lil' Tee headed back in the trap.

"Yeah, you do that! I ain't trippin'! I just snatched me a few bricks to hold me down. I knew it! Right on time for moments like this, you heard?" he said, to no one out loud. The block was quiet as a mouse. "That's why I ain't the plug. I'm the socket. Keep an opening for more than one plug! Street rules!" Lil' Tee looked around outside before he closed the door behind him.

E-Dub made it home in record time, finding the door to his mother's house hanging by the hinges. He ran in, going to check one of his unknown hiding places, flying right past his mom.

Chapter 13
Two Months Later
Dothan, Alabama
Farm Center the Fairgrounds

It was hot as hell outside and summer hadn't even come yet. It was Fourth of July. William Porter, who was known to the streets as Dreamer, had put together a mean car show.

Dreamer was the king of putting a car show together. Every year he made sure to pack the Fair Ground out. Always promising live performances from the hottest rap artist out. This year it was rough since the pandemic was still in effect and no one wanted but so many people to gather together. Since this was to be an outside event, Dreamer was able to pull it off. People showed up from all over the country. Who else could sell dreams better then Dreamer? No one!

This year Dreamer brought Moneybagg Yo down with Lil' Baby, and Da Baby. NBA Young Boy was supposed to be there but got scratched due to the feds grabbing him months earlier off a high-speed chase. He was replaced by Young Nudy, another street rapper that had the streets going crazy.

Dreamer had the super soaker wet T-shirt contest that would take place at one o'clock in the afternoon. Then it would be the loud music contest. After that would be the cleanest old school contest, and last but not least was the flyest car of the year award. There would be judges from each coast to make sure it went proper.

The reward was worth a hundred thousand dollars cash and would land a place in the hottest urban model magazine out called *E'legal Activity*. So you know everyone brought their best vehicles out to win that cash, girls, and a slot in next month's issue. Quiet as kept, supposedly the City Girls were going to grace the cover featuring Mulatto. That was WAP sho' 'nough. Wet ass pussy.

Freak Zeenie sat low on the passenger side of the pineapple-gold and black 2021 Convertible Corvette that Levi choose to bring out. He couldn't have picked a better day to do so than the Fourth of July at a car show. Freak Zeenie was observin' everythang. Freak

Zeenie knew it was the smallest detail that made the biggest difference. This was how he stayed on point, because before was how he had lost his life temporarily, not paying attention.

Levi had the top down, windows up, sitting on twenty-four-inch black and gold Forgiato rims. They were parked up under a shade tree making small talk.

"This bitch already thick as fuck, bruh! Look at the line of whips waitin' to get in this bitch!" Levi pointed to the line of cars.

Freak Zeenie sat up a little bit.

"Now that's a motherfuckin' Jeep right there, bruh! Look at that bitch! Them got to be thirties on that bitch, hun?" he said, pointin' to a 2021 Jeep Wrangler Rubicon. It had an outrageous orange wrap on it and was sitting on thirty-two-inch, all-gold Forgiatos. The Jeep was crawling slowly, swerving side to side.

"Hell yeah! That motherfucker wet, ain't it?" Levi said, smiling. Knowing all the while who was in the automobile. "Them 'bout some thirty-twos or better."

"Sho 'nough? Yeah, I'm probably gone have to gone snatch me one for the one time."

A pack of young females stampeded through the crowd, excited, passing by Levi and Freak Zeenie, who hadn't stepped out the vehicle yet.

"Girl...look at that bitch right there!" One of the females pointed.

"I see it, bitch!" another said.

"Bitch, that's motherfucking Cartier Jay fine ass, girl! Y'all late! He been all over the Gram showing his newest whip, hoe!" Freak Zeenie overheard one of them say.

Freak Zeenie looked over at Levi, who was textin'.

"Cartier Jay?"

Cartier Jay was swerving hard through the fair grounds.

"Man, Boo-Boo? Get your motherfuckin' ass up, nigga! All this WAP in this bitch! You trippin', homes!" Cartier Jay said, as a text came through his phone. Picking the phone up from off his lap, Cartier Jay read the text.

"Shiiid, Cartier Jay! Man, this wockesha got a nigga nodding, leanin', and some mo' shit, homes! Know what I'm talkin' 'bout? Hell yeah, you know?" Boo-Boo sat up and said, asking and answering his own question at the same time. He was lookin' 'round, holding on to the Draco that rested on his lap.

Kal-Kal sat in the passenger side beside Cartier Jay. He was high as hell off the loud. Kal-Kal had recently been released from out the State Prison in Alabama. Cartier Jay had his clique with him tough today.

"This what I'm talking 'bout, cuz! This bitch lit, yah heard?" Kal-Kal's head was everywhere all at once.

Cartier Jay's eyes came from off the phone screen. Scanning the rows and rows of cars, trying to spot his uncle's gold Corvette. Cartier Jay had the all-gold Cartiers on with the VVSs on the arms with a matching Cartier bust down watch. James Brown had nothing on the way the flawless diamonds were dancing. A smile came on his face.

"Man, Unk already out this bitch! Nigga just text me. Say pull up, he settin' out a whole bag of zar' on the strength!" Cartier Jay hit the gas hard then braked, causing the exhaust to scream on the Hemi motor. You could tell he had it geeked up straight running. Cartier Jay turned the sound system up, shakin' the ground drowning out everything 'round 'em.

Boo-Boo tapped Cartier Jay's shoulder, causing Cartier Jay to hit mute.

"Bruh, ma-ma-man, I-I-I'ma le-let th-the fi-fi-fireworks g-go if-if ah-ah ni-n-nigga g-get out-out of line n-n-now!" Boo-Boo said, out of nowhere, stuttering. He was wide awake now.

Cartier Jay busted out laughing at his partner.

"Already, Boo-Boo!" Cartier Jay released mute. Moneybagg Yo came blaring through the speakers. "Clear Da Air" from off his latest album, *A Gangsta's Pain*.

Nigga be lying like they raw/48 hundred my cough/Put my lil' bitch in a loth/keep yo' eyes on the bread, I toss/ I threw some diamonds in a Audemar, coulda went and bought a car/open that trophy bag full of zar'!

111

They were bobbing their heads to the music while they wore a unit (mean mug) on their face. The females who passed by Freak Zeenie and Levi a few minutes ago ran up on Cartier Jay's Jeep, hoping to get chose but got the gas hit on them, shooting the Jeep forward swervin' and curvin' them at the same damn time.

***

Minutes Later...

Inching through the lanes of cars, Cartier Jay finally pulled right up beside Levi's gold Corvette. Throwing the Jeep in park, Cartier Jay jumped out stupid fresh. Ignoring the passenger, he went 'round to the driver's side greetin' his favorite uncle.

Levi lifted the door up and stepped out, embracing his nephew.

"What's up, nephew? That bitch on somin' right there now! What? You putting it in the contest or somin'?" Levi looked past Cartier Jay at the Jeep. "Who that, Kal-Kal right there?" He pointed.

"You better say it!" Kal-Kal said, getting out the Jeep.

"Welcome home, lil' nigga! Stay the fuck out! This where it's at!"

"Got to know that!"

Freak Zeenie sat quietly, eyes hidden behind a pair of all-black Cartiers. Cartier Jay glanced in his direction. *Damn, this nigga look just like my gotdamn step-pops and shit! Fuck this nigga is?* Cartier Jay thought then quickly pushed the thought to the back of his mind.

"What's up with that smoke, Unk?"

Levi looked at Freak Zeenie.

"Aye, Freak? You heard him? Pull that shit out, bruh!" Cartier Jay looked at Freak Zeenie then back to Levi then back to Freak Zeenie again.

"Yeah, a'ight, Unk! I sit on the bench, homes! You know I don't play at all! Especially 'bout Pops, nigga!" he said, wearing a very serious expression.

Freak Zeenie let the door up on the Vett and stepped out.

"You ain't the only one who don't play, son," Freak Zeenie said, holding his arms open. "Bring it in, son!"

Ran off on the Plug

"Pops? Man, what the fuck? I mean, when you—? How you get—?"

Cartier Jay was running through different phases before he finally went to embrace his dad. "Damn, it's good to see you, ole boy!" Cartier Jay was feeling super good now.

"Look at you, son! Boy you have grew the fuck up, hun? You was a baby when I left!"

"Yeah, I know. I was nine. You taught me how to count that money before you left! I ain't never forget! Now I make that bag talk, Pop, I ain't lil' no mo'!" Cartier Jay made an imaginary bag talking demonstration.

"Nawl?" Freak Zeenie smiled.

"Yeah! My line up two hun-dun (2 hundred), Pops! I don't drip, I drench in this shit! Look at it! Ain't it stickin'? I ain't wastin' shit! I wish I would drip some shit for these thirsty ass motherfuckers to try to suck up, ya heard?" Cartier Jay said, looking down at himself.

"Hell yeah, son! Talk shit, boy! You killin' 'em! Freak Zeenie said, wearing a proud expression.

"How long you been out, Pops?" Cartier Jay went to thinking 'bout the past events that took place.

"Not too long, son."

"You talk to Moms and Grandmoms yet? 'Cause no one mentioned it to me." He was studying Freak Zeenie carefully.

"Nawl, no one knows I'm out. I'm going public today, I think. Haven't made my mind up yet," he said, glancing 'round the fair grounds. "I see Unk still coming out here with them fresh pork skins, homemade BBQ sauce, homemade bake beans, and that good sweet chip BBQ, hun?"

"Know Uncle James 'bout to be surprised like a motherfucker! Y'all come on right fast!" Freak Zeenie mobbed toward his uncle James's tent.

James had a line in front his tent that would put Krispy Kreme donuts to shame when the light on. James had the smoky pig sign all 'round the tent. James had barbeque sauce stains all over his apron, and you could tell he'd been hard at work. James had the big grill fired up. You know the one with the three different grills on it?

"Next! Come, come! Best BBQ in the south! Hun? Meat so tender it melt in yo' mouth!" Uncle James fake cleaned his fingers with his mouth.

"That's right! Let me get the works, Unk!" Freak Zeenie yelled over the crowd, making his way to the front of the line.

Uncle James looked up, recognizing a voice he'd longed to hear but hadn't in over ten years.

"Nephew? Boy-y-y, when you get out? Come on up here and bring it in, nigga!" Uncle James was smiling, holding his arms wide open.

Freak Zeenie made it 'round the crowd. Everyone started calling him 'cause he was the city for real for real. Freak Zeenie stiff armed them all as he dapped hard, head high. Everything he had on cost an arm and leg.

"Just some dap for now, Unk, you know, you been cookin' and stuff." Freak Zeenie shook his uncle's hand.

Uncle James had everything grilling on the grill. He took the meat cleaver.

"I know you ain't ate like this in Lord knows when. I got you the hook up! Un-n!" Uncle James said, making a Master P adlib, causing everyone to laugh. He began to chop into the grilled pork. After cutting up enough, Uncle James sprinkled some of his special seasonings on the meat along with his homemade BBQ sauce.

Levi and Cartier Jay were shaking their heads no. Levi never ate the pork from their family-owned business. He only ate the sides. Cartier Jay couldn't help but think back to the Big Man's incident.

Uncle James was putting pickles and the finishing touches together for 'em.

"You know, Unk, I'm good on that pork stuff! Ya know I don't eat that type of meat! That's why I keep telling you. You need to add some beef in there!" Levi said, looking at the grill like something else was to pop up on it or something.

114

"Hell nawl, nigga! The name of this business is Smoky Pigs, nigga! No add-ons or takeaways, fool!" Uncle James said, stoppin' what he was doing, looking upside Levi's head like he were crazy.

"Man, Unk, you late! I eat seafood only. I'm on my healthy shit now! Man, a nigga trying to live!" Freak Zeenie said.

"Yeah Unk, me too. Matter fact, I ain't even hungry! I ate before I left!"

"Si-si-since w-when?" Ca-cause w-we b-be t-together a-all day, n-nigga?" Boo-Boo said, looking at Cartier Jay like he was crazy for missin' out, and putting him on blast at the same damn time. "L-Let me-me g-get hi-his t-t-to then, Unk!" he stuttered.

"Yeah Unk, don't forget me too! Load me up! Extra pork, I don't know what they cappin' 'bout," Kal-Kal said, rubbing his stomach.

"Suit y'all selves. The plates were on me. Y'all weren't gone have to pay, with y'all lil' young broke asses!"

"Who? Stop it, Unk!"

"Yeah, a'ight old school, I heard you!" Cartier Jay started laughing.

"Everybody know ain't nobody got no money but my favorite nephew, Freak! Can't nobody do it like him!" Uncle James said, passing Freak Zeenie, Boo-Boo, and Kal-Kal a plate of chipped BBQ bake beans and country cut steak fries. "Y'all make sure to grab one of them ice-cold beers out the cooler!" Uncle James pointed toward the cooler.

***

Across the Fairgrounds...

Just thirty yards away, unbeknown to Freak Zeenie, was Cedrick Bellermy (Ced-B). Ced-B was another informant who had proffer on Freak Zeenie. Ced-B's name was all in his indictment.

Ced-B received a downward departure for turning over as much information as he could to the DA. He had been out and had got into sound production. Ced-B was the one in control of making sure the music had the perfect sound and microphones. Ced-B been doing pretty good for himself, you know. Keeping his dirty deeds undetected and the fact that he was a bigger cat than the Chucky Cheese Mascot.

Ced-B was double checking all the equipment, making sure everything performed correctly for the performance. Dreamer didn't even know 'bout Ced-B or he would have never fucked with him on no type of level. Since he didn't, Dreamer had paid Ced-B well to make sure the people enjoyed themselves.

Ced-B grabbed a microphone.

"Testin', testin', one-two, microphone check." He place the microphone back in its stand. "Yeah, she straight!" he said, going on to check the rest of the equipment.

The fairgrounds was so massive. Even with all the speakers and microphones, it still wouldn't reach across the whole land.

***

Thirty Yards Away from the Stage...

Freak Zeenie ended up accepting his plate that Uncle James forced on him. They all had grabbed a beer and were now headed back toward the cars. Freak Zeenie leading the pack. The people had grown impatient waiting to place their orders.

"What? They VIP or something, dang?" one of the awaiting customers blurted out.

"Yeah, we been standin' here way before any of them! My money spend just like anybody else's!" someone else said.

Boo-Boo turned around, stoppin' in his tracks overhearing the complaints assault his ears.

"Spend th-that sh-shit then! O-o-ole cr-crying a-ass m-m-mutherfucker! Sh-sh-shiiid!" he said, sending a menacing look over to the customer.

"Maw, calm down, bruh!" Cartier Jay said, right before his phone came to life interrupting him.

Boo-Boo heard Cartier Jay loud and clear but wasn't trying to hear what he was talkin' 'bout. Boo-Boo continued to stand there muggin'.

"Hell nawl! I-I-I got-got-got-got th-these meat-meatballs jah-jammed in-in this ba-bitch for ah-ah nigga wh-who hungry! Blow-blow they-they got-got-dam spa-spa-spaghettis th-th-the fu-fuck o-ou-out round-round th-this ba-bitch! Sh-shiiid!" Boo-Boo said, hoping like hell to provoke anyone to call his bluff so he could shut the life off and the fairgrounds down.

Freak Zeenie burst out laughing so hard he almost dropped his plate. He was in such good spirits that he walked over the front of the line.

"Ya right, miss lady, where my manners at? Ladies first. Here you go, beautiful." He handed his plate to a short, thick, dark-skin chick.

She blushed. "Thank you," she said, stepping to the side for her two home girls to place their orders.

Uncle James nodded his head, giving his approval.

"That's right, nephew! A real boss move!" he said, showing his pearly whites.

"You already know, Unk! Oh, yeah. You ain't never saw me either. No one know I'm out, yah dig?" Uncle James nodded his head, agreeing to his terms. Freak Zeenie looked at Kal-Kal and Boo-Boo. Boo-Boo had the look of death written on his face toward the people in line. "Man…y'all let these ladies have y'all plates! Where y'all niggas' manners at?"

Kal-Kal stepped up without hesitation, passing one of the females his plate. She tried to protest. "Nawl, I want you to have it," Kal-Kal explained, then finally, she accepted it reluctantly.

Boo-Boo had a death grip on his tray.

"Who-who? Sh-shittin' m-me! Th-th-the hell if-if I-I-I d-do!" he growled out.

"Man, stop playing, Boo-Boo, and let the pretty lady have it. We'll come back later, nigga! You trippin'!" Freak Zeenie said. Levi was cracking up laughin' on the side. Cartier Jay shook his head smilin' while he was in a serious conversation on his phone.

The last friend of the trio was super model fine.

"Nawl, I can pay for my own food! Thank you, though," she said, keeping it polit. She opened up her clutch. Boo-Boo finally

117

had a change of heart, eventually giving the female his tray. He looked her up and down, admiring her sex appeal for the first time.

Boo-Boo turned 'round, adjusting his fire arm before dappin' off toward the vehicle without further words, being the goon he was. Freak Zeenie 'em looked at Boo-Boo, shaking their heads smiling. They all knew Boo-Boo since his childhood and knew he was a loose cannon who needed close monitoring twenty-four-eight.

Cartier Jay was trailin' slowly behind them, still in conversation.

"A'ight, bruh, turn on Ross Clark Circle and pull up, you gone be at the fairgrounds. I'll meet you at the gate," he said, ending the call. "Oh now? I got to run right fast! Be right back y'all! Don't start without me!" Cartier Jay took off running toward the gate.

Lil' Tee was at the front gate by the time Cartier Jay made it there.

"What's up, my nigga? What it do? Shiiid, this bitch lit, hun? I would check this shit out a minute but I'm headed to the A' right fast! Check it out, though. I got two honey buns and a biscuit for yah! I need a ten-piece chicken nugget (10 kilos)!" he said, pointing to a medium-size duffle bag.

"A'ight, I'm gone do that for you this time, bruh, on the strength. Next time, though, you got to come correct, partner. I don't know how y'all rockin' down there, but this ain't that! This the Dot! We come correct in Bama, homie," Cartier Jay said sternly, then a smile plastered his face.

"But...ain't no pressure. Good lookin', my nigga!"

"It ain't 'bout nothing, just slide back through on your way back. I'll have it ready for you."

"Say no mo,'" Lil' Tee said, throwing the car in reverse after handin' Cartier Jay the duffle bag.

Cartier Jay half unzipped the bag, peekin' inside before zipping it back. It looked right from him eyeballing it. He'd count it later to make sure it was what Lil' Tee claimed it was.

"A'ight, boy. Be safe on that highway," Cartier Jay said, before beelining it back to where he had parked.

Freak Zeenie sat on the passenger side of the Corvette, rolling a cigarillo of zar up, contemplating if he would take a few puffs of the exotic trees or not. He looked up and saw a familiar face making his way through the fairgrounds, greeting the people.

"Man, who that? William Porter? Dreamer? That's you over there? Hell yeah! What's up, my nigga?" Freak Zeenie said, placing the blunt on the console before getting out the car enroute toward Dreamer.

"Who that, Freak?" Dreamer said, squinting from the strong rays of sun blinding him slightly in the angle he was standin'. Dreamer put his hand up over his eyes to shield the light.

"Hell yeah!"

Dreamer smiled, walking swiftly toward Freak Zeenie. "Man, when they let you out?" He dapped Freak Zeenie up, embracing him.

"Let me see." Freak Zeenie went into thought. "Hell, a slight minute, but best believe I'm out chere!"

"Shiidd, I definitely can see that! Lookin' like that whole thang!"

"Already! I see you got this bitch shaking though! Hun?"

"Say what?"

"Say you got them vibes out this bitch! Shakin' the room like RIP Pop Smoke night!"

"Yeah, they out here!" Dreamer said, laughing. "Nigga, talk that shit then."

"Dreamer, you know me, bruh! From out them slums running up funds ain't 'bout to give a bitch a crumb, you heard?"

"Got that right!" Dreamer said, looking at Cartier Jay who eased up, dropping off the duffle bag in the back of his Jeep. "Boy, Cartier Jay, ya got that bitch mounted up, ain't it? I'm gone tell you now, you 'bout to give it to 'em this year now, lil' homie." He walked 'round the Jeep examining it thoroughly.

Cartier Jay smiled at him. "Got to know that, Dreamer! You might as well go and get that trophy and gone put that bitch right here. To cut you some time, you heard?" Cartier Jay said, opening up the back to the Jeep, patting the space back there.

"I don't have a problem with it, only after ya win it though. You know its comp' out this bitch now?"

"Where? I don't see none!" Cartier Jay looked around like he didn't see all the other tricked-out cars out there.

"You looking at him, nigga! You know I'm bringing the green machine out this year, nigga!"

"Well, that's all good, old school! We'll let the judges seal the deal, but like I said, this new wavy, and I don't see no competition out chere...yah diggg?" Cartier Jay said.

Boo-Boo started laughing at his long-term friend's cockiness. He poured up a double cup of Wocky, sitting wedged on the passenger side of the Jeep with a blunt of zar dangling from his lips taking light puffs all in the same. Freak Zeenie was smiling at Cartier Jay and how much his son had grown up since he left.

Moneybagg Yo took to the stage dripping like chili and turnt the fuck up, performing tracks from off his latest album, *A Gangsta's Pain*. He had Big 30 with him. Big 30 had that fire on him up on stage, giving it to them. The Fair Ground was jumpin' off the meat rack by the time Young Nudy took the stage performin.' Young Nudy was high as elephant pussy in his element, rapping tracks from off his album, *Rich Shooter*.

Lil' Baby gave up a few exclusive tracks no one had heard yet but Dothan, Alabama. The wet T-shirt contest had already took place, and Lil' Baby had the winners on stage with him as he did the Woe on stage. Then Da Baby came on, said a prayer, and explained to the crowd about the situation he had just got out of by the grace of God that took place in Miami, Florida a good month ago. The crowd was fucking with Da Baby the long way. He put on a grand performance.

It started raining out of nowhere without a cloud in the sky, sending the crowd scattering for shelter. It only lasted a couple of minutes, just enough to cool things off to heat up for the car show. I guess the Devil whipped his wife quick.

The vehicles began to pull up and line up to be judged. Freak Zeenie, Levi, Boo-Boo, and Kal-Kal were in a respectable place to be in a safe distance and witness everything all in the same.

"Now check Lil' Baby out! Nigga done got in the gotdamn contest!" Freak Zeenie pointed, as Lil' Baby swerved his charcoal gray Rose Royce truck up, playing "Rags to Riches," a song he was featured on, by Rod Wave. "That bitch fresh as fuck now."

"Hell-Hell yea-yeah! Bu-Bu-But n-n-not as fr-fr-fresh as Ca-Ca-Cartier Jay sh-shit i-is th-though, sh-sh-shiidd," Boo-Boo slurred, stuttering from the wockesha.

"You know what to say now!" Kal-Kal said. Levi just nodded his approval. He respected it but could get any whip he wanted from off the CPN jug. Plus, he was high as a UFO off the zar.

"Hold on now! Shiiid, I see trouble comin'! Who the fuck is that, y'all?" Freak Zeenie said, pointing to a Maybach truck on all-gold, thirty-inch Forgiatos. "That's that new Maybach truck right there now! I know what the fuck that is. Nigga just disrespected that truck now! Oh now, Levi? You see that shit? Bruh, the nigga got thirty-fours on a mutherfucking Maybach truck! This shit crazy! A'ight, this shit gettin' good now, ha!"

"Yeah, that shit stupid!" Levi said, checking the truck out a little closer. They all got up and moved closer to check the exotic truck out. The Maybach truck was flipping four tropical colors as it took its place parking. Levi liked the truck, being it had not long hit the market.

An extremely black ass nigga jumped out in an all-white Dior short set with a Dior head band and some all-white low-top Dior shoes on with no socks. A female got out from the remaining three doors of the Maybach truck wearing matching powder pink Channel body dresses and low-top Channel shoes. The extremely black dude hopped out and walked off nonchalant, leaving the truck. As he began to put distance between him and the truck, the women who came with him ran up on him real aggressive.

"Fuck they got going on?" Freak Zeenie asked, as they witnessed the argument take place between the four.

The women were pointing their fingers in the extremely black dude's face, rolling their necks with their hands on their hips the whole nine.

"Ain't no telling. Look like he got hoe problems though," Levi said, shaking his head at all the new drama.

They were going so hard that it drew all the attention on them.

"Okay! Really, Blahza? We will see, bitch!" one of the females said.

"So, you think you the shit, hun?" another said, all in his face. Blahza had his hands in his pockets with a cool demeanor, until one of them tried to snatch his headband off.

"Stupid bitch! Y'all better get the fuck back! Hell y'all talking 'bout?" Blahza said, mushing the third one lightly from out his personal space.

"Yeah, yeah, yeah, you right, motherfucker! We got something for that ass, bitch!" The three women ran to the truck, pullin' out medium-size Super Soakers. Surrounding the Maybach truck, they all pumped their water guns. Blahza began to charge them, but he was a lil' too late. "Who the bitch now, mutherfucker? Hun?" They were spraying his truck with the water guns that were eating the paint from off it in patches as the unknown liquid hit it. Turning it a prime gray everywhere it touched.

Blahza had a murderous look on his face.

"Hell fuck nawl! Fuck y'all hoes doing? Got damnit!" They had fucked the expensive paint job all the way up. Blahza was chasin' them but couldn't catch 'em. The females had dropped the water guns, running for cover. Everybody was in awe and ooh'd as they all witnessed the horrific damage.

Security came to calm things down.

"Sir, you gone have to leave the premises if—"

"Yeah, bitch! Let me see you win the car show now, mutherfucker!" one of the females said from behind the security guard.

"Look y'all, look!" a kid yelled out, gaining everyone's attention. "Ooo, the paint coming back! Cool!" the kid said. Everyone looked at the Maybach truck, and the paint was coming back slow as it began to start flipping tropical colors again. "That's my car right there, Mommy!" the lil' boy said, pulling on his mother with joy.

All the girls walked back to Blahza's side, putting their hands on their hips. The phones came out flashing, taking pictures of the truck. The crowd went crazy in uproar with rounds of applause. The car show hadn't even started yet. Blahza smiled, shaking his head, knowing he had just killed anyone's chances of winning.

"Yeah, that nigga just killed it!" Freak Zeenie said, nodding his approval.

"G-Got tah-to kn-know th-that n-n-now!" Boo-Boo admitted.

Even Cartier Jay saluted Blahza. He wasn't no hater. He knew to come super stupid harder next year though.

The judges wasted no time. They didn't need to see nothing else. They put up all tens for the Maybach truck, And three tens and a nine for Cartier Jay. Three tens and a eight for Dreamer's green machine.

"Well, there you have it, folks! We have a winner! all the wayyy fromm! Hold on. Where you from, player?" Dreamer said on the mic, pointing to Blahza.

"Florida!"

"Florida y'all! All the way from Fl—"

Blocka, Blocka, Blocka!

Shots rang out, surprising the crowd, sending everyone scattering for cover.

"Go, go, go! Damn!"

Blocka, Blocka!

Freak Zeenie was running and thought he saw a ghost. He spotted Ced-B, and they locked eyes. Freak Zeenie was trying to say something, but his words were drowned out from the gunfire. He pointed his hand at him in a gun image, and as soon as he did, Ced-B drop dead. Ced-B caught a head shot, blowing his brains out as he fell by the stage from a stray bullet. Moneybagg Yo crunk up the red 2021 Corvette up and cleared it.

Freak Zeenie and Levi made it to their Corvette, crankin' up and leaving.

"Man, you ain't gone believe this shit, bruh! I just saw that bitch ass nigga Ced-B! Soon as I recognized him, he got hit in his head, boy! Hun? Krama ah mutherfucker!" he said, as they were on Moneybagg Yo's trail until they hit the highway.

"You better say it!" Levi said, navigating the sports car with perfection. Freak Zeenie felt a thousand precent better after seeing the outrageous orange Jeep Wrangler sitting tall following closely behind them. Freak Zeenie grabbed the cigarillo from out the console. "After seeing that fuck nigga get his top knocked out, I got to celebrate! Happy Fourth of July, bruh! A cat died today! On fair grounds!" Freak Zeenie started laughing at his own joke. "You get it, bruh? On fair grounds!"

"Yeah, bruh. You already know! Fair grounds. Anything goes!"

Freak Zeenie put fire to the spliff, inhaling the strong, sweet aroma letting, it relax his mind as he released smoke through his nostrils. Instantly, the zar had him high enough to soar in the clouds.

Levi took them safely home with Cartier Jay right behind them. Freak Zeenie was zoned out, replaying the look on Ced-B's face when he saw him.

Once they made it home, they enjoyed each other's company and festivities the remainder of the evening.

Chapter 14
Dothan, Alabama
A Day Later

Levi and Cartier Jay were in Brentwood about two streets over from his main house in the upscale neighborhood in Dothan, AL. Cartier Jay had counted the money twice that he received the day before from Lil' Tee.

Now he and Levi stood in the kitchen at the island.

"Shiiid, let's get to work Unk. The nigga just hit me letting me know he coming back today. So I want to be ready you diggg," Cartier Jay said, grabbing a few different items.

"Already, plus I got a few jugs of my own. So check it out. I'm 'bout to put you up on the no taste no smell game now right fast! This how you cap on these rookies out here nep," Levi reached over, grabbin' the no taste no smell, bringing it to him. "So how many the mark want again, nep?" he said, taking a puff of zar and passing it to Cartier Jay.

"Just a light tension!" Cartier Jay had a nonchalant expression about it. Rubbing his hand together anticipating the boss game from his uncle. He knew Levi hadn't lead him wrong ever. His favorite uncle had him playin' with figures on a grown man's level.

***

Across Town…

Freak Zeenie was up early out in traffic. Today his initial plan was to pull up and surprise his mom. Ms. Lois. Freak Zeenie's phone came to life.

"Who this?" He looked at the caller ID. "Oh, a'ight." Nodding his head, he pressed answer. "What's up, woman? What's-up-with-that-puss-say?" Freak Zeenie sung his words.

"Put this wap all on that bald head, nigga! But what's up with the tree business? Meads been blowing my shit the fuck up 'bout the wood, baby-y-y-y!" Khashia said. "Put me on FaceTime, so I can see your face. I'm gone be able to tell if you need some of this good cat or not, nigga," she said demandingly.

"I'm in traffic. But I can just tell you now, I been blowing yo' shit up too 'bout this wood! I need you. I'm ready to hog dog that wet, wet," he said, smiling.

"Hot dog me? Fuck is that, Freak? Khashia held a serious expression.

"Raw dog-g-g! A real nigga deep stroke! Come on now, you know!"

"No hell I don't. I thought you was talking 'bout puttin' it in a bun or some shit, nigga!"

Freak Zeenie burst out laughing.

"You wild, hell nawl. Check it, though. What else on your schedule for today?"

"I got to go sign the insurance papers and put up that, you know what, on Mister No Show! Ah bitch, a millionaire! Just call me Misses Million." Khashia was cheesing super hard as her pussy got gushy wet thinking 'bout the commas.

"We millionaires, woman! Look at you. Ready to get selfish on a nigga already, hun? I thought they said six months though?"

"No, I'm not! You right. They did, but I got a call this morning to come in, baby."

"I already know."

"So what you gone be doing, after you handle the tree shit first, nigga?"

"I'm going to see Mom Dukes, but since I know she headed to work, I'm gone go and check up on some of our real estate properties first."

"So what, we meetin' up later tonight?"

"Better say it." Freak Zeenie pulled up and stepped at the red light. He looked to his right and saw the Jeep he wanted. "You mine!" he blurted out.

"You got to ask?"

"What?"

"I said you have to ask me that?"

"Nawl, nawl, my bad. I was talking 'bout this black-on-black Jeep Wrangler I'm lookin' at over here at the lot." He glanced back at the car lot before pulling off from the light.

"Oh, you want me to grab it for you, baby, when I finish?"

"Yeah, do that for me if you don't mind."

"Anything for you, Freak Zeenie."

"Already, let me get off this phone though sexy," he said, finishing up his conversation with Khashia.

Freak Zeenie pulled up to one of their many properties. This one was just so happened to be in Brentwood. *Now what they got going on?* he thought as he killed the engine, getting out seeing his stepson's Jeep.

Levi had broken a brick down. Plastic covered the island. This was to keep the cocaine residue from leaving any traces of evidence behind.

"This how this shit go, nep. You snatch a nine piece from off each block, you heard? Then put ah nine back in of—"

"No taste, no smell." Freak Zeenie walked in, surprising the both of them out of nowhere. "Un-hun, caught y'all asses, nigga! Fuck y'all got going on? So, y'all just done turned this to a safe house or somin, hun? Where the cameras at? How I just crep' up on y'all then?" Freak Zeenie held a very serious expression, staring at Levi and Cartier Jay. They both remained silent. "Hold on, hold on, hold on, now. Let me get this shit right. Levi, bruh, why are you up in here showing my son how to finesse the dope game, nigga? Fuck wrong with you?" Freak Zeenie stood there waitin' on an explanation. "I'm talking 'bout now is the time to say somethin', 'cause I see what's going on, nigga! So, you can't lie…What's up?"

Cartier Jay looked at Levi then to his dad. He chose to speak for his own self. Cartier Jay been off the porch, little did Freak Zeenie know. Part of it was his fault.

"Because…Pops. I'm all in! You been gone. Food must still go on the table And we all know bills never stop. It's money to be made," he claimed. This hurt Freak Zeenie's heart tremendously. Seeing how his departure had affected his son's life from his lifestyle rubbing off on his son.

Levi took his chance to speak.

"Yeah, Freak, shit. I tried to keep him steered straight on the right path, but he was determined. So if he gone be in the game, I have to make sure he is aware of the rules, know how to apply them, and always stick to them no matter what! Boy gone be boys and men will be—"

"Men! So, Cartier Jay. You a D-boy now, hun? This is a nasty game you chose to play boy, y—"

"You played it!"

"And lost! An got life! Yeah, I played it The game got me LIFE in a VSP federal maximum PRISON! What? You ready, to do life now too, hun? Throw ya shit away. Leave your family out here that you trying to feed to starve! Who gone pay the bills then? I'm pretty sure it will still get done without you, son! Like it did without me!" Freak Zeenie explained. His heart was shattering by the second.

Cartier Jay wanted to speak, but the respect he had for his pops wouldn't allow him to. What Freak Zeenie had said made plenty sense to him. The fact still remained, though. He was committed.

"Y—" He caught himself.

Freak Zeenie pulled out his phone, unlocked the screen, and touched it a few times. Just thinking 'bout how his family's lives had been forced made him ready to kill each and every one of his co-dees who sold him out to the feds.

"Come here, man! Let me show you somthin', 'cause I don't think you really fuckin' understand the seriousness of this shit, boy!" Cartier Jay walked over to him. "Ya see this?" Freak Zeenie turnt his phone around so Cartier Jay could see it. "Look, all these peoples I fed. Look! Read that shit!" Freak Zeenie looked at Cartier Jay. "That's a lot of folks, right? Right, we were family. You reading it, right? See they faces?"

Cartier Jay read the indictment and saw name after name, face after face. Some he knew, some he didn't. He came across one who he had been recently dealing with but kept his thoughts to himself.

"Yeah, they all turned on me, nigga! Put your dad in a concrete casket, sealing it shut. Traded my life to save their own. My motherfuckin' first cousin told on me!" Freak Zeenie shook his head in disappointment. "Two sisters' sons. We slept in the same bed. You thank that mattered to him? Hell fuck nawl! I said this to say, if the time comes, and it will come, trust me, it's gone be the one closest to you that kills you. And nigga, they won't hesitate! So, before you jump out there, you need to be sure this is what you can endure," Freak Zeenie explained.

"I hear you, Pops." Cartier Jay paused, choosing his words carefully. "I'm definitely sorry that happened to you. It tore the fam' apart fo' sur'. The difference from then to now, though, is me and mine are blood in blood out. We murdering first and never asking questions 'bout it. Any weary feelings, and POW!" Cartier Jay made a gun sound with his right hand in a gun formation. "It's too late, I been out there since you left, Pops, for real. Top-lip deep! So where were we, Unk?" Cartier Jay stated his facts and opinions 'bout how he viewed it then turned his attention back to Levi.

"See there! You talk too much, son! Never speak about what you have done in the past or will do in the future. It might come back to haunt you one day and be used against you!" Freak Zeenie said.

He was now fire hot, but it was nothing he could do to change Cartier Jay's mind. He had witnessed that look that he saw in his son's eyes before. It was the same look he once had back in the gap. Only thing he could do now was give him all the boss game that he had accumulated along the way. So, hopefully, Cartier Jay wouldn't stumble along his journey in life making the same mistakes that he did. How could he tell Cartier Jay about the speck in his eye, when he had a whole log in his own?

Freak Zeenie took a deep breath, calming himself down a bit. He put his phone back in his pocket, shook his head, and walked over toward the island by Levi. Levi wanted to say somethin' to his older brother but at this point, it was nothing he could possibly say to change this situation. Life had taken its course. Now it had to be lived out to find out how it would turn out.

Freak Zeenie did something today that he vowed to never do again in life. He revealed some precious jewels on how to milk the game for all its worth. A sure blueprint to climb the ladder to the height of riches without a downfall. Things that Levi thought he knew but never had a clue 'bout.

Cartier Jay was all ears soaking up the format from his steppops and favorite uncle, with his own plans to surpass them both. Once he applied his sauce with what he picked up from the both of them. After two hours, Cartier Jay had a lifetime of game, along with seven bricks of raw and three of straight flex (fake dope).

Levi had whipped up twelve bricks of flex for his ordeal, mixing 'em in with twenty real bricks. He looked at Freak Zeenie and rubbed his hands together, smiling.

"Ooh wee...I'm 'bout to fuck 'em up with this one, nigga!" he claimed, thinking of all the free bands he was going to bring in from off this one play.

Freak Zeenie just shook his head in an aggravated manner at the both of them. Here he was, just beat a life sentence, trying to show the community how to win from off the land of the free, to get home and his fam' was still in the streets with no plans of changin' as he could see.

"So this how ya got all those foreigns and shit, bruh?" he asked, thinkin' 'bout the profit from the no taste, no smell. Almost lured him in, until the consequences quickly outweighed the profit by a landslide, causing his mind to only live life in reality.

"Nawl, that's another investment right there called CPN, tradelines. I'm living off the land, for the free! But that's a later on topic, big bruh. I got to hit the highway and get it my way!" Levi announced, packing the last of the thirty-two kilos into cardboard boxes. He had arms like an octopus, getting money from eight angles like an octagon.

"Oh, a'ight. Yeah, I know all about the CPN tradeline shit, bruh, I'm just trying to see. "'Cause it's a lot of secret shit going on 'round me that I'ont know 'bout. I got to be in the know, nigga! I ain't with all that tip-toe shit 'round me. I'm tellin' y'all now, better know what the fuck y'all doing!" Freak Zeenie said, turning on the balls of his feet, leaving abruptly without waiting for any further response from either of 'em.

Levi and Cartier Jay looked at each other.

"He mad, ain't it?! Cartier Jay said, grabbing his duffle bag full of bricks.

"I think so, but he'll be a'ight. He has experienced a lot dealing with this side of the game, so now he on his righteous shit. Let's get this money, nephew!" Levi started carrying boxes out to his Coca-Cola truck. Cartier Jay went and threw his duffle bag into his Jeep, pulling off leaving to meet Lil' Tee.

Levi finished putting the boxes in the back of the truck then pulled, off headed toward highway 231 in route to Atlanta, Georgia in his big rig that he had painted duplicating the Coca-Cola brand. This was how he trafficked his illegal item. He could operate just 'bout any kind of vehicle with no licenses to show. He learned to drive a stick shift at the age of six. Levi believed in risk taking.

Freak Zeenie was in traffic. He had to put some serious thought 'bout the peoples who he had around him. One thing for sure was, he would not end up in the position he had just come from up under. Family or not.

Paper Boi Rari

Chapter 15
Later That Afternoon

After checking on a few more real estate properties and putting everything in order with Meads and the tree business, Freak Zeenie headed to his mother's house to give her the surprise that she deserved.

"Yeah, it's been well overdue," he said aloud as he parked up the street a few houses away and waited in the car until she came home.

Ms. Lois had been calling Coleman Prison faithfully as she began to worry about her beloved only child. *It has been way too long since I heard from Deacon*, she thought to herself as she pulled into her driveway of her upscale home.

I pray all is well with my baby, Lord. Even you know he would have reached out to me by now. I think these nasty peoples are lying to me. Every time I call, they keep saying the prison isn't on lockdown or keep me on hold so long that I just hang up. Ms. Lois was running different situations through her mind as she unlocked the door to the house.

Ms. Lois threw her keys on the counter and rushed to the bathroom. Soon as she closed the door to the bathroom, her doorbell began to go crazy. She snatched the bathroom door open.

"Now who this at my door ringing the doorbell like they have escaped from a doggone plantation or somethin'," she said, as she briskly walked to the front door as the doorbell continued to sound off. "Hold on, hold on, I'm coming, just wait a minute!" she yelled, and seconds later, locks could be heard unlocking. She finally snatched the door open. "Ok, now what's the big emerg—" Ms. Lois stood there trying to let her speech catch up with her mind as Freak Zeenie stood there smiling. "Dec—"

"Yes, Momma. It's me! Surprise!" He embraced his mother as she squeezed his neck tightly. They rocked back and forth, enjoying the moment.

Ms. Lois released her son.

"Come on in!" Stepping to the side to let him enter, tears of joy cascaded down her face as she secured the locks on the door. "Why didn't the lawyer call me and let me know you were being released, Deacon, so I could have come and picked you up?" She stared at him as they walked toward the kitchen.

"Because, Mom, it didn't come from his end h—"

"Well, who did it come from then?" she said, not waiting for him to finish.

"God, Mom. He allowed me a second chance," he said, as he took a seat at the island clasping both hands together.

"I knew God would send my baby back to me, answering my prayers," she said, as she began to move expertly about the kitchen. "I got to cook you a homecooked meal right now!" Ms. Lois took out pots and pans, placing 'em on the countertop. "Don't break your promise with God now, Deacon, by the temptation of these wicked streets! I love you! The streets love no one. I pray you learn that from your horrible incident you've just experienced for a little over a decade, didn't you?" She stopped, glanced back at Freak Zeenie a second, then went to the refrigerator.

***

Meanwhile, Across Town...

Cartier Jay pulled up on the west side of N. Ross Clark Circle. Lil' Tee was waiting in the parking lot of a new venue that recently open in Dothan called Hanger 38. A family friendly arcade and full-service restaurant and bar.

The parking lot stayed crowded, which made it the perfect spot for if you wanted to go unnoticed to public eyes. Cartier Jay understood if you doing something you shouldn't, do it right under their noses because they would never see it. Cartier Jay threw the car in park, leaving it running.

The driver side and back window came down at the same time on Lil' Tee's car. Cartier Jay placed the duffle bag through the back window on the seat smoothly.

"You put somin on 'em and straight drop!" He stepped up, dappin Lil' Tee up. "Next time paid in full, ya feel me?" Cartier Jay wore a dead serious expression.

"Already. Ain't no pressure. Let me gone hit this highway. Twelve was already deep back up the way on four-thirty-one as I came through stoppin' everything moving, checkin' licenses and registrations and shit. Got to make a town down off this play. I'm in the red zone! 'Preciate the love, I'll hit you when I'm finished, maybe a couple of days," Lil' Tee said, fast talkin' Cartier Jay. He would try to short him chance after chance if he could. Lil' Tee threw the car in reverse, backing out slowly as he made his claim.

"A'ight. Be careful on that highway, hit me when you ready," Cartier Jay said, saluted Lil' Tee, and jumped back in his Benz. Cartier had switched vehicles on the way knowing his Jeep attracted too much attention as it was. He pulled out right on Lil' Tee's bumper as they made it to the exit. Lil' Tee went one way, Cartier Jay went the other.

***

Back at Ms. Lois's House…

Freak Zeenie was full as a stuffed turkey, relaxin' in his mother's den watchin' TV as he made light conversation with her.

"They finally made Juneteenth a national holiday, after all these years. Ain't that a blessing? The world's transitioning on our behalf," Ms. Lois said, placing a hot cup of coffee in front of Freak Zeenie.

"Thank you, Momma. Yeah, it's overdue. They ain't done nothing. President Biden just making up for all the damage he has caused to our communities in the past," he said. "President Biden ain't nothin' but a liar. If it was up to him, I'll still be locked up 'cause he still hasn't signed no bills to release nobody like he said and been in office almost a year!" Freak Zeenie was muggin' as he picked up the steaming hot coffee, taking a few light sips before placing it back down.

"I agree with you a hundred precent on that, Deacon."

"The world's messed up, Momma. You heard about Derick?"

"Who?"

"The officer who killed George Floyd!"

"Oh, yeah, say he got twenty-two years, right?"

"Only twenty-two years? For a cold-blooded murder! In front of multiple witnesses! I received a life sentence, for drugs that they say I had. They were told I had, they heard I had! Never got caught with even the slightest bit of residue! They oppressin' us, Momma. Now explain to me, how is that equal justice, Momma?" Freak Zeenie's phone lit up, interruptin' him. He looked at the screen, not recognizing the number but answering anyway. Freak Zeenie held his finger up for Ms. Lois, indicating for her to give him a second. "Hello?"

"This is a pre-paid call from 'Levi,' you will not be charged for this call. Press five to accept or nine to disconnect," the automated service said.

The color drained right out of Freak Zeenie's face once he heard his lil' brother's name come through a jail call. Freak Zeenie pressed five, thinking the worst already. "Yeah, hello, man what the hel—I mean, what you done did, man!" Freak Zeenie said anxiously.

"Man, I hit four thirty-one and all hell broke loose, bruh! Russell County Sheriffs on both sides. They got me on no CDLs license and traffickin'. Bond at a million! Go tell Remy Red I said do that thang I told her 'bout, use the reserve tank. She know what I'm ta—"

"Hello? Hello?" the jail phone disconnected. "Ump, ump, ump!" Mad couldn't explain Freak Zeenie's anger he was feeling at the moment.

Ms. Lois became alarmed noticing her son's demeanor transition from happy to mad in the blink of an eye.

"What's wrong, baby?"

"Nothing to worry 'bout, it's always something," he said, getting up. "I love you, Mom. I'm gone be using one of the real estates in Brentwood until I find me something. You know I'm coming to see you much as I can and calling every day!" Freak Zeenie hugged her and rushed toward the door.

"Deacon, don't go and get yourself into no more trouble now. You just came home. Stay home! We need you out here, I need you out here! Ms. Lois said, giving him the words of a loving mother.

"I know, Momma. I know! I'm not!" he said and took off in a sprint down the street toward his car. *See what I'm saying? See? This what I'm talking 'bout!* Freak Zeenie thought to himself as he made it to the car.

Freak Zeenie left his mother's house in deep thought, anger, and confusion but loyal to his family. He was all in.

Paper Boi Rari

Chapter 16
Tallahassee, Florida
The Next Day

Lil' Tee had just got off the phone with E-Dub with plans to meet up in the next day or so. According to E-Dub, he was gone come through and drop so much weight on Lil' Tee, that even Samson from out the Bible couldn't lift it all by himself.

That encouraged Lil' Tee just that much more to hurry up and get rid of the ten bricks he'd scored from Cartier Jay. He wanted to make sure he had his money right 'cause he was fluctuatin' between two consecutive plugs. Lil' Tee had tried to convince E-Dub to gone come through now, but E-Dub claimed he was in Marianna, Florida at his mom's crib, busy at the moment. Even though Lil' Tee was using reverse psychology, he never wanted to see E-Dub today from the start.

Lil' Tee made a few calls trying to get off his product and couldn't conduct one sale. Everybody he'd contacted had just purchased or just wasn't ready yet. What he really needed was the ice that E-Dub had, but he also knew E-Dub would also have coke to go with it. Becoming frustrated, Lil' Tee went through his whole call log.

"Man, I got to gone get this shit off real quick!" he said, talking aloud but only to himself. *Shit, I bet the fuck nigga Horse Head bitch ass ah buy all this shit right now!* he thought to himself. *I need a mediator, though, someone he could buy it from not know it's comin' from me,* Lil' Tee was thinking as he scrolled his call log for the second time when he came 'cross a name who could be the perfect candidate. "Motherfuckin' Main!" he said aloud. "Main would do it and I'll never be suspected of it. Thank God for family," Lil' Tee said, pressin' send, calling his cousin, Main.

"Y-yeah, wh-wh-what's, what's u-up, c-cuz?" Main answered, stuttering his ass off.

"Boy, I need yah one time, bitch!"

"W-w-what's hap-happenin'? Ta-talk t-to me, c-c-cuz," Main said. Lil' Tee went on to explain his master plan, cutting Main in on the play as he freestyled his play.

Lil' Tee impatiently waited for Main to call back. Becoming bored, he jumped in his whip to cruise through the city. He rode in deep thought. Lil' Tee thought about how his life was going. *How am I moving all the dope but still staying on the roughest side of town? I mean, I'm getting a bag, don't get it wrong. How am I still driving this Charger when this nigga switching foreigns and shit. I get my own shit! Everybody know Lil' Tee stay fly! I'll jack that fool before he bird feed me!* Lil' Tee's thoughts were running wild as he was trying to find fault against his main man, E-Dub.

Lil' Tee pulled up in the apartment complex called Hidden Village, right 'round the corner from Tallassee Mall. He was just out riding with no specific destination.

"Damn, that's…" he blurted out, bringing the car to a snail's creep. "Damn, show the fuck is them hoes," Lil' Tee said, making a complete stop, watching what they were about to do. "That's the lil' hoes me and E-Dub met. So he done hotdog both y'all, hun? Bingo!" he said, as he found a parking space and parked.

The two females were obviously tipsy by the way they clumsily walked to their car. Finally making it to their Model X Tesla, the taller one out of the two was the driver. She pulled out swerving at first before she got it together.

Luckily for Lil' Tee, he had the chance to see what apartment they came out of.

"Got to see," Lil' Tee said, and he waited for about five minutes. He got out, looking 'round. The complex was pretty empty for the most part. Lil' Tee went to his trunk, poppin' it. He grabbed a pair of gloves, a navy-blue skull cap ,that came with the bib, and a crow bar. Lil' Tee put the cap on pulling it down low, then pulled the gloves on. He looked 'round one last good time then headed to the door he had witnessed the females come out of.

Lil' Tee made it to the door, listening for a second after not hearing a sound. He knocked a few good raps just to be sure. Wasting enough time, he finally stuck the crow bar between the ledge of the door jam. Lil' Tee was inside the small apartment in under two minutes. Once inside, he moved like a professional burglar. In a matter of seconds, Lil' Tee found exactly what he was there for. "Damn, jackpot!" The middle room was compact with bricks. "Ole smart ass nigga, dumb as fuck!" Lil' Tee ran and snatched the sheets from off the bed and went to work. It was just too many. He would need a U-Haul truck or better to pack up all those bricks, so Lil' Tee just got what he could, making it out of there unnoticed.

***
Seven Minutes Later…

Soon as Lil' Tee made it back to Holton Street, his phone lit up.

"Yeah, what they do, bitch!" Lil' Tee answered excitedly.

"That's done, cuz, sh-shiiid, I-I'm on my w-w-way," Main said.

"Bet!" Lil' Tee ended the call. He knew he had to find somewhere to hide the bricks. His house wasn't a good spot. It would have to do for now. He would just have to keep any company away.

***
Two Hours Later…

Lil' Tee had gave Main $2,500 for handling the ten-brick transaction. Now two hours hadn't passed good before Main was calling him back

"Yeah, what's up, bitch!?" Lil' Tee answered, irritated.

"A-A-Aye, c-c-cuz. W-we g-g-got a-a pr-problem." Main was stuttering bad, speeding through his words.

"What's that?"

"H-H-Horse Head s-s-said th-that s-so-some of th-the stuff was-was n-n-no g-good! He wa-want h-h-his m-money b-back, c-cuz! Look—"

Lil' Tee disconnected. "Ain't no way I'm giving a nigga shit back! Dope sold, money fold! Fuck all that! Where they do that at?" Lil' Tee said aloud, scrollin' through his call log finding Cartier Jay's number. He pressed send, and it was answered after a few rings.

"Oh now?" What's up with it? You ready already, my boy? That's what I'm talking 'bout," Cartier Jay answered, and asked. He couldn't wait for this call.

"Naw, say, some of it wasn't right."

"What you mean, it wasn't right? Everything added up, didn't it?"

"Yeah, but it didn't come back? What we gone do 'bout that?"

Cartier Jay took the phone from his face and looked at it like he bit a sour apple. *What we gone do 'bout that? Fuck he mean? Like he pressing me or some stupid shit! Nigga, you was the fuck short in the first place, pussy! What ya thought was gone happen?* Cartier Jay concealed his thoughts. Barely. "Well, if it's taking too long to lock up, bring it back. You was short anyway, bring a stack! Nigga, you know how the song goes!"

Lil' Tee shook his head and smiled.

"Fuck it, tell you what. My bag long and strong, just put me another four piece together. Plus, I'm gone straighten up that lil' bit I was short on too. That way you can just tighten that up too at the same time, how 'bout that?" Lil' Tee said. Even though he didn't need the bricks, his pride and greed had him going. He was feeling himself from his earlier successful lick. "Plu—"

"Yeah, that's cool, bruh. We can do that. Good ya said that, 'cause you called at the right time. Matter fact, one of my lil' bitches down the way right now. Shiiid, she will bring you up here and shoot you back for me if you want! Gas on me, nigga. Where you want her to meet you at?" Cartier Jay said, knowing he wouldn't turn the opportunity down.

"Tell her to come to the Greyhound bus station. I'll be there."

"A'ight, I just texted. Oh, hold on. This her right here hitting back, bruh." He took a second to read her text. "Okay, check it. She say it's a go. Meet her there, don't beat her there. She right up the street at McDonald's on Tennessee Street, homes."

"One hundred, I'm on the way. What she on?"

"A blue Karma Revero GT."

"A who?"

"A car you never saw before, nigga." Cartier Jay hung up.

Lil' Tee took all the dope in the house after drivin' 'round to the back so he could be discreet. Once he put everything up, Lil' Tee quickly headed to the bus station. He wanted to get ghost anyway, knowing Main would soon be pulling up looking for him to straighten up the misunderstanding. That he had no plans of doing.

***

Two Hours Later
Dothan, Alabama

"What's up, homie?"

"I'm out here." Lil' Tee sat in the car hitting ignore on his phone, not answering Main's call. He had called him over two hundred fifty times and countin' in the last four hours.

"Oh, alright." Cartier Jay looked out the blinds. "I see you, come on in." He ended the call.

Lil' Tee saw him in the blinds and got out. Soon as he closed the door, the female pulled off.

The front door came open on the house.

"Come on in, partna, so I can hook you up and get you back on the highway. She coming right back after she hit the store for me." Cartier Jay stood two feet back from the door. There was thick plastic covering the entire floor.

Lil' Tee noticed plastic on the floor as he made his way up the steps.

"What's with all the plastic? Y'all painting or some shit?" Lil' Tee took a few more steps. "'Cause that's wha—"

Blocka!

Boo-Boo pulled the trigger one time from the Glock 45 soon as Lil' Tee broke the door seal, blowing blood and brains all over the front door and floor. Lil' Tee collapsed, crumbled up on the floor, barely in the door. They both grabbed one of Lil' Tee's legs, draggin' him further into the house.

Cartier Jay closed the door as Lil' Tee's blood oozed down the door.

"Wrap this snitching ass nigga the fuck up, bruh! Whatever's in his pockets yours, yah heard," he instructed Boo-Boo to do.

"A-already r-r-ready, b-bruh." Boo-Boo went to work, tucking his gun in the small of his back.

Cartier Jay went and grabbed the chemicals to sanitize the front door. After checking to make sure they cleaned up everything, Cartier Jay and Boo-Boo carried Lil' Tee's corpse to the bed of the stolen hearse. Spinning rocks out the driveway, Cartier Jay was headed straight to Web, Alabama. To the hog farm. "Bitch ass nigga told on Pops! Small world, stupid muthafucker! Feed his bitch ass to the hogs."

***
Webb, Alabama
Twenty Minutes Later…

Cartier Jay parked and laced Boo-Boo up on what was about to transpire. Boo-Boo put two and two together and liked to vomit thinking 'bout how close he almost came to consuming the food at the fairgrounds on the Fourth of July. Then got mad 'cause of how Cartier Jay was just gone allow him to eat it without warning. They got into a light argument for a minute, but Boo-Boo quickly got over it.

They got out, both working diligently through the night to get rid of Lil' Tee's remains. Just like Levi told him not to do without his permission.

But Levi wasn't here now, was he?

Chapter 17
Marianna, Florida
The Next Day

E-Dub had been calling, calling, and calling, blowing Lil' Tee's phone up trying to reach him. He did the same to Main's phone. E-Dub couldn't reach neither one of 'em to no avail.

"Fuck!" He threw his phone down out of frustration. "Damn man! Loss after got damn loss!" he hollered through the house. E-Dub had just gotten back from the college girl's house. They called him last night, but he couldn't make it because he was out of town. Finding out this morning that he took a good hit on his bricks had him heated. *At least they didn't clean me out*, he thought. E-Dub had to pack the remainder of the kilos home with him. He couldn't take the chance of them coming back for the rest of them.

Moments later, his mother entered the house, fresh in from her F-Bop job.

"Hey son, can't believe you still hangin' 'round these parts of the woods," she said, as she headed down the hall straight toward her room, preparing for her shower.

Needing time to clear his mind, he switched the TV on the Dothan, Alabama news station.

"Dothan's crime rate has sky rocketed in this first half of year. The homicides have increased tremendously. Just last week marked over two hundred homicides. On the Fourth of July at the fairgrounds, a middle-aged man by the name of Cedric Bellermy was found and pronounced dead on the scene with a gunshot wound to the head. The murder is being investigated but unfortunately, is still unsolved. Another man is still missing, folks, who was strongly involved in the community. Sad but true, the authorities are starting to assume he is also dead, but the hope is still there. Everyone knows him by Marcus Wright."

"What? Marcus Wright missing? Big Man? I didn't know that! Ced-B dead? Damn! Shit crazy," E-Dub talked to the TV.

He didn't catch another word the news reporter said after that. With the news he just received and worried about his own situation,

145

E-Dub was only one setup from going back to the feds. He knew if he didn't make these busts for the Marshals, he could kiss the streets goodbye. E-Dub had the setup part down pat. He had the Gucci belt with the mic in it that he already had used to hit a couple of his victims with, but they were just add-ons. E-Dub's real lick was Denise up in Atlanta, Georgia.

E-Dub had already made his mind up that he was going to bring Denise and his homeboy, Lil' Tee, in, to trade them for his own freedom. *Damn! Where that lil' bitch at? See, they fucking with my plans and shit. I got to fatten Lil' Tee ass up with bookoo kilos right. Yeah, then turn the feds on to him. 'Fore they get him, get that money from him, turn 'round go shop with Denise, get her voice on the recorder. Then turn that shit in. Hell yeah! I got to do this*, E-Dub was thinking to himself.

He knew if he pulled it off, he was for sure a free man after he worked his move. E-Dub had only one, well, two problems.

One, the dope had been tampered with and wasn't all there for the most part. Two, Lil' Tee hadn't picked his phone up yet. E-Dub put his hands in his face, taking a deep breath. He picked up his phone in another attempt to reach Lil' Tee.

E-Dub's mother came in, sitting on the couch across from him.

"You alright, Eric?" she asked.

"Yeah, Mom. Just been a lot taking place lately. Look, you need anything before I get ready to head to Tallahassee?"

"Nawl, baby, I'm good. Thank you, though. You be safe out there, Eric," she said, getting off the couch walking behind him.

"I will, Mom, don't worry," he said, walking in a daze.

"Oh yeah, Eric? I knew it was something I was meaning to tell you," she said in a matter fact tone.

"What's that, Mom?" E-Dub stopped and faced his mother.

"You know your boy ah, Early Barbers, out, right?"

"Say what?" E-Dub's ears lit up like a deer's as his stomach dropped.

"Yeah, he got out a few months ago to be exact! Compassionate release. Ain't that something?"

146

"Yeah, that's something, Mom. Thanks, Mom, I love you!" Out of everything he had recently found out, this was some of the worst news ever by far. The dope being stolen was a small fragment to this newly discovered news. E-Dub was now scared shitless with his skittles ass self.

E-Dub drove back to Tallahassee, Florida, replaying the names he heard earlier on the news. *Cedric Bellermy and Marcus White?* he thought to himself.

"Could it be? One missing and one dead. Both have to be tied to one another. I don't believe in coincidences. It has to be you, ain't it, Freak Zeenie? Yeah, I know your work, nigga!" E-Dub was checking the mirrors now every two seconds out of paranoia, thinking Freak Zeenie could be following him. If nobody knew, E-Dub knew how pernicious Freak Zeenie could be when crossed. "Oh!" E-Dub swerved, crossin' over the land, barely missing an oncoming car head on. He thought he saw something in his peripheral vision, but it was only a group of birds. "Damn, I'm trippin'."

E-Dub pulled his phone out, wasting no more time. He called the Marshals explaining his made-up theory to them about Freak Zeenie being responsible for the two murders, well, one murder and the other missing. E-Dub explained to the Marshals about how they were all on a conspiracy case together and they all debriefed on Freak Zeenie, causing him to receive a life sentence. And now that he was free, all of a sudden, people who were responsible were missing now or either dead. E-Dub was trying to give as much as he could to secure him a spot in the free world instead of a federal prison.

The Marshals jumped right on this new information form E-Dub. They trusted his words as if they came from one of their own officers. After a few strokes of computer keys, they quickly found out that Earlie Barber had been released a while ago.

The Marshals instantly contacted Dothan Police Department, briefing them with the information received from their high-profile informant.

Chapter 18
The Next Day
Phenix City, Alabama
Russell County Jail

Freak Zeenie, Remy Red, and Poochie were at Russell County Jail. They all were waitin' to meet up with a bond lady from triple-A-bonding. Freak Zeenie was already skeptical about attempting to make a million-dollar bond for his brother, Levi, being that the news was blowing the lucky bust all the way up. Playing it back to back on the morning, noon, and night Channel 12 News like they were breaking a new hot record or somethin'.

Freak Zeenie tried to convince Levi that this would be a dumb ass move. Not only was he risking losing his money, he was risking the county to turn his case over to the feds also. Since they both had experienced the feds in the past, Freak Zeenie knew that the feds would be the last person either one of them would want to see. Of course, Levi didn't want to hear none of what his older brother was talking 'bout, he wanted out. After all, he was the one who was locked up, not Freak Zeenie.

After sitting in the jail's parking lot for nearly twenty unwanted minutes, a silver Mercedes S-class Benz pulled up and parked. A middle-aged woman stepped out elegantly dressed. She moved with precision. Freak Zeenie got out and met her before she could reach their vehicle.

"Hi, you must be…Mr. Barber?" the middle-aged woman said, holding a well-manicured, delicate hand for him to shake.

"Yes, nice to meet you, Ms. Jackson," he said, accepting her hand and shaking it firmly. "We bought what you asked a—"

"Well, yes, that part. We have a big problem," she said, just as Remy Red and Poochie made it alongside Freak Zeenie. Ms. Jackson was looking nervous all of a sudden.

"What's the problem?" Freak Zeenie said sternly as he put his hands in his pockets, looking directly in her eyes.

"First off, your brother's bond is set at a million dollars cash! He's allegedly charged with trafficking over thirty kilos of cocaine.

I'm not a lawyer, but even I know that it would be a bad move for him to try and make a bond of that kind. It's just not smart, know what I mean?" Ms. Jackson held her arms up and hunched her shoulders. "But, if ya just want to donate some money, then it's on you!" Ms. Jackson put her hands on her hips and stared at all three of them while she waited to hear his response.

Freak Zeenie blew out a whiff of frustrated breath. He looked at Remy Red and Poochie to feel a reaction, but they had a poker face.

"So how long you think we gone have to wait?"

"Quiet as kept, he'll go to arraignment next month. From there, the county gone turn this case over to the feds. This is the biggest drug bust in Phenix City's history!" she said, looking at them, feeling a pang of sympathy for her young Black people. "I'm so sorry, sweetie. I'm not even supposed to be mentioning this to y'all for real. Just look at the bright side, though. At least I didn't trick you all out the money knowing in advance that they would place a federal hold on him, right? Like most these wicked peoples out here would have done with no regrets," she said.

"You right, I was afraid of all this. Thanks a lot, Ms. Jackson," Freak Zeenie said, extending his hand for a departing handshake. Ms. Jackson shook his hand and said her goodbyes and good lucks to the women with him. Then she proceeded on toward the county jail to carry out her business.

Freak Zeenie, Remy Red, and Poochie jumped in their car, crunk up, and shot back down 431 hwy, headed to Dothan, Alabama. They all knew Levi would be mad, worried, and depressed once he received the recent news. Freak Zeenie was mad already. He had already warned him And his stepson of these possibilities. Freak Zeenie hated to admit it, but it was true. One day you here and the next day ya gone. Like UGK them said many years ago.

Levi paced the small dorm floor back and forth anxiously with his hands behind his back. Wondering what was taking Freak Zeenie so long to get him the hell out of there. Levi gave his dinner tray away. He would eat on the other side. He walked over to the

150

phone about to call his big brother, but the CO cut it off, calling for them to lock down for count and shift change.

Levi was mad as hell. He cussed all the way to his single-man max cell. Too bad he didn't know, but he would soon find out. The hard way.

As of right now, Levi's ass was stuck like Chuck. Ya heard?

Chapter 19
Two Weeks Later
Detroit, Michigan

The next two weeks passed by swiftly. Today the wind blew the muggy air that was so thick it would take a chainsaw two and a half blades to cut through it. Cars could be seen cruising up and down Jefferson Street. Car horns could be heard, as the police sirens howled in the distance along with ambulance sirens blaring. People moving along up and down the sidewalks were carrying on with light conversation. None of this distracted them because this was the norm in Detroit, Michigan. A treacherous city, home to pimps, players, robbers, prostitutes, hustlers, Mo-Town, and Motor City.

With Levi incarcerated and no clue of his release date, he had to sign the power of attorney contract over to Freak Zeenie. Once Levi caught wind that the feds were lookin' to intervene, he jumped on top of everything. Trying to sell anything that they may try to confiscate or siege.

Freak Zeenie had to catch a flight to Detroit so he could hopefully tie up some loose ends on a piece of property that Levi had out by the airport. It was an offer on the table for a substantial amount. The city wanted it for a commercial development. This was the second time that Freak Zeenie would try to seal the deal. The first time didn't go well. Being the businessman he was, Freak Zeenie turned the offer down. The offer didn't satisfy Freak Zeenie's financial appetite. See, Freak Zeenie knew the offer should have been in the double mens (Millions). Instead, they insulted his intelligence with a measly five hundred thousand dollars.

When Levi discovered the news, he went ape shit on Freak Zeenie for not taking the deal, knowing that he only purchased the piece of property for a steal. Levi had only paid thirty-five thousand cash for it in the first place. They way Freak Zeenie figured it was, the city not only wanted the location, they needed it. See, but the way Levi saw it, though, was fuck all that shit Freak Zeenie was coppin' 'bout. Get what you could before it was found out about, and they lose it without nothing. That debate ended between the two with Freak Zeenie ending the call on Levi before the call was up. So you know Levi broke the jail phone on the wall from not being in control wanting things to go his way. Plus breakin' an inmate's jaw along with it for speaking on him breaking the phone. Straight to the SHU he went.

So today he would not have a say so in the business. Freak Zeenie was in a barber shop that sat on Jefferson. Freak Zeenie got up after the barber finished checkin' out his face in the mirror. Went in his pocket pulling out a blue hundred-dollar bill.

"'Preciate that, bruh!" he said, handing the barber the currency. "Keep the change," Freak Zeenie said as he made his way toward the exit.

The barber smiled.

"Good looking, but that was the price, dawg," he said, pocketing the money poppin' the barber bib out.

I already know, nigga! I ain't got shit extra for a nigga, fool! Fuck you talkin' 'bout? Freak Zeenie kept his thoughts quiet as he walked out the barber shop. Making his way out the barber shop, Freak Zeenie bumped into a lady who was busy talking on her phone plus trying to talk to her pre-teen at the same time. "Oh, damn, my fault, Ms. Lady! I got it. Damn!" he said, as he bent down picking up her phone from off the ground.

"Nawl, you need to watch where the fuck y—" Her words were cut short. "Freak?" she said and asked at the same time, in her Detroit accent. Squinting her eyes, she didn't believe them at the same time. "Boy-y-y, what you doing in the city?" When the fuck you get out?" The pre-teen boy was looking back and forth between the two, looking confused.

"Denise! Damn, who would have ever thought I would have bumped into you out of all peoples," he said sarcastically.

"What you mean by that?" she asked, with much attitude in her voice.

"Girl, stop playin'! How you all happy to see ah nigga all of a sudden. When ah nigga wrote you, I'ont 'member you respondin'." Freak Zeenie had a serious mug on his face as he rubbed his freshly trimmed beard.

"Well, first off, you d—" Denise didn't get a chance to finish her statement. Freak Zeenie walked off, stiff arming her, leaving her words to hang in the air. He didn't stop until he entered his new triple-white Rolls Royce Dawn. Freak Zeenie let his top down and turned up the sound system. Moneybagg Yo could be heard clearly. If pain was a person. Waiting for the lane to clear, Freak Zeenie got in traffic. He was running a couple minutes behind to complete the deal on the property. Denise wasn't talking 'bout nothing far as he was concerned.

Denise's pussy was wet as the seven seas as she corrected herself. "I was trying to tell you...that—" She looked at her son, who was looking at her, also trying to figure out what they had going on. Denise decided to keep her words a secret like she had done for over the last decade or so.

Chapter 20
Days Later
Dothan, Alabama
Police Convention

Police officers from the surrounding counties gathered together today showing unity. They were participating in different competitive activities. Challenging counties for rewards as they performed, showing off their good-guy duties. Who could outdrive the next, the best shooter in target practice, the mile run. Things of that nature, with plenty refreshments to enjoy.

Officer Duke was sweating profusely as he sat in the white fold-up chair under the shade tree along with two more officers. Officer Duke was sipping an ice-cold Coca-Cola as his breathing returned to normal from the mile run. He was the chief over in Bakersville, Alabama.

Officer Duke took another sip of his beverage then sat it down on the grass between his legs. Grabbing his phone off his waist reading a text, Officer Duke started texting back while he quietly listened without trying, to the two officers who sat next to him who were on the drug task force in Dothan, Alabama.

"If only he would have let us execute the warrant, then we would have already locked that maggot Maddox under West Jefferson Maximum Prison!" the bulky white officer said, leaning to the side spitting out a wad of tobacco juice onto the grass.

"Tell me 'bout it. Now we have allowed Russell County to lock up and grab one of the biggest busts Alabama has ever witnessed!" the lanky officer responded, patting his forehead with a face towel containing the sweat.

"I know that mutherfucker Levi Maddox wasn't as clean cut as he presented to be! And it's very sickening just to think of him living eight houses away from me. I fucken knew it!" He punched his hand for emphasis.

"Such a shame." The lanky officer shook his head. "Knowing we should have been jumped down on him. Now they say the big boys are involved. Making us look like wussies down here."

"Yeah, I know." The bulky officer dropped his head in disappointment. "But on another good note, though, Chief gave us permission to start an investigation on his older brother. Earlie Barber."

"What about him?"

"What about him? What about him?" The bulky officer jumped up out his seat, almost knocking it over.

"Listen, I been on the force over twenty years! Now this mutherfucker, Barber, who goes by Freak Zeenie! What kind of gotdamn name is that anyway? Hun? But like I was saying, though, he was slicker than a can of oil. Tried everything to bust him, but I can't lie, he had his shit extra tight! Plus, he comes from a family of wealth. He was too big for Dothan. It took for the feds to bust that thug. Get this, not even a federal agent neither!" he said.

"Who then?"

"Fucking Northern Division of Florida. Some fucking rat inside of his own team took him down. Ain't that ah bitch? Anyway, he ended up with a lengthy life sentence, but after thirteen short years, he has somehow returned. Chief said he recently received a call about him a few days ago. Claiming that he is somehow behind the disappearance of that other shit eater, Marcus Wright, and a few others." The bulky officer walked back and forth as he explained the details.

Officer Duck could not believe his ears. He sat there until the officers finished all the details about Freak Zeenie. It was enough that he just found out that Levi had been taken off the streets, who he was sure moving dope in the surrounding areas like he was a CVS. If that wasn't shocking enough, then the news of Earlie Barber's freedom was. Officer Duke didn't know that, and on top of that, he already was back on the laws' top ten list.

Before they ended the police festivities for the day, they all were briefed on Earlie Barber BKA Freak Zeenie and his capabilities. Warned to shake him up, mostly careful not to blow the investigation because as of right now, it was only a tipped hunch. Which was called a criminal complaint. They would have to build the case.

Freak Zeenie was now a potential candidate to Dothan Law Enforcement and surrounding areas.

Chapter 21
Days Later
Tallahassee, Florida
Holton Street

E-Dub pulled up right after Main pulled off, missing him and all the action by minutes. First thing E-Dub witnessed was that Lil' Tee's door was hangin' only by the hinges. Fear and worry started to set in on him.

E-Dub threw his whip in park but left the engine running as he examined the house, dialing Lil' Tee's number in the same moment.

"I'm sorry—" E-Dub ended the call after getting Lil' Tee's voice mail.

"Fuck!" Not wanting to be a witness or better yet, a suspect, E-Dub eased off, pressing speed dial on his touch screen. The phone began to ring.

"Hello, what's up, E?" a female voice came through on the other end of his phone.

"What's up, D. Shiiid, I'm on my way," he said, sounding a bit down.

"Okay, waiting on you. See you when you get here," she said.

E-Dub ended the call as he got into traffic headed to Atlanta. He was feeling some type of way. One of 'em were confused and angry because he couldn't locate his main man, Lil' Tee. Which he had started to think Lil' Tee was behind his dope missing. Until he'd just witnessed Lil' Tee's door hangin' by a thread. Then he had another thought. Just then, he picked his phone up, calling Leon County Jail.

After a few minutes of holding on, E-Dub found out that Lil' Tee wasn't incarcerated either.

"Damn! I don't know!" He couldn't help but think the worst. Then he thought of Freak Zeenie. Shit was falling apart around him quickly.

That thought became short lived because his own problems quickly haunted him. Threatening to put E-Dub behind bars for an eternity, eating disgusting food. Now he was left to do what he did best. Tuck his tail like the bitch he was and set someone of value up to escape with his freedom. This was his reason for the trip to Atlanta, Georgia.

As E-Dub passed through Houston County, he couldn't help but think about Freak Zeenie. *I wonder did they pick his fuck ass up yet?* E-Dub's thoughts were running a hundred miles per hour. He got the eerie feeling that someone was watching him. E-Dub got on all his mirrors and hit the gas a little more, trying to hurry up on through a county he had begun to hate so much.

***

Somewhere on the Southside
Tallahassee, Florida…

Main was smiling like a Cheshire cat. He had just come up on a super lick.

"A'ight, my-my-my b-b-bad, b-b-bruh! I-I-It's a-all th-th-there. F-F-from now on, y-y-you c-can cop st-straight f-from me-me th-though, i-it's gone be j-just like that, ev-ery ti-time," Main said, passing Horse Head a few stacks of money and a quarter key of cocaine extra to help make it right from the bad dope the first time.

"A'ight, Main, good looking. Ain't no pressure, ya a real one. The rest of them niggas ya be fucking with be on some ole flaw shit! Straight floggen. If this is what you say it is, then I'll spend somin." Horse Head dapped Main up, went and jumped in his whip, and peeled off.

After attempting to contact Lil' Tee to no avail, Main went over to Lil' Tee's a few times. Each time Lil' Tee wasn't there. This time, Main kicked the door in and ransacked the houses, coming across so many bricks that he could build a single-family home. Well, maybe not that many, but you get the picture. Main was set, plus he came across a few good racks also.

Main walked in his house.

"I-I-I'm b-b-bout ta-ta-to t-t-turn th-th-the f-fuck u-u-up ou-o-out here!" he finally managed to get out as he closed his door, lockin' it then putting the chain on. Main went and peeped out his blinds one last time before pullin' the curtain closed. Main had become 'noid. For some reason, when you got them free bands off the lick, it always seemed to have that effect on you. I don't know why. It just do.

Paper Boi Rari

Chapter 22
Dothan, Alabama

Today, Freak Zeenie was high off life and his accomplishments. Everything was on the high rise for him. The only side effect was that Levi wasn't out here with him to celebrate the success.

After Freak Zeenie returned from Detroit, Michigan, he moved himself and Khashia into one of the family's real estate homes out in Brentwood. Khashia was overjoyed with Freak Zeenie's new transition he'd made. Not only did she purchase him the black-on-black Jeep he'd requested, Khashia took matter a lot further.

"Where are you taking me, woman? You know I don't like surprises now," Freak Zeenie said, as he relaxed on the new leather seats of the passenger side of his SRT-8 Wrangler Jeep. Khashia had the exhaust system howlin' away in traffic.

"I got this, nigga," she claimed, peekin' out the side of her Chanel frames at him.

"You trust me, don't you?"

Freak Zeenie played with that question for a second. Thinkin' of all the peoples who had crossed him in the past that he'd once trusted.

"You already know. I'm just saying…shiidd—" Freak Zeenie stop talking as Khashia pulled into a parking lot of a building. The parking lot was vacant except for their vehicle.

"Well, we're here!" she said, unstrapping her seat belt, exitin' the Jeep. Khashia looked at Freak Zeenie, who was still just sitting there. "Well… you comin' or not?"

"What is this? A B&E or something?" he asked, as he unfastened his seatbelt then exited the Jeep.

"A what, Freak?" Khashia stopped to see what he was talkin' bout.

"A B&E! Breaking and entering," he claimed, as he made it to the front door of the building with her.

"Stop it!" Khashia unlocked the door and they stepped inside of the dark building. It was very cool on the inside. "Just give me a sec', let me find the lights. They're somewhere over here." She fumbled 'round a split second.

"Wel—"

"Surprise!!!" came simultaneously as soon as the lights popped on, catching Freak Zeenie by surprise. He stepped back a few feet, getting in a defensive stance. Once he recognized a few familiar faces, Freak Zeenie couldn't help but smile before bustin' out into laughter.

"Man, what's this 'bout?" he asked, walking over embracing his mother. "You behind this, ain't it?" His whole family was there, all his kids and aunties. Unfortunately, there were a few important people missing, like his brother Levi and one of his uncles.

"Baby, me and Khashia went in and purchased this building for you. This way you could gone start up your Change of Heart program. The community need to hear from you, and we need more peoples out here like you," Ms. Lois said, with a warm, motherly smile.

"Oh yeah…!" he said, looking at Cartier Jay. "So you knew 'bout this all this time and didn't lace me?"

"Nawl, Pops. I'm just as surprised as you are," Cartier Jay said, holding a poker face.

All six of Freak Zeenie's kids rushed him, hugging him in a group hug and hitting him with question after question. This was their first time seeing him since he had been out. Ms. Lois had kept his freedom a secret from everyone. So this was a surprise for everyone all in the same. She had them all thinking something different from the other.

"Man, I'm speechless! Thank y'all!"

"Me too, nephew!" one of his aunts said.

Khashia and Ms. Lois gave Freak Zeenie a walkthrough of his new building as they made plans of how he could decorate the inside for public speeches.

Ms. Lois's sister walked up.

"Come here a minute, Lois," she said, cutting the tour short.

"Alright," Ms. Lois said, looking at her son, touching his arm. "I'm so proud of you, son!" she whispered before going to see what her sister wanted.

Freak Zeenie and Khashia continued to make small talk as they watched Ms. Lois and her sister carry on with an intense conversation. A few minutes passed before Ms. Lois and her sister ended their conversation. Ms. Lois seemed rather worried for the remainder of the day.

As the day unfolded, everybody enjoyed themselves as they ate good and congregated among one another. No one even noticed the slightest difference in Ms. Lois's mood. She was good at showing no emotion.

Ms. Lois was good, but nothing got by Freak Zeenie's keen eye. Freak Zeenie had picked up on it from the moment his aunt started speaking to his mom. The way they kept looking back over their shoulders and at him caused him to be alert.

After watching Ms. Lois for a while, Freak Zeenie walked up on his mother.

"What's the matter, Mom?"

"Oh, nothing, Deacon, just kinda tired, son," she said. Freak Zeenie always could tell when his mom was hiding something from him, but since everyone was enjoying themselves, he decided to play it cool, going along with the flow of things.

"Well, thanks again, Mom, for all this." He waved his arms around. "So I guess we can gone and retire for tonight. I think we all had a great time today, and no one appreciates it more than me, Mom. If something is wrong, make sure you let me know, Mom. Most likely I can help," Freak Zeenie said, trying one more time to get Ms. Lois to express herself to him. He gave his mother a big hug and kissed her on the cheek, still coming up with nothing from her.

"Thanks, son. You know I will. You just keep doing the right thing and make a difference out here for the ones who need you. Son, you are a born leader. So lead! The right way! God has something special for you in the end," Ms. Lois said. She walked off with her shoulders saggin' because she already knew how argumentative her son could become at times. Ms. Lois also honestly didn't believe that her son was involved in anything illegal. How could he be? He just got out after coming from up under a life sentence. It was just a mother's instinct.

***

Dothan, Alabama/Brentwood...
Later On...

Later that night, Freak Zeenie laid up in bed thinkin' about his first speech he would present to his community. Khashia was fast asleep. After she presented Freak Zeenie with some fire head, he returned the favor by fucking her into a baby coma.

I wonder what's up with Mom and my aunt, though, for real. Freak Zeenie's thoughts were turning. He glanced at the nightstand.

"Shit, I might as well," Freak Zeenie got up and picked his laptop up and went to work on his presentation. He wanted his first appearance to be his best appearance at his Change of Heart program.

Freak Zeenie worked on his program diligently well through the night until the wee hours of the early morning.

Chapter 23
Atlanta, Georgia
The Next Day

E-Dub had put everything in place. He would meet his cousin Kendall with 40 kilos of ice alone with another 60 kilos of cocaine. E-Dub had Kendall waiting for him in an apartment complex near Martin Luther King Junior Boulevard and Maple Street in Atlanta, Georgia.

E-Dub was a couple steps ahead of the law. He had Reneesha meet him so they could switch vehicles. Reneesha transported the money from Tallahassee, Florida all the way to Atlanta, Georgia for E-Dub in a hidden compartment of a cream-colored 2021 Toyota Camry. E-Dub didn't want everything in one car, so he had them drive separate cars there but turned right around and changed patterns, making plans to send them back down the highway together. Even though it didn't make sense to Kendall or Reneesha, they never stopped to question his decisions. Why would they, when he was paying for their services?

Reneesha pulled in the parking lot where E-Dub was already waiting. She pulled up and got out. E-Dub was antsy.

"A'ight, Reneesha, good looking out. Here you go. This won't be more than an hour or so. Kendall waiting for you over on Martin Luther King Junior Boulevard," E-Dub said, as he handed her fifteen hundred dollars for driving the car for him.

"Ok, E-Dub. Thanks, be safe. Yeah, he called me already. So, I'm on my way over there now," Reneesha said, as she put the small bag of money on the passenger seat of his Range Rover. Reneesha walked swiftly to the driver side, jumped in his truck, and pulled off.

E-Dub waited for a second until he was satisfied with Reneesha's distance as he sat in the trap car. E-Dub finally eased into traffic on his way, in deep thought. *Somebody going to prison, but if I got anything to do with it, it definitely won't be me*, E-Dub thought before picking up the phone, touching the screen a few times.

The number started to dial a moment later.

After a few seconds of rings, the phone was answered.

"Hello?"

"Yeah D, pulling up in seven," he said, turning on his signal light. E-Dub dropped his right hand holding the phone close to his lap, making sure to get as close to the belt with the built in recorder that the feds gave him.

"A'ight, E-Dub, come on through. Everything's in order," Denise claimed, in her most assured sexy voice.

E-Dub put the phone back to his ear after being sure to capture her voice on the recorder for the life of his own future. He felt no type of way 'bout his pussy ass ways. E-Dub had pulled some of these same stunts back in 2004 and 2005, taking down some foreigners down South Florida. He had done this so many times the shit just came natural to him.

"Say no mo'," E-Dub said, but not meaning it. What he really wished for was for Denise to say something incriminating to sink her own boat. "You heard?" he asked, but Denise had already hung up, and the line went dead. E-Dub dropped his phone back in the console.

I'll get her to talk more once I get there, better know that, E-Dub thought to himself as he navigated through traffic.

***

Seven Minutes Later…

E-Dub was greeted at the front door by Denise. Denise stood in the door in a sheer, white lace nightgown, barefoot on the cherry oak hardwood floor. Denise made sure to leave nothing for E-Dub's imagination. E-Dub stood there soaking in every sexy inch of Denise's tasteful body. Denise's hips were bowed out, showing off her smooth, flat stomach to go with her nice pretty titties. That sat up like cantaloupes with big brown circles around her extended nipples.

Denise bit down on her bottom lip and grabbed two handfuls of her titties, pushing them up, squeezing 'em at the same time.

"Well, E, do you like 'em or what?" she asked, staring directly into his eyes. E-Dub was caught by surprise and had yet to move from off the front porch into her house.

His manhood rose to attention. Denise was everything he'd imagined she'd be, a straight dime piece.

"Hell fuck yeah," E-Dub said. Denise reached out, snatching him by his belt buckle into the house. She closed and locked her door as E-Dub was rubbing all over her soft body.

Denise went to sucking on his neck as he lifted her up onto the wall. She fumbled with his belt until his pants were down 'round his ankles. "Ahhh!" She let out a whiff of air as E-Dub found her soft openin', pushing his full length all the way to the hilt as her wetness enveloped him completely.

Denise had straight pressure. That juice box was slippery wet. E-Dub only managed to get off a short session of good, strong pumps. Within moments, he released himself all up in her womb.

"Got-Got-Good-Gotdamn!" E-Dub stuttered but managed to get out as he slowly eased Denise down.

They both were breathing hard from the good sex.

"I-I don't know where that came from, E," she said, as they gathered themselves. E-Dub couldn't complete his sentence.

Denise escorted him into the living room, and they took a seat on her love seat. "So, E, after this baby you gone have to give me a minute, because this the last of this shipment," she paused, letting her words sink in as she was observing him as well. "My connect has caught a traffickin' charge. So I'm 'bout to get ghost until I'm sure they don't flip and snitch me out," Denise claimed, before going silent.

E-Dub's heartrate seemed to be beating a thousand miles per hour. At first, he almost caught a second nut on himself from how Denise was saying all the right language that he was sure would soon be used against her in federal court. Until he heard her say she was 'bout to get ghost and vanish.

E-Dub didn't really care 'bout the re-copping part because after he got back to Florida and turned the recorder in to the feds, he would be expecting for them to look Denise up, and he had hopes to be done with the drug game. E-Dub had plans of getting his citizenship in another country. He knew he'd burned his name and reputation up in this one.

"Damn, so, I must make the most of this then. When you ready, though, just let me know, 'cause I'll be ready," he said, trying to keep her talking. Wishing the feds would come now and bust 'er.

Denise took a deep breath before speaking. Truth was, though, Denise's connect hadn't been hemmed up by the law. In fact, she never had a connect. Denise's closest cousin had gotten assassinated and left on the side of the highway in another state. Denise used to hold all his drugs and a lot of money for him at her place. Once she found out he was deceased, Denise went to work with what was left like a Mexican on a construction site in the United States who had just crossed the broader.

"You already know, E, you have been a very profitable, loyal customer. That's why I had to give you a little going away present to remember me by," Denise said, then she got up and walked E-Dub to the front door. "Everything's already in place out there." She pointed toward the car. "Drive safe out there. I'll keep in touch with you, maybe we can link up and do this again sometime." She touched E-Dub's arm, searching his eyes for assurance.

This was pernicious to E-Dub's operation, but he still had faith in his plan.

"Sounds like a plan to me," E-Dub said, hugging her and grabbing hands full of juicy ass. E-Dub turned 'round, stepping in full stride. Suddenly, he stopped, turnin' 'round. Denise was still standing there watching him.

"Hey, D?"

"Yeah?"

"'Preciate it!" E-Dub said, before getting in the Toyota, cranking up, and leaving.

Denise closed the door, never really knowing what he appreciated. The drugs, the money, or the pussy. She went in the house wondering. If only she knew, it was none of the above. E-Dub was talking about all the incriminating confessions he had just captured on the hidden recorder to help him help the feds help free him.

No sooner than E-Dub made it up the street, four black identical Range Rovers pulled up into Denise's driveway. Denise came back to the door only to be greeted by some very well-dressed Mexicans.

Denise barely got the door open.

"May I h—" The group of Mexicans entered, walking straight past her without invitation. "Ah, excuse me?"

***

Back on Martin Luther King Junior Boulevard and Maple Street...

E-Dub swapped vehicles out with his cousins, Kendall and Reneesha, giving them the dirty Toyota loaded with a 100 kilos. He hopped in his Range Rover that was clean as a whistle.

Denise's assistant had retrieved the money from out the stash spot. Putting as many kilos into the stash spot as possible, which wasn't many. So the some went on the back seat with a sheet over them and the rest went into the trunk.

"A'ight, y'all already know what to do! Once we make it to the city, I'll finish cashing y'all out. I'll be twenty minutes behind y'all this time instead of being in the front, yah dig?" Be alert cuz!" E-Dub said, out the driver side window.

"Already, bitch. Meet me there. Don't beat me there!" Kendall said, pulling out. He looked back in the back seat.

"Look at this shit! We good, though," he said, more to himself than to Reneesha, even though she looked back there anyhow and shook her head, keeping how she felt silent. She cared only 'bout her cut. Money had that effect on people who were in need of it. They made wild decisions without serious thought.

E-Dub sat there for a few seconds in thought. *Man... Fuck all that! I can't do her like that. Shit, I know she strapped! Denise going*

173

with me! She say she about to vanish anyway, we might as well go together, E-Dub was thinking to himself.

E-Dub took his belt off, got out his truck, and put the belt under the back tire of the truck. Then he jumped back into his truck, putting it in reverse, slowly backing over the belt buckle and crushing it under the tire. He rolled the truck over it twice more just to be sure. *All these niggas I got for them. They should be happy, fuck they talking 'bout,* E-Dub thought to himself as he pulled out the parking lot enroute back to Tallahassee, Florida.

E-Dub picked his phone up, calling Denise. He let it ring until it went to her voice mail. Trying again only to get it again. *Damn, I'll just keep trying,* he thought to himself.

E-Dub called another number.

"Hello? Agent Kane here. Talk to me. I'll talk back," Agent Kane answered.

"Everything in motion. I'm straight dropping," E-Dub cheered, pushing end on his phone. Dropping it in the console, he set his truck on cruise control at eighty miles per hour.

E-Dub made it to Spalding County, Georgia. The interstate was lit up like the Fourth of July at Walt Disneyland. Traffic was backed up for miles. Black Track Hawks with flashing headlights, state troopers, and local police could be seen on the side as E-Dub and the rest of the traffic inched their way through.

As E-Dub passed by, he made eye contact with Kendall, who sat in the back of a police cruiser. E-Dub just shook his head. The officers were pulling kilo after kilo from the back seat and the trunk of the Camry. Reneesha was in a separate car crying her eyes out.

E-Dub finally made it through the thick of the traffic stop, picking back up his speed. *Cousin or not, nigga, I'm straight drop, fool!* he thought to himself. E-Dub was already formulating his next plots. He grabbed his phone out the console once again, calling a few more numbers. Lil' Tee was one of them, only to get his voice mail.

***

Later That Night…

Griffin Spalding Narcotics Task Force Office

"Kendall Odale and Reneesha Hunts were arrested in Spalding County, Georgia after a traffic stop was tipped off by an anonymous caller, revealing that a cream-colored 2021 Toyota Camry was transporting approximately 100 gross kilograms of powder cocaine and methamphetamines. Forty of 'em ice and sixty of 'em cocaine! Well, folks, it's been a great day for Spalding County. They might not ever see the streets again," Agent Kane proclaimed sarcastically, holding an imaginary mic in his hand, imitating a news reporter. He was working on Reneesha first.

Reneesha was still trying to squeeze out tears by crying but by now, there was just no more water in her to release.

"All I did was drive for Eric! I swear on my life!" Reneesha said, calling E-Dub's government name to Agent Kane.

"How much, how many times, what was your cut, where is this Eric now?" Agent Kane shot a rapid fire of back-to-back questions at her. Reneesha answered as best she could, but what little info she gave on E-Dub had the Northern Federal Division on his team. "I wish I could help you, but this just won't free you as of yet. If you can think of anything else, don't hesitate to contact me." He slid her his business card, tapped the table twice, then got up. "A'ight, Reneesha, take care."

Agent Kane looked at the officer who stood in the far right corner. "She's ready," he said, and walked out the interrogation room. Reneesha dropped her head as tears finally formed in her eyes. The officer took Reneesha straight to jail.

Agent Kane made it to Kendall. "You want to go to jail or you want to go home?" Agent Kane asked, coming through the door quoting a famous line of Denzel Washington's from the movie *Training Day*.

"Home!" Kendall said, searching Agent Kane's eyes to see if he was pulling his leg or not.

"A'ight, I need something I don't know about all this, and it better be good, because I'm missing a good shot of pussy right now, which could be my chance of making another good agent in this corrupt world such as myself." Agent Kane pulled the chair out and sat down, pulling his pen and pad out along with a recorder.

Kendall made a mess with it. He started his proffer in summary, hold on, let's read it and see what he said:

On September 5, 2021, Kendall and Reneesha Hunt were arrested in Spalding County, Georgia after a traffic stop revealed that they were transporting 100 gross kilos of cocaine and methamphetamines in a 2021 Toyota Camry. Kendall operated the vehicle while Reneesha Hunt was the passenger in the vehicle, Kendall told SA Kane and JCDTF Captain Rabs.

Kendall said, he is an associate of Eric Horne BKA (E-Dub). Kendall said, he spent the night of September 2, 2021 at Horne's residence, which is located at 999 Burnt Leaf Lane in Tallahassee, Florida. Horne woke Kendall up on the morning of September 4, 2021 and informed Kendall that Kendall and Reneesha Hunt would be traveling to Atlanta, Georgia the next day, in different cars, in order to obtain cocaine and ice meth from a person, who Kendall didn't personally know. Reneesha was to transport the money of Horne's that was claimed to be $1,500,000 in United States currency inside a hidden compartment, which was located inside the 2021 Toyota Camry, prior to Kendall and Hunt leaving for Atlanta, Georgia.

According to Kendall, his original job was to be a "lookout" for Hunt. Then, on the way back to Tallahassee, Florida, Horne (E-Dub) claimed there was a problem with one of the other cars, so E-Dub instructed Kendall and Hunt to ride in the same vehicle. Both Kendall and Hunt were aware of roles in the act. Kendall went on to say that Horne (E-Dub) also had included his live-in girlfriend, Toyka John. Claiming that she rode in the same car as E-Dub. That they were but twenty minutes behind them and he had witnessed them pass by as he sat in the back of the police cruiser while they searched the vehicle.

Kendall stated that the two cellular telephones taken from him by law enforcement authorities at the time of his arrest had not only Eric's number stored in it but other resourceful information also.

Last, Kendall went on to include that Eric (E-Dub) was his cousin, and he'd mentioned that Freak Zeenie had recently been released and Eric thought that Freak Zeenie was behind crimes in the surrounding areas. He gave the names of Big Man, B-Love, and Ced-B.

Kendall signed and dated his proffer agreement, then pushed it toward Agent Kane. "This the truth so help me God, and if I could be released, I'll help bring them all in!" he said, with his hands clasped together.

"Damn! Now that's what the fuck I'm talkin' 'bout! You want a motherfuckin' job, boy?" Agent Kane said, jumpin' up from excitement. "You got damn right, you going home. Tonight! Try anything stupid and you'll be underground in Colorado, sir!" Agent Kane said, then left and went to get permission to free Kendall.

***

Hours Later
Tallahassee, Florida

E-Dub had just left the gas station headed home. Moments later, Chico Dee and his brother and sister pulled into the same gas station, in the side parking lot, and waited. They had been coming to the store in hopes of finding E-Dub. Chico Dee had got word that E-Dub frequented this very gas station.

After a few moments, their answer came to life.

"I knew it," Chico Dee said, cocking his pistol, ejecting one in the head. "There that bitch ass nigga go right there," Chico Dee pointed, as the dude stepped out the white Camry.

The dude turned around and put the gas pump into his gas tank after swiping his card. The pump started up.

"Fuck ass nigga thank he slick! Don't nothing beat the cross but the double cross, and the triple cross beat the double. Yeah, E-Dub, I'm the triple cross, nigga. I got somin' for his ass,"

"Arrgh!" Chico Dee hit the dude in the back of the head as hard as he could, knocking him out cold on impact. The dude never knew what hit him as he went down and crumbled up.

Chico Dee and his brother got him into the back seat of the white Toyota Camry and pulled off. They would not take the same chances of E-Dub getting away this time. They drove until they were enveloped by the darkness of the interstate.

"Wake your pussy ass up, old ratting ass nigga!" Chico Dee said.

Kendall stirred to life with an excruciating concussion.

"Man…what, th—"

BOOM!

Chico Dee sent one shot straight through the center of his forehead, blowing a giant hole out the back. Blood oozed everywhere on the back seat of the Toyota.

"Fuck ass nigga! Told on Pop-Pop! Won't tell shit else!" Chico Dee said as they drove to a secluded area. Chico Dee searched him. He pulled out his wallet, reading his license. "Man, what the fuck!" His face frowned up.

"What's up, bruh?" his brother asked, coming 'round to the back of the car while their sister was up the highway looking out.

Chico Dee shook his head in disbelief.

"This ain't him, bruh!"

"What? Ain't No way."

"Nawl, this ain't E-Dub, bruh!"

"Shit. He look just the fuck like him to me. What are you talking 'bout it ain't him, nigga?" his brother asked, irritated.

This is Kendall Odale, bruh, by his ID. Anyway, this must be his gotdamn cousin!" Chico Dee said, pulling a childhood picture of Kendall and E-Dub out Kendall's wallet, studying it. Chico Dee read the address on the licenses. "I got another idea, though, bruh!"

Chico Dee and his brother left, following each other with plans to look into the address. If you can't find who you looking for, you make them find you.

E-Dub made it home, feeling himself. *Two down, a few more to go*, he thought to himself. E-Dub pulled his phone out, calling Lil' Tee's number only to get the voice mail again.

"Damn, fuck he at?" he said, putting his phone on silent before he prepared for bed.

Chapter 24
The Next Morning
Dothan, Alabama

Freak Zeenie woke up with the business on his mind. After consuming a strong shot of Folgers, Freak Zeenie was moving a hundred miles per-hour.

It was only 6:53 a.m. and he had accomplished a great deal of important factors. His first one was fucking Khashia back to sleep. After that, he placed a couple phone calls. One to his cousin, Dr. Tony Burts, who was the director of Freak Zeenie's Change of Hearts program. Dr. Tony Burts also had recently completed a novel 'bout Freak Zeenie's life-changing events called *Man in the Mirror*. Freak Zeenie also had talked to his aunt Doris, agreeing to meet both of them today, who resided in Atlanta, Georgia.

Freak Zeenie also made plans to stop by Russell County Jail and drop a few dollars on his brother Levi's account. Grabbing his keys from off the counter, Freak Zeenie headed out the front door. Freak Zeenie was in love with his new Jeep Wrangler. He jumped in and crank it up. The pipes growled loudly a second before idling down a bit.

Once the garage door rose, he backed out slowly. First thing he noticed was a patrol car parked across the street from his residence.

"Fuck they got going on?" he said, looking both ways before letting the Jeep back in the street. A white officer sat there with a scowl on his face.

Freak Zeenie didn't acknowledge the officer at all. Putting the Jeep in drive, he took the winding road out the upscale neighborhood doing thirty miles per hour until reaching the main highway. Freak Zeenie kept peeking in his rearview mirror making sure the police officer hadn't jumped behind him. Already knowing that this wasn't a neighborhood that the cops frequented or did stake outs, this had him puzzled. Once he didn't think he was being followed or harassed by the officer, he relaxed a bit.

Freak Zeenie jumped into traffic, pressing down on the gas feeling the power of the straight eight motor. A couple minutes later, Freak Zeenie pulled up to the family-owned restaurant Smoky Pigs. Freak Zeenie wanted to holler at his favorite uncle, James, before he pulled out and headed to Atlanta, Georgia.

Finding a parking spot, Freak Zeenie jumped out, going inside.

"What's up, nephew? Boy, look at you! Up early, looking good. Good to see you! Man, I heard 'bout your Change of Heart demo! Damn sho' need to change a few of these knuckleheads' hearts around here," Uncle James said, as he sat the two plates down on the counter for the two white police officers. "Here y'all boys go, sir! Hope y'all enjoy it! Now, eat up!" he said, as he returned his attention back toward his nephew, Freak Zeenie.

Freak Zeenie was now standing at the end of the counter.

"Yeah, Uncle, everything going good on my end. I just wanted to stop by and see you, my boy. Matter fact, I'm on my way to the A' to meet Tony and Aunt Doris about the program now," Freak Zeenie said, glancing at the two white officers. The officers were chowing down on the freshly cut bacon, eggs, and cheese grits along with toast on the side. Even though they were eating, they also were all ears too, listening to Freak Zeenie's every word.

As the two officers ate, they also couldn't stop shooting mean mugs at Freak Zeenie.

"Man, James...you got the best got damn bacon and pork in the south! If you ask me," one of the officers said, still chewing a mouth full of food.

"Damn sho' does... James, how come your pork taste so different from everyone else's 'round these neck of the woods?" the other white officer asked, real country like. "What the hell you feeding them there hogs?" he said, sucking his fingers clean before grabbing the napkin to dry his hands.

Cartier Jay walked in on the last part.

"What's up, Dad? Morning, Unk!" he said, walking up shaking Freak Zeenie's hand and giving Uncle James a head nod.

Uncle James turned his attention back toward the officers.

180

"Man, it's not the feed! It's the sauce!" Uncle James said, wiping his hands on a towel as he slid back like James Brown. "I got the ...sauce, yah dig? Flavor! And if I tell yah, then...I'll have to kill yah. I'm taking the secret to the grave," he said, real smooth-like, looking at the two cops.

The officers both started laughing at Uncle James's humor.

Cartier Jay looked over at the officers.

Yeah, eat up! You bitch ass pigs! The secret is pussy ass snitching fuck niggas! They taste better dead, hun? Cartier Jay thought to himself then bust out laughing at his own inside joke.

"Hell wrong with you, son? You kinda late on the all never mind," Freak Zeenie asked.

"Hun? Oh, man, Unk think he still young! Crazy old head!" Cartier Jay said, feeding off Uncle James's comments.

"Yeah, Uncle James something serious, boy." He looked at his uncle. "Well, Uncle, I got to get going!" Freak Zeenie said, putting his arm 'round Cartier Jay's neck before turning to leave. "Stay out of trouble, son. See what happened to Levi, didn't it?" he whispered in his ear.

"Alright, Freak! Yeah, nephew, don't be no stranger now you here," Uncle James said, as he turned his attention back on his cooking. The two white officers left their tips and got up and left out the door.

"Yeah, Pops! You know I'm on point," Cartier Jay said. He took a seat, pulling his phone out. He was feeling himself knowing he was killing all rat niggas, leaving no room for evidence. The community was eating up everything without the least bit of a clue. So he heard Freak Zeenie but was hardly listening. Freak Zeenie shook Cartier Jay's hand then left.

By the time Freak Zeenie made it back outside to his Jeep, the two officers were already sitting in their car waiting on him. Freak Zeenie didn't pay them no mind.

Jumping in his Jeep, Freak Zeenie headed toward 231 highway. After making it a few miles up the highway, Freak Zeenie noticed the cops from Smoky Pigs were trailing him.

"Now what the fuck they on? Fuck is they keep following behind me for?" he said, looking in his rearview. Freak Zeenie switched lanes. So did the cops. He sped up a little. So did the cops. "Yeah, they following me," he said, assuring himself.

Just as he was almost out the city limit, the lights came on. "Fuck!" Freak Zeenie yelled, reluctantly pulling over with a menacing mug on his face. Freak Zeenie grabbed his COVID mask from off the mirror, putting it on. He had all kinds of thoughts running through his mind. *Man, these crackers already killing all these black folks. I'm telling you now!* he was thinking as he placed both of his hands on the steering wheel, careful not to give the police the wrong impression.

The officers had their guns drawn already as they approached Freak Zeenie's Jeep.

"Step out the car for me, sir?" one of them asked.

"What I do?" Freak Zeenie said, keeping his hands safely on the wheel, eyes straight ahead for the police body camara just in case something went wrong.

"I said, step the fuck out the got damn vehicle! Now!" one of the officers said, sweat forming on his brows.

"Man, what I—" Freak Zeenie cut his words short and got quiet. Even though he didn't want to, he went with what the officers had instructed him to do. People whizzed by in their vehicles on the interstate but were trying their best to be nosy.

Freak Zeenie made sure to move slow. Careful not to spook the white trigger-happy officers. Knowing in these days and times, cops, especially Caucasian ones, were dying to catch a body and kill a black man. He had witnessed it too many times and it was just too many to name.

"Turn around and put your hands on the hood! Do it now!" one of the officers yelled, face becoming beet red.

Freak Zeenie shook his head. *Racist ass crackers! Boy I tell yah!* he said in his mind but did as he was forced to do. One of the officers patted Freak Zeenie down then placed him in a pair of handcuffs while the other officer kept his service weapon trained on him until his partner had finished.

After getting Freak Zeenie cuffed, they placed him into the back of the patrol car. That's when Freak Zeenie went straight crazy, knowing they weren't following the proper procedures.

"I can promise y'all this! Once I finish with you pecker woods, the both of you will not only be fired, sued, and embarrassed! You won't be able to hold another job here in the dot, motherfuckers!" he yelled, as the cops slammed the door in his face.

"Yeah, buddy, you do that!" The officers left and went to search Freak Zeenie's Jeep for longer than they should.

Oh, hell fuck nawl. They done fucked up. Man, they shouldn't even be on the interstate pulling folks over anyway. Hell nawl. Where are the state troopers at? I got they stupid asses, Freak Zeenie thought to himself as he watched them as best he could from his position.

Freak Zeenie's whole mood changed from good to bad after they let him go. He was back in motion on the interstate, talking on the phone.

"Man, Momma, I'm telling yah! These police just had me on the side of the interstate. Searching my Jeep for a hour! Ain't even nothing in the Jeep but the registration!" He was constantly looking in his mirrors as he talked.

"Baby, we will call the lawyer and see. Don't get your blood pressure all up and stuff now. Just try to calm down. You need to call your uncle," Ms. Lois said, feeling bad for not telling him what her sister had already explained to her.

"Mom, I just left Uncle James! See, you aren't even listening to me," he said, frustrated.

"Not James, baby, I'm sorry. Call your uncle Duke. He wanted to come to the Change of Heart gathering but couldn't make it.

"Oh, what he want?" Freak Zeenie didn't want to talk to his uncle Duke. He thought his mom was trying to get his mind off the incident that had just taken place and she didn't want to talk about it. Or wanted him to calm down.

"Just call him, and he can help you with all this," she said.

"Mom, I don't need him on this! I need a lawyer. I'm 'bout to sue both them crackers! Plus the police department too! I know they don't like me as it is, but what's his number?" Freak Zeenie programmed his uncle Duke's number in his phone, but he didn't call him. He was too riled up off the traffic stop harassment, and that's all he wanted to talk about at the time. *Fuck ass cops, ol' pussy ass bitches! This shit crazy!* he kept thinking to himself after hanging up with his mother.

***

Fifteen Minutes Later
Russell County Jail

Freak Zeenie was walking out of Russell County Jail. He dropped a thousand dollars on Levi's books to hold him down while he was in there. Keeping it real was a must. Something they both understood, because it's not until you are in a situation or gone when you find out that the people who you loved and thought that they felt the exact same way for you were just riding the wave for as long as they could. Once the wave wiped out, so did they.

***

Four Hours Later
Atlanta, Georgia

After Freak Zeenie met his cousin and aunt, he stopped by Lenox Mall while he was still in the city. Freak Zeenie was strolling through the mall when all of a sudden, he saw Denise.

"Damn! What? You following me or something?" he said real harshly, mean muggin'.

"Hold up! Who is you to follow, nigga? I'm thinking the same thing!" Denise said, putting her hands on her hips.

"Yeah, alright. Let me find out!" he said, as he walked right past her, continuing to carry on with his business.

"Freak?" Denise called out. Freak Zeenie stopped in his tracks.

"Yeah, what up?" He turned around facing her.

"I need to talk to you a minute, for real," Denise said sincerely, as she thought about her encounter with the Mexicans the other day.

Denise knew if anyone could help her it had to be him or E-Dub. Knowing Freak Zeenie was that nigga before he left to do his bid, that's exactly was she needed at this moment. A well-groomed, seasoned nigga such as Freak Zeenie. "Can I buy you a bite to eat, so we can talk please?" Denise swallowed her pride and asked.

Freak Zeenie looked at this watch as he thought quickly. "Yeah, you got ten minutes, that's it!" he went on and agreed.

Making it to the food court, they both ordered Chinese food, sat down, and began to talk. Denise explained to Freak Zeenie about how the Mexicans had stopped by her place. That they were there to retrieve their product that her cousin Dee had left behind with her. The Mexicans claimed that they knew Denise was holding their product because her cousin admitted it before his consignment. She said she had denied their accusation at first. Until they provided old pictures of her cousin Dee carrying bags into one of her older residences when he was alive. On many different times.

There was now a problem. Denise no longer had their drugs. She had sold it all. Denise admitted to Freak Zeenie that she did have the money, most of it anyway. Freak Zeenie wanted to know what all this had to do with him. Then Denise explained that the Mexicans explained in order for her to keep her life and her only child that now she decided was the perfect time.

"Freak," Denise looked him dead in the eyes.

"Yeah?"

"My son is also your son too," she said. Denise went on to explain to him that the Mexicans wanted her to work off the debt by selling their drugs or else. Denise made him take her number down.

Freak Zeenie didn't want no dealings with that 'cause he had changed his life from that area of the game. Denise noticed the stallment he was providing her. So she made him a multi-million-dollar proposition that almost had him about to give it a try. Until Denise mentioned one of her other clientele members that she was strongly thinking 'bout bringing in.

Freak Zeenie din't know why he even asked, but he did.

"Who?"

"E-Dub," she said, clasping her hands together like she just killed the game with her response.

"Who?" Freak Zeenie asked again, thinking he had heard her wrong. "E-Dub who?" He just had to know.

"E-Dub, you probably don't know him, Freak. He from—"

"Florida?"

"Yeah. How did you guess?" she asked, shocked that he knew.

"Man, that hot ratting ass fuck nigga! Are you for real? Bitch ass nigga the one who got me a motherfuckin' life sentence! You fucking with him?" Freak Zeenie's face was screwed up.

Denise had butterflies in her stomach now. She went to thinking all kinds of shit.

"Well, yeah. He has made me some good, good money! And I didn—"

"Hell fuckin' naw!" Freak Zeenie cut her off. He jumped up from the table and left abruptly without another word, leaving Denise right there. If he wasn't mad about the traffic stop this had taken the cake. Freak Zeenie couldn't believe his ears.

Here it was Denise needed Freak Zeenie's help to keep her life. Plus, she had tried to convince him that her son was his son. Then to make matters worse, tell him that she had been dealing with the nigga who had tried to leave Freak Zeenie to die inside a federal prison cell.

Freak Zeenie headed back to Dothan, Alabama in a daze. *Fuck, I tripped the fuck out. I supposed to had got that shit from her fuck ass and ain't paid that bitch shit!* Freak Zeenie thought to himself as he rode down the highway. He really wanted to kill her and him. Ain't no way he would be alive and free knowing that E-Dub was still alive and hadn't paid for his fraudulent and unforgivable sin he had committed. It was a must that E-Dub pay.

The world was just too small for the both of them to be roaming at the same time. Freak Zeenie wouldn't be happy until he was sure that the bitch ass nigga was in a casket or somebody's ditch somewhere. It really didn't matter to him long as E-Dub died.

Chapter 25
A Few Days Later
Tallahassee, Florida

E-Dub sped through the heavy rain like Bobble the race car driver going for first place. E-Dub's grandmother called him early this morning stuttering and fumbling over her words, all hysterical. Waking E-Dub straight up with her concerns. Whatever she did say had E-Dub visibly shaking. Chill bumps were running up both of his arms. E-Dub's hands were trembling against the steering wheel as he mumbled some inaudible words.

E-Dub made it to his grandmother's residence in record time, which was off highway 90, located at 990 Burnt Leaf Lane. First thing E-Dub saw when he pulled in was a smoking casket that was sitting up on a slab of cement.

"Man, hold up now, what the hell's going on?" E-Dub slammed the vehicle in park, hoppin' out.

His grandmother stood back in her house coat and house slippers on, with a head full of multicolor rollers. E-Dub's two uncles stood a couple feet back from the casket, still holding on to fire extinguishers. White smoke was rising from the casket heavily, making it hard to see how much damage had been done.

Everyone had their eyes on E-Dub as he slowly approached his grandmother.

"Grandma? What's going on? Why is there a casket in the front yard, and why was it on fire?" E-Dub asked question after question before she could even answer the first one.

E-Dub's grandmother handed him a piece of paper.

"This was taped to my front door, Eric. Maybe you could help me and everyone else figure the answer to your question out too," she said, as she studied E-Dub closely. After a moment, she said, "What are you doing out here in these wicked streets, grandson?"

E-Dub heard his grandmother but didn't answer. He was still reading the piece of paper that had his full attention, which read:

Pussy ass E-Dub, in the world that we live in, all rats must die! Even you, Master Splinter! This was a mistaken identity, but you are next. Open the casket! Hope you like it, talking 'bout the color of the casket, it was all red. I hope y'all caught the fire. I chose that color 'cause your bitch ass going to hell, fuck nigga! Open the casket, it's a surprise in it, well, two of 'em.

E-Dub's mind was running faster than a Bugatti as his heart almost jumped out his chest from pounding so fast. He read the letter twice like the message would change from the first time.

"I said, what are you into out there, grandson?" E-Dub's grandmother repeated, after snapping her fingers twice in front of his face, bringing E-Dub back and out of the trance he'd fallen into.

"Hun?" E-Dub responded, looking from the piece of paper back and forth from the casket to his grandmother. "Aww, Granny, I'm not into nothing," he lied.

"You doing something, damnit! People just don't put burning caskets in other people's yards unless…" She paused, trying to control herself. "I'm going to just say this, from the looks of it, you have ran your big ole mouth too much on the wrong ones, grandson. I will always love you, but I didn't raise you or no one in our family to be no damn snitch, boy!" She was staring upside his head like he was crazy, her lip trembling. "Eric, no one likes rats. Unless you ah snake! I mean, no one, not even me!" E-Dub remained silent. What could he say? He knew his grandmother was correct. "Now you don't got shit to say, boy? Which speaks volumes to me. You should have been kept your big mouth closed, hell… It's too late now! Ain't no tellin' what's going to happen with your telling ass!" she said, leaving E-Dub standing there dumbfounded. She walked toward her two sons. Even though it wasn't a laughing matter, her sons couldn't help but laugh from their mother's last statement.

Two Leon County Sheriffs pulled up just as the casket had finally started to cool down. They got out the patrol car.

"Morning, y'all! What seems to be the problem?" the lead officer asked, stepping up to the casket pointin'.

"Well, we know as much as you do. I woke up after I heard consistent knocks on my door this morning. I get up and go to my door, opening it. All I see is a big ball of fire in my front yard and a car pulling off," E-Dub's grandmother explained, as she looked over at him before giving her attention back to the officers. "That's all I know, sir. I called my two sons to come put the fire out, which you see. Then I called my grandbaby."

"Okay. What kind of car was it? Do you know?" the lead officer asked.

"It was a gray truck, a Chevy if I had to take a guess, an updated one," she said.

"I thought you said a car, ma'am?"

"Well, I did say that but I meant a truck. How the hell will someone haul a damn casket in a car, sir?"

"In a hearse, ma'am."

"Yeah, well it wasn't a damn hearse. It was a gray truck! What are you saying? That I'm sitting here lying or something, sir?" She had a scowl on her face toward the officers.

"Not at all, ma'am. We just are asking the questions trying to put the pieces together and make some sense of all this, ma'am. I have to ask these kinds of questions. They're protocol."

"Un…Hun," she said, putting her hands on her hips.

"Officer Long, could you grab a crowbar out the trunk for me please? So we can open this thing. Let's hope it's just a prank and no one's in there."

"Yes sir, I'll get it." Officer Long turned around, leaving to retrieve the crowbar from out of the vehicle.

E-Dub's grandmother looked over at him. E-Dub was 'bout to turn the note over to the law as evidence. She took a deep breath, shoving the paper deep down in her pocket on her housecoat. She shook her head at her grandson. *Now, didn't I just explain about how I feel about snitchin' to this slow ass boy?* she thought to herself, keeping her hands in her pockets.

"Looks like the sky 'bout to fall out at any given moment, y'all!" the lead officer said, looking up, noticing how dark the sky had become out of nowhere. He reached out, grabbing the crowbar from his partner. The lead officer went to work prying the thick, three-inch nails out the casket.

***

Fifteen Minutes Later…

The lead officer had completed the task.

"Well, let's see what we have here," he said, grabbing a hold of the top half of the casket. Everyone took a few steps closer so they could see inside the casket also. The lead officer lifted the door.

"Oh my God, Kendall!" Nothing could prepare E-Dub's grandmother for what she had just witnessed. These were here last words. She passed out cold.

Kendall laid there, eyes wide with a single hole in the center of his forehead. It was big enough for a grown man's thumb to fit in it. The cushion Kendall laid on had a pile of dried blood everywhere. His lips were blue from days of being dead.

Everyone was shocked in their own way. E-Dub, because he thought Kendall was still locked away in Georgia. His uncles because they didn't know what to expect to find inside, and the officers, well.

The officers looked from Kendall to E-Dub 'bout three times.

"Is this your brother, son?" they both uttered at the same time.

"No. He's my first cousin," E-Dub said, eyes still glued on Kendall's corpse. It was a single piece of paper laying on Kendall's chest. E-Dub reached to grab it.

"Hold up! Don't touch that! Don't touch nothing! It's evidence. We have to get it tested for fingerprints," the officer said, reaching in his pocket, pulling out another pair of latex gloves because the ones he had on had torn.

Pulling the new set of gloves on, the lead officer reached in the casket, grabbing the piece of paper off Kendall's corpse.

"We won't miss next time, fuck nigga!" The lead officer read the note three times over and over to let it sink in. He looked at E-Dub. "Let me take a guess. This for you? Well, I mean, this should have been you?" he asked, stuffing the note into a plastic evidence bag, sealing it shut.

The lead officer's partner radioed the incident in to the homicide department and called for a hearse so the corpse could be transported to the laboratory for examination and autopsy. This way they could determine the cause of death and how long Kendall had been dead.

By the time the hearse and all the cops came out to highway 90, E-Dub's grandmother had finally come back around. She was a crying mess.

E-Dub's grandmother was just too upset.

"You are not welcome here anymore! Get your ass from off my property, Eric! And don't you ever come the fuck back!"

"But Gr—"

"I said, leave! Now!" she screamed on him. She didn't want to hear another word from him. For all she knew, he was responsible for her grandson's death for telling on the wrong person. In her house and family, they didn't raise their kids to be rats.

E-Dub was the first one of his kind in their family. E-Dub had embarrassed his whole family in her eyes. His grandmother had to cut him loose for his fraudulent ways. "My damn momma and father got to be turning over in their graves right now!" she said, with her arms folded over her chest. She turned her back to E-Dub, dismissing him. Her oldest son rubbed his mother's back trying to calm her down a bit, knowing that she already had high blood pressure.

E-Dub left with his head hung low and eyes moist, feeling hurt from his favorite grandmother's harsh words. E-Dub looked back out of curiosity, but the only thing he caught was the door slamming shut. He was hoping his grandmother had a change of heart, but he was wrong.

Paper Boi Rari

Chapter 26
The Next Day
Dothan, Alabama

Freak Zeenie was so mad the only thing he could see was red. He sat in his den going through his black book, in deep thought. He had been this way for the last couple of days after he'd finally spoken with his uncle Duck, finding out that one of his co-conspirators who had got him a life sentence in the feds hadn't stopped. He was now trying to place Freak Zeenie right back inside the concrete graveyard. That last piece of news was it for Freak Zeenie. He'd had enough.

In the last few weeks, Freak Zeenie had heard more than he cared to about E-Dub for his liking after a few moments of scrolling down the list of names in his black book. He came across a name and number that he was looking for.

"I hope this nigga number hasn't changed! He told me it never would." Freak Zeenie picked his phone up, dialing the number then listening. "Okay!" he said, after hearing it ring. "That's a good sign," he said, face still balled up.

The phone rang a few good times.

"What they do?" the voice answered on the other end.

"Shiiid...seeing shit clearer through these Cartier lenses, nigga!" Freak Zeenie said, with a sinister smile plastered on his face quoting one of his old famous lines.

"Freak Zeenie? Who this? Freak? Hun?"

"You better say it! What's happening? Long time no see, Paco! Boy, I see this number still the same, my nigga! Man, it's good to hear your voice, bruh!"

"Man, I been out a cool second, you know, getting my shit in order."

"Oh yeah...What that ticket, you know I want in?"

"Nawl, I gave that up, bruh! I'm into uplifting the community now."

"Oh, bet that. Ain't nothing wrong with that."

"Right now, though, I got a bone to pick with a low-down dirty dog, but I can't seem to locate the motherfucker! So…I figured maybe for the right price you could do something nice, feel me?"

"Shiiid, you got to know that! Who is it, so I can get on it right away?"

"I got an—" Freak Zeenie stopped. "Just say he the reason I fell down for life, feel me?" he said, refraining from what he was about to say first.

"Man, say no more! This one on me. For free! I already know what you talking 'bout. I know where he lay his bitch ass head at right now! So shiiid, when you want it done?"

"Nawl, fam, I got to do this one myself, fool! I just need someone to share the location, feel me? Like Meek Mills 'em."

"Oh, yeah, a'ight, but we might as well go together, 'cause the nigga on the list anyhow. Things just been kinda backed up for us, but homes been fouled out! So, he cut from the team and his balling days are over within this city anyhow. So, what's up?" Paco claimed, as he pulled up parking at the Shell gas station across from Florida State.

Freak Zeenie went quiet for a few seconds. He didn't really want to chance dealing with any more co-dees, especially after coming from under a life sentence. If no one knew what could happen, Freak Zeenie knew firsthand. "Fuck it, I ain't trippin'! I'll be your way in a couple days anyway, bruh."

"Already, shiiid, the homecoming for FAMU this weekend. We can gone make it pop!" Paco said.

"Bet that, see you then. What's up with Horse Head?"

"Running up a check! Nigga, ain't shit change now but the years fool, one!" Paco hung up.

Freak Zeenie sat the phone down, feeling a lot better now that he put a bullseye on his worst enemy with just a little effort. Quickly changing his mind, Freak Zeenie started formulating all kinds of plots.

Everyone who ran off on him would straight drop. They would have to feel the wrath. One way or another, eventually.

Since she played me, watch this. I got her fuck ass too! Freak Zeenie thought to himself, picking the phone back up. He placed a call to Denise.

Chapter 27
The Next Day

Freak Zeenie found a used car lot in Savannah, Georgia. He needed a whip that wouldn't trace back to him. Today he had Remy Red and Poochie riding with him since he needed someone to drive his vehicle back home.

Freak Zeenie swung his Jeep up into JJ's car lot. There were at least sixty used cars on the lot, all makes and models. He parked, and they all exited the Jeep and instantly began to browse the rows of cars.

A few moments later, a medium-size, middle-aged white guy came outside from the small office. He was dressed in the latest top-of-the-line urban fashion. He stood there for a second, puffing the last few puffs of his cigarette before thumping it through the air.

The white guy walked out to where Freak Zeenie them were.

"What's up y'all? How may I assist you all today if I may? I'm JJ, the owner, salesman, buyer, hustler, all that and some! Whatever you looking for, I'll show it to you. What you ain't, I'll make sure you never see it. Talk to me, baby. Talk to me!" JJ said, smiling as he spread his arms, looking over his eyeglasses. Everybody knew JJ in his city. JJ was universal, kept his hands into many different hustles and stayed under the influence. JJ reported to no one, he was the CEO.

"As a matter of fact, JJ, yeah you can. I'm looking for something small but sporty, fast, and powerful. Good on gas, low key. You know, that will blend in with the public?" Freak Zeenie said, as he watched JJ. He could smell the alcohol reeking from his pores. "While you at it, pour me up a few of them shots you been on, too, my man!" Freak Zeenie smiled at JJ.

"Aw yeah, I gotcha! I got the perfect car for you! Right this way!" JJ said, as he led them in the opposite direction of all the cars on the lot.

"Where we going? The cars are out there," Freak Zeenie said, pointing.

"Just chill, this ain't for everybody's eyes right here! I just got this, this morning to be exact. I was thinking 'bout keeping it myself, to be honest," JJ said, laying it on thick. Knowing damn well everything he bought was for a markup. He had to gain a bigger profit for it.

After a short walk, they finally made it to the back of JJ's office building. JJ pulled down his COVID-19 mask.

"Be careful! This bitch is more contagious than the Delta variant! There is no vaccine for her either. If you don't know what you doing with her, she'll kill you!" he said, looking Freak Zeenie in the eyes with a serious expression.

"Man, come on now! Ain't no way! What the fuck is this?" Freak Zeenie said, after JJ snatched the car cover off of the vehicle. Freak Zeenie walked around the small muscle car, examining it carefully.

"What? You don't know?"

"Hell fuck nawl!"

"This right here! This right here." JJ pointed toward the car. "This is good on gas, it's super-fast, known but low key! It's everything you looking for, I can tell you that!" JJ paused, letting his words take root.

"This is the famous Nissan Z! Come on, let's take a look at the inside." JJ opened the driver side door for Freak Zeenie. "Get on in, my man." He held the door for Freak Zeenie. Freak Zeenie got behind the wheel, and JJ closed the door behind him. JJ walked around and got into the passenger side, leaving Remy Red and Poochie standing there observing the situation. "Go 'head, start her up!" Freak Zeenie crunk up the car, falling in love with the sound of the exhaust pipes instantly. JJ nodded his head in approval, knowing he just made another sale. "Yeah, powerful right. Let me explain this beauty. She employs a strong and smooth three-point-seven liter V6. It delivers quick acceleration and res—"

"I want it! How much?" Freak Zeenie said, cutting JJ off from the rest of his sales pitch.

"Well…for you, give me seventeen-five my man, and we got a deal!" JJ said, stone face.

Freak Zeenie took a deep breath. He looked at the mileage, which was fair. "I got fifteen cash that's a—"

"Sold! Now come on. Let's get the paperwork out the way and have a few shots that you asked about earlier while we at it," JJ said, getting out the car heading to the front of his office building.

Twenty minutes later, Freak Zeenie walked out with the keys and jumped into his new slider.

"I'll meet y'all back in Dothan. I need to shoot to the A' right fast," he said to Remy Red and Poochie before he pulled the car door shut, and they all departed.

***

A Few Hours Later
Atlanta, Georgia

Freak Zeenie convinced Denise to invest a few millions back into the drug exchange. Which was easy being that she was in a life-threatening situation. This way she could start paying the Mexicans back with the profit and never subtract from her principal.

It wasn't hard to convince Denise since she knew Freak Zeenie was super familiar with the game. She agreed to his terms with pleasure. Which were simple, deal with him only. If he found out differently, then the contract would be void.

Freak Zeenie sat in his car off of Martin Luther King Blvd., waiting on Denise. A few moments later, Denise pulled up in a triple-white Mulsanne. Freak Zeenie popped his trunk as two sexy females placed three duffel bags in his trunk, gently securing the trunk back. Then they strutted back to the big boy Bentley, getting into the driver and passenger side.

Seconds later, the back door of the exotic vehicle came open. Denise stepped out in a triple-white business mini-skirt suit with matching white Jimmy Choo sling-back heels.

Stepping like a supermodel, Denise walked over and slid into Freak Zeenie's car. "It's all there. Three-point-five, just like you asked. Let's make this shit pop!" she said, rubbing her Frenchpedicured hands together. "So, how fast your flip gone be?" Denise asked, studying Freak Zeenie's body language.

That question rubbed him the wrong way.

"Look, Denise, this shit dead serious! Less talking the better. Just know I got you! You don't need to worry! I'm him! Now let me slide down this highway and make this shit come together like Voltron, ya heard?" Freak Zeenie said, never changing his facial expression.

Denise smiled, becoming turned on from Freak Zeenie's masculinity.

"Okay, Freak Zeenie, just call me when or if you need me. I'm here for you," she said, then got out of the car and got in her exotic sedan, pulling off.

What she said that for? That show nuff seals the deal, Freak Zeenie thought to himself as he pulled off.

"Yeah right! If you here for me, then Popeye a sissy! Bitch, you gone wish you were there for me after this though," he said aloud, pulling on the interstate headed back down the highway toward Dothan, Alabama. Freak Zeenie looked in his rearview mirror. "Damn, boy! You still got it! Shiiid…Got her! Free bandz, rubbing without the strap! Bad motherfucker, I am straight drop! Bringing it all back with extras! I ain't never needed a handout! Just a blueprint and bet I stand out!" he said, riding back home 3.5 million dollars richer than he left this morning.

Freak Zeenie was on his best bullshit, and everybody was gone pay back their debt that was owed to him. Be it with money or their life. It didn't matter, whichever one, long as it covered what they owed to him.

Chapter 28
The Next Morning
Dothan, Alabama

At the police precinct, the chief had just got off the phone with Sheriff Duke.

Sheriff Duke spoke on Freak Zeenie's defense, clearing up all the false allegations. Sheriff Duke was well known everywhere as well as respected. If he stated something, it was stamped and taken at face value. Luckily, Sheriff Duke had a side piece who just happened to be a secretary in Tallahassee, Florida, in the Northern Division of Florida. Otherwise, he might have been visiting Freak Zeenie in a prison again somewhere across the country. Sheriff Duke helped get the Dothan Police Department off of Freak Zeenie's trail. Plus, the lawsuits that were placed on them from Ms. Lois also helped make up their minds to leave him alone until he got caught red handed doing something wrong.

Right after Sheriff Duke got off the phone with DPD, he called his connects down at the federal building in Tallahassee, Florida. Once he finished there, he tried to contact his nephew, Freak Zeenie, but got the voice operator. If he would have called the day before, Sheriff Duke might have had the chance to talk to him.

Freak Zeenie changed his number yesterday as soon as he made it home with them free bandz.

***

Tallahassee, Florida
Federal Building, Northern Division

The agent had just gotten off the phone with his college buddy, Duke, who was now a Sheriff in a very small town in South Alabama. The agent had just received some very disturbing news about one of his most valuable informants. The agent was heated because he just knew after this case he would be running for mayor.

Finding out that E-Dub had been giving him false information not only pissed the agent off, it broke E-Dub's proffer agreement and broke their once long-term bond. The agent was now ready to get E-Dub off the streets forever. E-Dub was now useless to him. The agent had no choice but to use what he already had and let the chips fall where they may.

Chapter 29
Marianna, Florida

Freak Zeenie made it to Tallahassee, Florida late Friday night, meeting up with Paco and Horse Head. Now the plan originally was they all were gone ride in one car, but they ended up revising it. Freak Zeenie was in his Nissan Z. Horse Head took a chance and brought his Porsche Panamera back out. He'd change the color after the incident. He didn't want to get rid of the car because it had sentimental value to it. Plus, it was a turbo S, the one that came with the red letters, super-fast, sure to get you out of tight situations.

Since the homecoming wasn't until Saturday, Freak Zeenie didn't want to miss his chance to serve E-Dub with a cold dish of revenge. Which would come with a gang of .223 chopper bullets. Freak Zeenie wanted E-Dub to enjoy a closed-casket funeral. No one needed to see a snitch's face anyway unless they were alive, right?

***

The Next Morning

Freak Zeenie met with Paco and Horse Head early Saturday morning, 'round 5 a.m.

"Check it, we don't even have to enter the house. Since the last break-in, they ended up putting more cameras 'round that bitch than Fort Knox has!" Paco claimed.

"I ain't even trippin', shit. That's what this is for anyway." Freak Zeenie held up his AR-15 with the scope. He pressed a button revealing a green laser beam. "Yeah...take his mask off! FUTURE!" Freak Zeenie nodded. "So, what, it's a wood line out there or something?"

"Already." Paco clapped his hands together from excitement. Horse Head was quiet. He just wanted to get it over with. Horse Head had his eye on taking over the city, but as long as E-Dub was living he was in his way, because E-Dub had an unlimited supply of drugs. The one whose money was the longest lasted the longest, usually.

"Say no more then. Shiiid, let's hit it!" Freak Zeenie slowly pulled onto the highway enroute to Marianna, Florida. Murderous thoughts trampled through his mind along the way. Horse Head and Paco trailed him with identical thoughts. Energy worked like that in the universe. What you put in was normally what came out.

***

Marianna, Florida

E-Dub was up early. Ever since he saw his cousin in that casket, he couldn't seem to get any sleep. Not from his death but because he had wished he'd got a time cut from off of him on the Spalding County, Georgia traffic stop. Now that he was dead, E-Dub started having second thoughts about how things would turn out over there. E-Dub had hopes of getting all the many federal agencies to come together and work for him in his favor. *Maybe they gone put it all on Reneesha, I hope!* E-Dub's thoughts encouraged his way of thinking. *Fuck! Almost everybody I had lined up is either dead or fucking missing!* E-Dub thought about his man Lil' Tee 'cause Lil' Tee still hadn't surfaced yet.

That's alright, though. I keep a plan for a plan to free the man! That's why I lined Horse Head and Paco 'em up. Oh, oh, and the nigga Freak Zeenie too! Bye, Freak Zeenie! Yeah. Fuck it, I might have to double back and bam Denise too! Shit, since when hoes stop going to prison? NEVER! Fuck that bitch! E-Dub's thoughts had begun to take root.

E-Dub's girlfriend, also his baby mother, entered the room interrupting his thoughts.

"Morning, baby, we still having family day today, right?" Toyka said, knowing that today was FAMU homecoming and the city would be stupid lit.

"Hun? Um, it's tomorrow I thought," he said.

"No, baby. It's today! That's what you told us last week," she expressed with much attitude, putting her hands on her hips.

"No, I didn't! Why would I say some stupid shit like that, knowing today is homecoming? I think you must have misunderstood what I said."

"Yes, you did, Eric! Oh, so you think that spending time with your family is stupid now, hun?" She stared daggers through him.

"Nawl, I never said that! You putting words in my mouth now, T," he said, following behind her, leaving out the room where the security cameras were located.

"Nigga, yes the fuck you did, you just said it!" She was fuming mad. "Fuck you, Eric! You is a lying piece of shit!" Tokya ran to the room and started packing her things, shutting and locking the door behind her. Leaving E-Dub on the other side trying to explain himself.

***

Marianna, Florida.
Outside E-Dub's House, the Woodline

Freak Zeenie, Paco, and Horse Head had parked their cars about a half a mile down the highway. They all footed it to the treeline edge of the woods. Which was less than thirty yards away.

Freak Zeenie scaled the tree and got comfortable. He checked his view through the scope on his AR-15.

"Hell yeah! This bitch fire!" Freak Zeenie said, after aiming it at the door through the garage where he was sure E-Dub would come out. Even though it had been years since Freak Zeenie had seen E-Dub, he would never forget how E-Dub looked.

Paco and Horse Head took ground positions as they were only there to assist Freak Zeenie anyway. The both of 'em wanted E-Dub also but not as much as Freak Zeenie did. Their job was to shoot only if Freak Zeenie missed and E-Dub seemed like he would get away. Paco and Horse Head were cool with that, and that's exactly what they planned to do.

***

Fifteen Minutes Away

Marianna, Florida

Black Track Hawks were approaching Marianna, Florida at a very fast pace. Blue and white lights were flashing but had no sound behind 'em. Agent Simpson and his first cousin, Michael Simpson, who was also the assistant US attorney and who was also over this ongoing case, rode shotgun together leading the way.

"Yeah, cuz, this lying motherfucker been slithering through the cracks for decades! I want ya to throw the whole federal guidelines book on him, Mich," Agent Simpson said, through clenched teeth.

"You know we got to make our mommas proud. That's all they ever wanted is for us to keep the community drug free. Especially after that sissy got turnt out and started stealing everything that wasn't bolted down!" Assistant US Attorney Simpson said, shaking his head in shame, bringing back memories of his now deceased sister. "So, yeah, Eric has told his last tale. He fucked up with me when he didn't get the female out in Atlanta, Georgia."

"Right! The dirty dog don told his tail off, ain't it?" They burst out laughing as they turned into E-Dub's driveway, speeding, until they came to a screeching halt.

Chapter 30
Marianna, Florida
Inside E-Dub's House

With all the commotion that Tokya and E-Dub were making, they eventually awoke E-Dub's mother and son up. E-Dub was adamant about going to the homecoming today and taking his family out tomorrow. Tokya just wasn't having it though. Tokya had a suitcase in one hand and a blow dryer in her other.

"Hell fuck nawl, Eric! You can go to the homecoming, the freaknik, South Beach! Hell, you can go to hell for all I care! But your dog ass gone wish you had listened to me, just watch!" She pointed the blow dryer at him.

"Tokya!" E-Dub's mom hollered. "Don't talk like that in front my grandbaby, girl!"

"Nawl, this mut—"

Boom!

The doors came crashing in all at once, catching them all by surprise.

"Freeze! Everyone put your hands up where I can see 'em!" Agent Simpson said, first thing through the door.

Tokya must have not heard him right, 'cause she spun around holding the blow dryer. "What th—"

Pop! Pop!

Two shots dropped her in her tracks.

"Nooo!" E-Dub screamed, running to her aid, only to be shoved to the floor and handcuffed.

***

Marianna, Florida.
Outside at the Woodline

When Freak Zeenie spotted all them unmarked police jeeps, he couldn't get down the tree fast enough. Paco and Horse Head had already gotten a head start, but even with that they weren't fast enough. Freak Zeenie caught up with them and passed them.

Making it to their cars, no words were needed. Freak Zeenie crunk up his Nissan Z, headed to the highway with Horse Head on his bumper. They turned out, heading back toward Tallahassee, Florida.

Only two minutes had passed by when Freak Zeenie brought his car to the regular speed limit. Horse Head flew around Freak Zeenie Nissan Z in a blur. Seconds later they were passing by a gang of police cars and an ambulance headed in the direction of E-Dub's house.

"Man, slow this bitch down, nigga! We straight!" No sooner than Paco's words left his mouth, two of the police cars' brake lights came on, and a heap of white smoke came from the tires as they bust a U-turn, turning on their sirens.

Freak Zeenie's heart rate sped up by a hundred. He didn't know what to think or do.

"Damn, damn, damn!" Freak Zeenie said, looking at the AR-15 that rode shotgun beside him over in the passenger seat. Knowing that just the gun along with his record would get him ten more years at the least. Freak Zeenie had a quick thought. He put his right signal light on, whipping up in the next driveway he came to just as the two cop cars closed in on him. Freak Zeenie threw the car in park and squeezed his eye shut tight. "God, PLEASE!" he mumbled a quick prayer. By the grace of God, the cop cars kept going, picking up even more speed. Freak Zeenie opened his eyes. "Thank you, thank you, Lord!" he looked to the sky and said.

Seconds later, a frail, hunch-back, elderly white woman opened her front door.

"May I help you, sir?" she said, with a nasty tone.

Freak Zeenie let his window down. "Is Shan here?" he said, asking the first thing that came to mind.

"Who?" the elderly lady said, adjusting her glasses to get a better view.

"Shan. Is she here?"

"Don't no Shan stay here! Now get the hell off my property!" The elderly white lady said, pointing a 20-gauge at the windshield of his car.

208

"Oh, wrong house, ma'am, wrong house!" Freak Zeenie crunk up and threw his car in reverse, backing out faster than he had come in.

"You doggone right, wrong house," she said, slamming her door shut as he was backing out.

***

Five Minutes up the Highway...

Freak Zeenie had to slow down to pass by the police, who were directing traffic.

"Damn!" Freak Zeenie said, as he witnessed the Porsche Panamera on its side in the ditch. Horse Head was bleeding from the head, flat out in handcuffs, face down. Paco was cussing as he was being placed in the back of the police car. Soon as Freak Zeenie made it through, the last thing he saw was the officer pulling two assault rifles from out the Porsche with latex gloves on. Freak Zeenie shook his head but kept it moving. There was nothing he could do to help them now anyhow.

Freak Zeenie headed back to Dothan, Alabama mad and disappointed. He had come way too close to finally getting the person responsible for his long incarceration, to only miss his opportunity to the feds.

"Fuck ass cops! I hate 'em!" he said.

"This is why, because they always blocking what a nigga got going on! At the wrong damn time! Bitch ass niggas! Now this ratting ass nigga done got the fuck away! Again!" he said, as he headed home. "Plus got my homies into some shit, boy, got to be more careful."

Freak Zeenie rode home deeply in thought 'bout how his life was going. Desperately trying to figure out how to perfect any and every imperfection. Now that everyone who did him dirty had been taken care of, Freak Zeenie could focus on himself.

I don't know where your fuck ass at, Big Man. You still out there some damn where, ain't it? Better keep your snake ass head down, bitch! 'Cause if or when you stick that big ass head up, I promise you, I'm going to knock that bitch the fuck off for you, fuck nigga! Freak Zeenie was thinking as he entered Alabama's state line. He thought about Khashia fucking with his opps. The more he thought about it the more his heart became numb for her. *I ain't tripping, if you play you lay!* Freak Zeenie thought, riding in silence for the remainder of his drive home.

Chapter 31

E-Dub was on his best fuck nigga shit. He began to proffer even while his girlfriend was in and out of consciousness. Before E-Dub left his residence, he had convinced Assistant US Attorney Simpson to allow him to make a few phone calls regarding people he knew seeking to purchase or sell drugs.

Even though Assistant US Attorney Simpson didn't trust E-Dub, he still allowed him one last chance to help himself. It was just a cop's way of life. Assistant US Attorney Simpson went along but had no intentions of crediting E-Dub with the time cut in the end. Since E-Dub reneged on his end about giving him the Atlanta connect, then so would Assistant US Attorney Simpson when the time presented itself.

E-Dub was motivated. He recorded drug conversations with eight sets of persons seeking drugs. He was able to lure six sets to meetings, which was approximately $80,000 in drug funds seized. E-Dub did not actually meet with any of these persons, because his history of flight made that an unacceptable risk. Those matters were still under investigation and were likely to result in several state court prosecutions.

E-Dub agreed to cooperate against them all. He was giving up as many names as he possibly could and making it like they were big-time drug dealers. Bigger than himself. E-Dub provided information and made recorded telephone calls concerning other drug traffickers, particularly including a few people he outgrew but kept for these reasons only. A set of drug suppliers in Atlanta (responsible for the eleven kilograms seized in this case) and a set of Spanish drug suppliers in South Florida.

"You did very good, Horne, thanks a million," Assistant US Attorney Simpson said, patting E-Dub on his back.

"Yeah, sorry for shooting your baby mother, man. I thought the blow dryer was a gun! When doing this kind of work, you can never tell. Especially in the moment, know what I mean?" Agent Simpson said, walking E-Dub to the awaiting police Jeep, placing him inside. Agent Simpson hit the top of the Jeep twice. "A'ight, take 'em away!" He looked to this first cousin. "So, you gone agree for him a time cut for real?" Agent Simpson looked concerned.

"Hell nawl, even though he did a meritorious job. Given the amount of corroboration which is available from other witnesses and evidence, it is reasonable to expect further prosecutions to follow. Prosecutions may also be had, in either state or federal court, of some of Horne's customers, depending upon resources and availability of corroboration," he said, as they both headed to the black Track Hawk, getting in and heading back to the federal building in Tallahassee, Florida.

***

Seven Months Later...

E-Dub sat in court with his head held high with the confidence of Donald J. Trump. His lawyer had assured him that he wouldn't serve any prison time, not after all the people he had brought down. They had E-Dub in the SHV back at the federal Tallahassee holdover. It was at least one person in each pod who he had a 5k1 on.

Paco didn't make it no better because he was lacing everyone up on how E-Dub been a fed and how he had gotten his partner Freak Zeenie a life sentence back in the day. E-Dub didn't care about none of that. If he did go to prison, he was going to an informant's yard anyway. So to hell with what anyone thought was E-Dub's thoughts.

Assistant US Attorney Simpson stood up and began to speak. He cleared his throat.

"In most respects, Horne appears to have been fully and completely candid since the day of his arrest. Unfortunately, his cooperation has been flawed by his failure to be truthful about the criminal involvement of Toyka Jackson, his now deceased girlfriend and mother of Horne's child. Although Horne denies that Ms. Jackson actually did anything in the drug business, at least four other witnesses say that she did.

"Clearly, Ms. Jackson lived off the proceeds of drug dealing for a period of around two years. And lived in the house where this business was transacted," Assistant US Attorney Simpson scratched his chin and said. He looked over to where E-Dub and his lawyer sat. "A hundred seven thousand dollars and remnants of four kilograms of fake drugs were found in the house at the time of Horne's arrest. Horne's mother was also arrested but later released. The house has been seized in the process.

"Moreover, Ms. Jackson was the owner of the vehicle where the eleven kilograms were seized, hidden in a secret compartment operated remotely. The government recognizes Horne's desire to protect the mother of his child but cannot condone any lack of condor by a government witness." Assistant US Attorney Simpson paused a second to catch his breath.

"Horne faces risks similar to but greater than those faced by most other incarcerated defendants. The risks are magnified both by the number of persons against who he has cooperated and by the levels at which they operate. So, with that said..." Assistant US Attorney Simpson glanced over at E-Dub. "His 5k1 is deemed as a breach. The government will not be filing for a 5k1 in Mr. Horne's interest, sir," Assistant US Attorney Simpson said, then waited for the judge. E-Dub couldn't believe his ears. He wore a blank expression.

"Well, Mr. Horne, looks like you really did it this time. I am truly sorry for your loss, speaking of your child's mother. Now even though she has passed, someone must pay for these crimes. You had everything going in your favor as far as the 5k1 goes. You possibly would have walked a free man today, Mr. Horne. But once you lied about one thing, it all became a lie. You understand?" E-Dub's eyes became moist, but he nodded his head in agreement.

"However, the government sees the most serious flaw in the defendant's cooperation as his failure to be candid about Ms. Jackson. So, the court denies the 5k1 motion. With that said, today we will just have to sentence you by your PSR, sir." Judge Walker took a few minutes to read over the documents. He took a sip of water then cleared his throat.

213

"Ok, yes. Mr. Horne, the United States…" E-Dub's stomach tightened up. Even though his baby mother had died on him, he thought his plan would be Gucci. But it ended up being the knock-off version. "Sentences you, Eric Horne, to the high-end range of the guidelines, which is three hundred sixty-five months, with ten years of supervised release! Do you wish to file a direct appeal? If so, discuss it with your lawyer. It must be filed within twenty-eight days. Hope you decide that selling drugs isn't the life to indulge in, sir. It never has a good ending. Have a nice day," Judge Walker said.

E-Dub's lawyer pinched the bridge of his nose as he frowned his face up. "Got damnit!" he said, almost knocking the chair over to get out his seat as he looked at E-Dub.

E-Dub had lost his meal. He defecated all in his orange jumpsuit. The judge had just handed down a thirty-year sentence to him with no instructions on how to do it. E-Dub knew that going home was out. With that amount of time in the B.O.P, E-Dub knew that going to a low-security prison was now out. He would have to work his way down. The only thing he felt good about was he knew he would be going to a snitch yard. That way he wouldn't have to face his past or any of the people he cooperated on.

***

Forty-Five Days Later…

A month and a half passed by in a blur for E-Dub. Today E-Dub had that uneasy feeling in his stomach. You know the one when something isn't right. That's the one E-Dub was experiencing at the moment.

E-Dub stepped into B-unit at Coleman USP with great confidence on the outside, but he was a nervous wreck on the inside. *Man, this ain't no damn yard for snitches like they promised me!* E-Dub said in his head. He had been repeating that line over and over since he pulled up this morning on the blue bird bus. What E-Dub didn't know was once his 5k1 motion got denied, all deals were off also.

I got to call my lawyer. I heard something 'bout I-Block on the way in. I don't know why they didn't put me over there, E-Dub thought to himself as he observed all the eyeballs on him and the other three inmates who came with him.

"A'ight, you can go up to room two seventeen, sir," the CO said, after taking the ID card from E-Dub.

"A'ight, bet." E-Dub picked up his mat.

"What's up, bruh? Where you from?" one of the inmates asked him.

"Florida, bruh!" E-Dub said, keeping it brief.

"Me too, here, let me help you," the dude said, grabbin' E-Dub's mat, carrying it to the cell for him.

"Where bruh from?" Dude said, who was on the phone.

"He the homie, Hotboi," the dude carrying E-Dub's mat spoke up as they passed by.

"A'ight, I'll spit with 'em when I'm up off the phone," Someone came rushing over to Hotboi, whispering in his free ear. Hotboi nodded in agreement, but he never took his eyes off E-Dub them the whole time until they entered cell 217 deep in the corner of the unit.

COVID-19 was back in full swing, and E-Dub couldn't recognize anyone because mostly the whole unit was behind a mask. E-Dub had gotten blessed to have his own cell. E-Dub threw his mat on the bottom rack, making it up swiftly. The knocks on his cell door quickly got his attention. Bringing him from out his thoughts of how his mother wouldn't be able to visit him for the next three years, due to her knowing about his illegalities. On top of that, she also lost her job. Plus, his grandmother didn't come to court in his support and she hated his guts.

E-Dub took his time to turn around to acknowledge the person at his cell door. He didn't want to be bothered for real. His mind was also on his child's mother, who had been killed by the law at the time they were arguing. He could never correct that wrong. On top of that, he'd told on a slew of people to still receive thirty years. Now he had been sent to a maximum USP where everyone hated snitches. Showing your paperwork was a must in order to be able to walk the yard. A knock came again, then his door opened.

"What's up, partna? I'm Hotboi. I'm from the O. What they do?" Hotboi extended a hand. E-Dub shook it without thought. In actuality, though, Hotboi did this because it's a sign of I don't fuck with your kind. If a person give you their left hand, that's not gang related. Watch out, because they fake kicked it.

"Yeah, I'm from Marianna, bruh, ain't shit to it," E-Dub said, posting up between the locker and the bunk.

"Shiiid, bruh them 'bout to bring you a care package. It should hold you until we go to the store, feel me?"

"Yeah, good looking out, but I'm good though. I should be straight," E-Dub said, not really wanting to accept anything from anyone.

"Nawl, ain't no pressure, bruh. That's on the house. You don't owe us nothing, bruh. That's what we supposed to do, feel me?"

"Yeah?"

"What size shoe you wear?" Hotboi looked down at his feet. "We got to get you out them there, my man." Hotboi pointed down at the blue bus shoes E-Dub was wearing.

"Ten."

"A'ight, dog rock that size, you good. So how much time you got?"

E-Dub didn't like that question. He instantly started to feel uneasy. Hotboi was digging too much with all the questioning. "Thirty, bruh. Look, you got a pair of shower shoes?" I'm trying to base right fast before chow, you dig," he said, trying to get the attention off him.

Two more dudes walked in without knocking before Hotboi could answer.

"What's up, Hot? Who bruh?" one of 'em said, without acknowledging E-Dub at all. The other dude stayed quiet with a unit on his face.

"Oh, this." Hotboi looked at him. "What they call you, my bad, bruh."

"E-Dub," he said, looking at all of them at once.

216

"E-Dub," Hotboi looked at his partners and said. "Man, Arron, give bruh the care package, don't just hold it. Horne says he needs a shower 'for chow."

"Here." Arron handed E-Dub the net bag. It had soups, crackers, chips, sodas, lotion, grease, shower shoes, and soap in it.

E-Dub examined the bag carefully. "Good looking out, bruh. Shiiid, I'll replace all this when we catch store, y'all," he said, placing the bag on the bed, grabbing what he needed for the shower. "A'ight, I'll fuck with it in a second. Let me handle this right fast!" E-Dub said, walking toward the door.

Hotboi, Arron, and Jeff walked out in front of E-Dub. By the time they made it downstairs, they were approached by a group of Spanish guys.

"Here it go right here!" The older Spanish guy handed Hotboi a thick folder with a ton of papers in it. Hotboi opened it up, and the first thing he saw was E-Dub's government name and his alias beside it, which read Eric Horne a.k.a. E-Dub. It went on stating that E-Dub had cooperated against him on a case out of South Florida. When Arron heard the name Eric Horne, he remembered the name for being in his cousin Freak Zeenie's paperwork.

Hotboi looked at the Cubans. "Don't worry, bruh. I'll take care of it, okay?" he said, looking the Spanish guy in the eyes. The Cuban nodded his head in agreement then turned, leaving them still standing there as he spoke in Spanish to his entourage.

"Hot ass bitch! I knew I knew that fuck nigga, bruh!"

"Yeah?" Hotboi said.

"Hell yeah! That's the same nigga who got my cousin, Freak Zeenie, that life sentence! Ya remember, bruh!"

"Oh yeah, you talking 'bout homes who left on compassionate release, ain't it?"

"Fuckin' right! Don't trip, I got this one. Y'all gone to chow and I'll be behind y'all shortly, my nigga," Arron said.

"A'ight, it's your call, just make sure it's handled, and be careful, nigga!"

"I'm good, you forgot the system down?" Arron said, talking 'bout the cameras didn't work.

E-Dub came out of the shower and went to his cell. "Let me put this up." He put his towel over the window for privacy while he got dressed.

"CHOW! Chow call! You get seven minutes!" the CO yelled out to the unit, unlocking the front door to release B-unit inmates to chow. Everyone was rushing out. It was Tuesday. Chicken sandwich day.

"Damn. Let me hurry the fuck up!" E-Dub said, facing the window, watching his unit head toward the chow hall. Before he realized it, someone rushed in, pulling the door up behind him. E-Dub couldn't tell who it was because the gray toboggan was covering the dude's face like a ski mask. "Man, what the fuck you d—"

E-Dub's words were cut short. The masked man moved with great speed. E-Dub tried to weave the left hook that the masked man threw, but the left hook was really just a diversion. E-Dub weaved right into the seven-inch ice pick. The masked man pushed it with all his might into E-Dub's side, causing it to go all the way in like a butter knife slicing butter. E-Dub couldn't holler because the ice pick had punctured his kidney and lung simultaneously.

Arron pulled back, and the pierce was so fast that the pick didn't have a drop of blood on it. E-Dub released urine as he slowly began falling to the floor. Arron took the ice pick and quickly pushed it through E-Dub's neck with professionalism. Blood skeeted across the room, splattering against the lockers. Arron pushed E-Dub's head hard toward the ground and jumped back, careful not to get any blood on himself.

E-Dub was dead before he hit the floor as he laid face first, eyes wide shut.

"Bitch ass nigga! All hot niggas get straight dropped, pussy ass nigga! That's for cuz and all real motherfuckers," Arron said. He rinsed the ice pick off in the sink then took it safely away. Arron cracked the door, peepin' out. First thing he saw was Hotboi waving for him to come on out. Arron knew it was all clear. He still was cautious though. Holding his head down, he dashed out, closing the door up behind him. Taking off the homemade ski mask, Arron looked himself over one last time.

"You straight," Hotboi assured him.

They made it downstairs just as the officer came from outside.

"Last call! Last call for chow!" It was at least twenty people in the unit leaving out going through the metal detector.

Arron and Hotboi blended in and headed out the unit to the chow hall.

***

Eight Minutes Later...

The CO made his rounds after locking the door for B-unit to go to chow, making it to 217.

Knock! Knock!

"You a'ight in there?" the CO asked, waited for two seconds, then knocked again, repeating himself. He didn't get a response, and the towel was still covering the cell window. The CO snatched the cell door open. "Oh shit, oh shit!" He hit the deuces, which was a panic button for the Cos, or a distress button. The sirens went off, and officers from all over the compound ran toward B-unit.

Hotboi and Arron wore a knowing smirk, but words weren't needed.

***

Twenty Minutes Later...

The nurses were rushing, pushing a covered up body on a stretcher passing by the chow hall. A female LT unlocked the chow hall door, rushing in.

"A'ight! Everybody back to your unit! Lock down, lock down!" she said, letting the inmates out the chow hall.

"Damn! Man, fuck! We was just 'bout to make store! Fuck!" one of the inmates yelled out of frustration.

"Aye, LT, what happened?" one of the inmates asked.

"Don't worry, you'll find out! Now keep it moving!" she said, waving them along. "Come on, come on! Let's go! I know y'all can move faster than that."

Just as LT had promised, before they made it to their unit, the news had begun to spread.

"Someone gutted that boy! We gone have to rewind the cameras," the captain said, as he talked on his cell phone.

***

Moments Later...

"Sir, we have a problem," the maintenance man said.

"I don't need no problems at this time. But what is it now?" the captain asked.

"The cameras are down, and been this way for a week or so, sir! The people should be here today to be exact to fix 'em."

"What?" How did this happen?" The maintenance man hunched his shoulder in an *I don't know* manner. "Well, shit! They will be locked down so long someone will tell something eventually," the captain said, becoming worried, because he knew if it got out that the cameras were down while someone got killed, that was the end of his career, plus more lawsuits on top of the ones the Coleman complex was already dealing with.

***

Later That Night...
Coleman USP 1

Arron wrote a letter to his aunt, Ms. Lois.
Auntie,

How you doing? Tell Cuz that I said, when the time is right everything will straight drop! It's a season to everything. The leaves drop in the fall, tell him I said put a lil' something on my books for me another one!

> *Love,*
> *Arron*

220

Arron put his letter in the door and laid down, thinking 'bout the look on E-Dub's face when he entered the cell. "All rats must die! Even Master Splinter," he quoted a bar from off of Lil' Wayne's album from back in the day. Arron went to sleep feeling great, knowing his cousin was going to be super happy once he found out that E-Dub had been murdered at Coleman USP in B-unit.

Arron knew that Freak Zeenie would put it together. Everyone knew about Freak Zeenie's situation at USP Coleman one. No one said a word.

E-Dub's snitching days had finally caught up with him, bringing his life to an end. He died like the coward he was.

Paper Boi Rari

Chapter 32
One Week Later
Dothan, Alabama

Freak Zeenie had just picked up a letter from his mother's house. It was from his cousin Arron, who was doing time at a USP maximum prison. The same one Freak Zeenie had been released from.

Freak Zeenie put the letter on the passenger seat of the Wraith. Today he was in one of Levi's cars. He was truly missing his lil' brother.

Freak Zeenie headed to meet Khashia over at Westside Construction. The construction company that Marcus a.k.a. Big Man owned. After his disappearance, Khashia recently found out that the company now belonged to her also since she helped co-sign for it with Marcus.

Khashia had just beat the Delta variant, so she wanted to get active. Once she studied the financial statements of the construction company, she was eager to get the business back up and running. Which wouldn't be hard since it already had a structure and formula to a billion-plus annually. Khashia just needed her nigga's insight. She knew Freak Zeenie would be sure to know how to get some paper.

***

Minutes Later...

Freak Zeenie pulled into the parking lot, killing the engine. He got out, strolling through the entrance. Looking 'round, he didn't see Khashia but knew she was there because her car was parked out front.

Freak Zeenie headed to the lounge and got comfortable. Turning the TV to HLN, Freak Zeenie took a seat, opening up his cousin's letter. Just as he started to read it, Robin Meads captured his attention.

"Breaking news! This is so sad to hear, y'all, but it's my job to report it. This morning, a white Bentley Mulsanne was pulled from

out Lake Burton. This is hard to deliver, but it must be announced one way or another. Please be aware, this is gruesome to even hear.

"A woman was found inside beheaded, and as investigators have it, placed in the driver seat with her hand wrapped around her head! We do know that her name is Denise Jones. No one seems to have seen anything. If you know of anything, please don't hesitate to call Crime Stoppers at one-eight hundred-crime stoppers. There's a fifteen-hundred-dollar reward out leading to an arrest. Now, for other news." Robin Meads paused. *"Coleman US Penitentiary is currently still on lockdown and under investigation.*

"An inmate who had only been there less than twenty-four hours was found stabbed to death in his cell. Eric Horne, a black male who had been recently sentenced to thirty years. The government is looking into this matter further. Now we know that they claimed that this Eric Horne was a high-profile informant who never should have been housed in that type of environment in the first place. To make matters worse, it's said that the cameras in the unit had been down and didn't work! Ain't that something, y'all? Cameras not working, inside a federal institution! Now we know, someone is about to be in big trouble!" she said.

Freak Zeenie couldn't believe his own ears.

"Say what?" He leaped up from his chair, hitting his two step. "Straight drop! Bitch ass nigga!" He looked at the TV then to the letter that he still held in his hand. He sat back down to read the letter from his cousin. "Fuck that bitch too! Fuck wrong with y'all. How you gone run off on the plug when bitch, I'm the socket?" he said, talking 'bout Denise too as he read his cousin's letter. He knew instantly what took place. "I got you, cousin! I'm gone fill your shit up today!"

Khashia came marching in the lounge area. Right behind her were four Mexicans. The first one had a very powerful aura about himself.

"Hey baby, these are men who said that they are friends of Marcus's," she said, with a confused look on her face.

"Okay. Marcus's friends are his, not mine. Fuck that got to do with anything?" Freak Zeenie said, getting to his feet.

224

"Well, everything," the first one said, with a powerful presence. "You see, me and Marcus ran a very successful business together. At the time of his disappearance, he had just received tons of product." The Mexican paused, studying Freak Zeenie to see if he understood. "Product that has never been found or repaid. See, this product must be repaid one way or another. Now, I understand that Khashia here is now over most of Marcus's property. So I have a proposition for her. I made her an offer of a lifetime. She directed me to you," he said, pointing at Freak Zeenie.

"Is that right?"

"It is."

"What you have in mind? I'm listening," Freak Zeenie said, looking at his watch.

"Well, since this has been a drop-off since day one, I figured, why change it? I could still put the product here and me and you use the trucks to move it. Trust me, Freak Zeenie, I've done my homework. I know you are capable. If you say yes, then the debt is paid and from here on out, we can just get money together, my amigo."

"If I say no?"

"Then, who knows what may happen. Maybe Marcus won't be the only one who's missing. Get my drift?" The Mexican stared Freak Zeenie down. Khashia was shifting from foot to foot.

"Not really, but when you talking about billions of dollars, then I'm not the one to argue."

"I like that answer, Freak." The four Mexicans turned to leave. "Our first shipment will be here in less than a week," the short Mexican said, without ever breaking stride.

"What was I supposed to do?" Khashia asked, getting a strange look from Freak Zeenie.

"Nothing. What could you do? We locked in! Thank you, you just got me back in the drug game. Something I wanted no more parts of," Freak Zeenie said, walking out, leaving Khashia to talk to his back.

She let him go, knowing how he felt 'bout the dope game. After coming from under a life sentence where the majority of his co-dees cooperated against him, to say he was mad would be an understatement.

Freak Zeenie made it into the warehouse section.

"Ump, ump, ump!" he muttered aloud, thinking of all the disadvantages this game came with.

This bitch stupid! Stupid bitch! She got to go! Ain't no way! he thought as he lifted up the back door to one of the big rigs. He saw a trailer full of boxes. Freak Zeenie jumped up onto the trailer, opening up one of the boxes. His eyes got huge as flying saucers, lighting up like a set of headlights. "What the fuck? Nawl!" Freak Zeenie checked a couple more boxes to see the exact same thing.

He jumped down, going to another big rig. After checking that one and finding the exact same thing, Freak Zeenie went to the next truck. Lifting the door, he saw the same boxes, coming to the conclusion that they all were filled with tons and tons of kilos. *Why they didn't check this shit then? Damn, they probably already did.* His thoughts began to turn.

"Freak?" Khashia startled him. "What are you doing? Don't be mad at me, baby. I'm sorry, I just didn't know what else to do," she said, walking toward him.

"Hun?" He turned around. "Oh, nothing." He turned and jumped down out of the truck, pulling the door shut with him. "No, no, I'm not mad! I just don't like how they had the straight drop on me like that…"

To Be Continued…
Ran off on the Plug 2
Coming Soon

Lock Down Publications and Ca$h Presents assisted publishing packages.

BASIC PACKAGE $499
Editing
Cover Design
Formatting

UPGRADED PACKAGE $800
Typing
Editing
Cover Design
Formatting

ADVANCE PACKAGE $1,200
Typing
Editing
Cover Design
Formatting
Copyright registration
Proofreading
Upload book to Amazon

LDP SUPREME PACKAGE $1,500
Typing
Editing
Cover Design
Formatting
Copyright registration
Proofreading
Set up Amazon account
Upload book to Amazon
Advertise on LDP Amazon and Facebook page

***Other services available upon request. Additional charges may apply
Lock Down Publications
P.O. Box 944
Stockbridge, GA 30281-9998
Phone # 470 303-9761

Ran off on the Plug

Submission Guideline

Submit the first three chapters of your completed manuscript to ldpsubmissions@gmail.com, subject line: Your book's title. The manuscript must be in a .doc file and sent as an attachment. Document should be in Times New Roman, double spaced and in size 12 font. Also, provide your synopsis and full contact information. If sending multiple submissions, they must each be in a separate email.

Have a story but no way to send it electronically? You can still submit to LDP/Ca$h Presents. Send in the first three chapters, written or typed, of your completed manuscript to:

LDP: Submissions Dept
Po Box 944
Stockbridge, Ga 30281

DO NOT send original manuscript. Must be a duplicate.

Provide your synopsis and a cover letter containing your full contact information.

Thanks for considering LDP and Ca$h Presents.

229

NEW RELEASES

MOB TIES 6 by SAYNOMORE
A GANGSTA'S PAIN 2 by J-BLUNT
TREAL LOVE by LE'MONICA JACKSON
FOR THE LOVE OF BLOOD by JAMEL MITCHELL
CONCRETE KILLA 3 by KINGPEN
RAN OFF ON DA PLUG by PAPER BOI RARI

KINGPIN KILLAZ IV

STREET KINGS III

PAID IN BLOOD III

CARTEL KILLAZ IV

DOPE GODS III

Hood Rich

SINS OF A HUSTLA II

ASAD

RICH $AVAGE II

By Martell Troublesome Bolden

YAYO V

Bred In The Game 2

S. Allen

CREAM III

THE STREETS WILL TALK II

By Yolanda Moore

SON OF A DOPE FIEND III

HEAVEN GOT A GHETTO II

By Renta

LOYALTY AIN'T PROMISED III

By Keith Williams

I'M NOTHING WITHOUT HIS LOVE II

SINS OF A THUG II

TO THE THUG I LOVED BEFORE II

IN A HUSTLER I TRUST II

By Monet Dragun

QUIET MONEY IV

EXTENDED CLIP III

THUG LIFE IV

By **Trai'Quan**

Ran off on the Plug

THE STREETS MADE ME IV
By **Larry D. Wright**
IF YOU CROSS ME ONCE II
By **Anthony Fields**
THE STREETS WILL NEVER CLOSE IV
By K'ajji
HARD AND RUTHLESS III
KILLA KOUNTY III
By Khufu
MONEY GAME III
By Smoove Dolla
JACK BOYS VS DOPE BOYS II
A GANGSTA'S QUR'AN V
COKE GIRLZ II
By Romell Tukes
MURDA WAS THE CASE II
Elijah R. Freeman
THE STREETS NEVER LET GO II
By Robert Baptiste
AN UNFORESEEN LOVE III
By **Meesha**
KING OF THE TRENCHES III
by **GHOST & TRANAY ADAMS**

MONEY MAFIA II
LOYAL TO THE SOIL III
By **Jibril Williams**
QUEEN OF THE ZOO II
By **Black Migo**
THE BRICK MAN IV
By King Rio

VICIOUS LOYALTY III

By Kingpen

A GANGSTA'S PAIN III

By J-Blunt

CONFESSIONS OF A JACKBOY III

By Nicholas Lock

GRIMEY WAYS II

By Ray Vinci

KING KILLA II

By Vincent "Vitto" Holloway

BETRAYAL OF A THUG II

By Fre$h

THE MURDER QUEENS II

By Michael Gallon

THE BIRTH OF A GANGSTER II

By Delmont Player

TREAL LOVE II

By Le'Monica Jackson

FOR THE LOVE OF BLOOD II

By Jamel Mitchell

RAN OFF ON DA PLUG II

By Paper Boi Rari

<u>Available Now</u>

RESTRAINING ORDER **I & II**
By **CA$H & Coffee**
LOVE KNOWS NO BOUNDARIES **I II & III**
By **Coffee**
RAISED AS A GOON I, II, III & IV
BRED BY THE SLUMS I, II, III
BLAST FOR ME I & II
ROTTEN TO THE CORE I II III
A BRONX TALE I, II, III
DUFFLE BAG CARTEL I II III IV V VI
HEARTLESS GOON I II III IV V
A SAVAGE DOPEBOY I II
DRUG LORDS I II III
CUTTHROAT MAFIA I II
KING OF THE TRENCHES
By **Ghost**
LAY IT DOWN **I & II**
LAST OF A DYING BREED I II
BLOOD STAINS OF A SHOTTA I & II III
By **Jamaica**
LOYAL TO THE GAME I II III
LIFE OF SIN I, II III
By **TJ & Jelissa**
BLOODY COMMAS I & II
SKI MASK CARTEL I II & III
KING OF NEW YORK I II,III IV V
RISE TO POWER I II III
COKE KINGS I II III IV V
BORN HEARTLESS I II III IV

Paper Boi Rari

KING OF THE TRAP I II

By **T.J. Edwards**

IF LOVING HIM IS WRONG…I & II

LOVE ME EVEN WHEN IT HURTS I II III

By **Jelissa**

WHEN THE STREETS CLAP BACK I & II III

THE HEART OF A SAVAGE I II III

MONEY MAFIA

LOYAL TO THE SOIL I II

By **Jibril Williams**

A DISTINGUISHED THUG STOLE MY HEART I II & III

LOVE SHOULDN'T HURT I II III IV

RENEGADE BOYS I II III IV

PAID IN KARMA I II III

SAVAGE STORMS I II III

AN UNFORESEEN LOVE I II

By **Meesha**

A GANGSTER'S CODE I &, II III

A GANGSTER'S SYN I II III

THE SAVAGE LIFE I II III

CHAINED TO THE STREETS I II III

BLOOD ON THE MONEY I II III

A GANGSTA'S PAIN I II

By **J-Blunt**

PUSH IT TO THE LIMIT

By **Bre' Hayes**

BLOOD OF A BOSS **I, II, III, IV, V**

SHADOWS OF THE GAME

TRAP BASTARD

By **Askari**

236

THE STREETS BLEED MURDER **I, II & III**

THE HEART OF A GANGSTA I II& III

By **Jerry Jackson**

CUM FOR ME I II III IV V VI VII VIII

An **LDP Erotica Collaboration**

BRIDE OF A HUSTLA **I II & II**

THE FETTI GIRLS **I, II& III**

CORRUPTED BY A GANGSTA I, II III, IV

BLINDED BY HIS LOVE

THE PRICE YOU PAY FOR LOVE I, II ,III

DOPE GIRL MAGIC I II III

By **Destiny Skai**

WHEN A GOOD GIRL GOES BAD

By **Adrienne**

THE COST OF LOYALTY I II III

By Kweli

A GANGSTER'S REVENGE **I II III & IV**

THE BOSS MAN'S DAUGHTERS I II III IV V

A SAVAGE LOVE **I & II**

BAE BELONGS TO ME I II

A HUSTLER'S DECEIT I, II, III

WHAT BAD BITCHES DO I, II, III

SOUL OF A MONSTER I II III

KILL ZONE

A DOPE BOY'S QUEEN I II III

By **Aryanna**

A KINGPIN'S AMBITON

A KINGPIN'S AMBITION **II**

I MURDER FOR THE DOUGH

By **Ambitious**

Paper Boi Rari

TRUE SAVAGE I II III IV V VI VII
DOPE BOY MAGIC I, II, III
MIDNIGHT CARTEL I II III
CITY OF KINGZ I II
NIGHTMARE ON SILENT AVE
THE PLUG OF LIL MEXICO II

By **Chris Green**
A DOPEBOY'S PRAYER
By **Eddie "Wolf" Lee**
THE KING CARTEL **I, II & III**
By **Frank Gresham**
THESE NIGGAS AIN'T LOYAL **I, II & III**
By **Nikki Tee**
GANGSTA SHYT **I II &III**
By **CATO**
THE ULTIMATE BETRAYAL
By **Phoenix**
BOSS'N UP **I , II & III**
By **Royal Nicole**
I LOVE YOU TO DEATH
By **Destiny J**
I RIDE FOR MY HITTA
I STILL RIDE FOR MY HITTA
By **Misty Holt**
LOVE & CHASIN' PAPER
By **Qay Crockett**
TO DIE IN VAIN
SINS OF A HUSTLA
By **ASAD**

Ran off on the Plug

BROOKLYN HUSTLAZ

By **Boogsy Morina**

BROOKLYN ON LOCK I & II

By **Sonovia**

GANGSTA CITY

By **Teddy Duke**

A DRUG KING AND HIS DIAMOND I & II III

A DOPEMAN'S RICHES

HER MAN, MINE'S TOO I, II

CASH MONEY HO'S

THE WIFEY I USED TO BE I II

By Nicole Goosby

TRAPHOUSE KING **I II & III**

KINGPIN KILLAZ I II III

STREET KINGS I II

PAID IN BLOOD **I II**

CARTEL KILLAZ I II III

DOPE GODS I II

By **Hood Rich**

LIPSTICK KILLAH **I, II, III**

CRIME OF PASSION I II & III

FRIEND OR FOE I II III

By **Mimi**

STEADY MOBBN' **I, II, III**

THE STREETS STAINED MY SOUL I II III

By **Marcellus Allen**

WHO SHOT YA **I, II, III**

SON OF A DOPE FIEND I II

HEAVEN GOT A GHETTO

Renta

GORILLAZ IN THE BAY **I II III IV**

TEARS OF A GANGSTA I II

3X KRAZY I II

STRAIGHT BEAST MODE

DE'KARI

TRIGGADALE I II III

MURDAROBER WAS THE CASE

Elijah R. Freeman

GOD BLESS THE TRAPPERS I, II, III

THESE SCANDALOUS STREETS I, II, III

FEAR MY GANGSTA I, II, III IV, V

THESE STREETS DON'T LOVE NOBODY I, II

BURY ME A G I, II, III, IV, V

A GANGSTA'S EMPIRE I, II, III, IV

THE DOPEMAN'S BODYGAURD I II

THE REALEST KILLAZ I II III

THE LAST OF THE OGS I II III

Tranay Adams

THE STREETS ARE CALLING

Duquie Wilson

MARRIED TO A BOSS I II III

By Destiny Skai & Chris Green

KINGZ OF THE GAME I II III IV V VI

Playa Ray

SLAUGHTER GANG I II III

RUTHLESS HEART I II III

By Willie Slaughter

FUK SHYT

By Blakk Diamond

DON'T F#CK WITH MY HEART I II

Ran off on the Plug

By Linnea
ADDICTED TO THE DRAMA I II III
IN THE ARM OF HIS BOSS II
By Jamila
YAYO I II III IV
A SHOOTER'S AMBITION I II
BRED IN THE GAME
By S. Allen
TRAP GOD I II III
RICH $AVAGE
MONEY IN THE GRAVE I II III
By Martell Troublesome Bolden
FOREVER GANGSTA
GLOCKS ON SATIN SHEETS I II
By Adrian Dulan
TOE TAGZ I II III IV
LEVELS TO THIS SHYT I II
By Ah'Million
KINGPIN DREAMS I II III
RAN OFF ON DA PLUG
By Paper Boi Rari
CONFESSIONS OF A GANGSTA I II III IV
CONFESSIONS OF A JACKBOY I II
By Nicholas Lock
I'M NOTHING WITHOUT HIS LOVE
SINS OF A THUG
TO THE THUG I LOVED BEFORE
A GANGSTA SAVED XMAS
IN A HUSTLER I TRUST
By Monet Dragun

CAUGHT UP IN THE LIFE I II III
THE STREETS NEVER LET GO
By Robert Baptiste
NEW TO THE GAME I II III
MONEY, MURDER & MEMORIES I II III
By **Malik D. Rice**
LIFE OF A SAVAGE I II III
A GANGSTA'S QUR'AN I II III IV
MURDA SEASON I II III
GANGLAND CARTEL I II III
CHI'RAQ GANGSTAS I II III
KILLERS ON ELM STREET I II III
JACK BOYZ N DA BRONX I II III
A DOPEBOY'S DREAM I II III
JACK BOYS VS DOPE BOYS
COKE GIRLZ
By Romell Tukes
LOYALTY AIN'T PROMISED I II
By Keith Williams
QUIET MONEY I II III
THUG LIFE I II III
EXTENDED CLIP I II
By **Trai'Quan**
THE STREETS MADE ME I II III
By **Larry D. Wright**
THE ULTIMATE SACRIFICE I, II, III, IV, V, VI
KHADIFI
IF YOU CROSS ME ONCE
ANGEL I II
IN THE BLINK OF AN EYE

Ran off on the Plug

By **Anthony Fields**
THE LIFE OF A HOOD STAR
By **Ca$h & Rashia Wilson**
THE STREETS WILL NEVER CLOSE I II III
By **K'ajji**
CREAM I II
THE STREETS WILL TALK
By **Yolanda Moore**
NIGHTMARES OF A HUSTLA I II III
By **King Dream**
CONCRETE KILLA I II III
VICIOUS LOYALTY I II
By **Kingpen**
HARD AND RUTHLESS I II
MOB TOWN 251
THE BILLIONAIRE BENTLEYS I II III
By **Von Diesel**
GHOST MOB
Stilloan Robinson
MOB TIES I II III IV V VI
By **SayNoMore**
BODYMORE MURDERLAND I II III
THE BIRTH OF A GANGSTER
By **Delmont Player**
FOR THE LOVE OF A BOSS
By **C. D. Blue**
MOBBED UP I II III IV
THE BRICK MAN I II III
THE COCAINE PRINCESS I II III IV V
By **King Rio**

KILLA KOUNTY I II III
By Khufu
MONEY GAME I II
By Smoove Dolla
A GANGSTA'S KARMA I II
By FLAME
KING OF THE TRENCHES I II
by **GHOST & TRANAY ADAMS**
QUEEN OF THE ZOO
By **Black Migo**
GRIMEY WAYS
By Ray Vinci
XMAS WITH AN ATL SHOOTER
By Ca$h & Destiny Skai
KING KILLA
By Vincent "Vitto" Holloway
BETRAYAL OF A THUG
By Fre$h
THE MURDER QUEENS
By Michael Gallon
TREAL LOVE
By Le'Monica Jackson
FOR THE LOVE OF BLOOD
By Jamel Mitchell

BOOKS BY LDP'S CEO, CA$H

TRUST IN NO MAN

TRUST IN NO MAN 2

TRUST IN NO MAN 3

BONDED BY BLOOD

SHORTY GOT A THUG

THUGS CRY

THUGS CRY 2

THUGS CRY 3

TRUST NO BITCH

TRUST NO BITCH 2

TRUST NO BITCH 3

TIL MY CASKET DROPS

RESTRAINING ORDER

RESTRAINING ORDER 2

IN LOVE WITH A CONVICT

LIFE OF A HOOD STAR

XMAS WITH AN ATL SHOOTER